THE MISSING LINKS OF TANNADEE

THE MISSING LINKS OF TANNADEE

MAURICE GRAY

Troubador Publishing Ltd
Unit E2 Airfield Business Park,
Harrison Road, Market Harborough,
Leicestershire LE16 7UL
Tel: 0116 279 2299
Email: books@troubador.co.uk
Web: www.troubador.co.uk

ISBN 978 1 80514 381 9

British Library Cataloguing in Publication Data.
A catalogue record for this book is available from the British Library.

Printed and bound in Great Britain by 4edge Limited
Typeset in 11pt Minion Pro by Troubador Publishing Ltd, Leicester, UK

Matador is an imprint of Troubador Publishing Ltd

To Eddie and Dixon

CHAPTER 1

Sometimes the world is more than just a friend: sometimes it is your lover. This is a fact that Chizzie Bryson was in a position to confirm as he sat on a bench by the River Tay one glorious afternoon in late summer. He closed his eyes and gave way to the warmth of the sun's body on his skin. The river breeze cooled his brow while the fragrant breath of the hills carried away every care. In the garden of his Highland home in Tannadee he could've given way completely to blissful dreams. But he wasn't there: he was on a public bench in Perth, and his schoolteacher instinct told him that the instant he became a slumped and slumbering heap, some pupil would leap out of nowhere and howl, 'That's my teacher!' Eyebrows would jump, lips would curl, and letters to the headmaster would follow.

Another passer-by would point to the unconscious lump, and inform the world, 'That's the guy that runs the Tannadee Hotel!', thus causing occupation rates to dive and never recover.

Unfortunate though these exclamations might be, they nonetheless would be true, for Chizzie Bryson was both a part-time teacher and part-owner of a hotel. As such, he had reputations to consider. He looked around to see if anyone was near, and that's when his eyes met the familiar

1

figure of young Billy Pung running towards him with a small grey dog in his arms.

Billy came to a halt and sat down on the bench, still clutching the bewildered-looking dog. He explained how a big man had earlier taken hold of the dog and whacked it with the lead before dragging it by its collar towards a big blue car. People had groaned but no one had moved. So, Billy had grabbed the dog. And here he was, looking for Chizzie to sort things out.

Chizzie was used to young people presenting him with problems that the training college and textbooks had never prepared him for, but dog rescue was entirely new. He ran his fingers through his hair and took a deep breath. 'Let me see,' he said. 'When I saw you last, you'd gone off to buy a chocolate sponge, and now you're back with a hot dog.'

Billy was small and stocky, and so rugged and raw that on one occasion he'd been mistaken for part of the Caledonian pine forest. His chief assets were physical strength and speed. These, alas, were inversely proportional to his mental qualities. 'No choice,' Billy replied. 'We was all wonderin' what to do, when the big man pushed me an' a wee woman out the way. Then he whacked the dog, shoutin', "I'll murder you!", an' that's when I grabbed it.'

'Wouldn't happen to be the big man who's just got out of a dark blue car over there and is heading this way?'

'Oh, bollocks!' yelped Billy, and he got up and ran off with the dog under his arm.

The big man came running up, his face blazing with more than sunburn. 'Who's that lad?' He snarled. 'What's his name?'

2

'Never seen him before,' replied Chizzie. 'Tried to sell me a dog. What's up?' A spontaneous response that he considered a remarkable feat for a Scotsman in twenty-five-degree heat.

It certainly had the desired effect. The big man turned and ran back to his Maserati, leaving a whiff of sharp deodorant in the air. Billy, with the dog now over his shoulder, was sprinting at top speed towards the railway bridge, but the Maserati would surely catch up if the man gunned it.

Fortunately, or perhaps unfortunately, a police patrol car came by before the Maserati could pull out. If the man caught the attention of the police and reported the theft of his dog, Billy could be in big trouble. But the man reported nobody. He just crept along at twenty miles an hour behind the police car. This was also serious. If the man would not report the theft of his dog when he had the perfect opportunity, what did that say about him? And as if that wasn't enough, there was the possibility that Billy might turn to the police for help and get himself arrested. Even if Billy didn't turn to the police, they might just book him for exceeding the twenty-mile-per-hour speed limit.

Chizzie's mind swirled with possibilities. With no idea what to do, he could only look on helplessly as Billy ran up the steps leading to the narrow public footway on the railway bridge while the big man parked his Maserati. On the bridge, Billy overtook two golfers who were pulling golf trolleys, slipping past them with a neat swivel of the hips; then he weaved through a young family carrying little buckets and spades. Would Billy run the full length of the bridge, or would he run down the steps onto the

3

island and disappear into the golf course? He might even make for one of the little beaches on the island and swim to the other side of the river.

There was no time to find out. Chizzie got into his car and drove off towards the nearby road bridge about three hundred yards away. Approaching the road bridge, he glanced over to the railway bridge, and saw Billy take the stairway onto the island, while farther back there was a big man throwing a golf trolley into the river. At least it wasn't Billy. On the other side of the river, Chizzie swept into the car park, jumped out of the car, and ran to the riverside, hoping Billy would come towards him at the end of the island where there was a rough boulder-strewn causeway. To his great relief, he saw Billy heading towards the causeway. Relief turned to worry, though, when he saw Billy stop to allow some small boys to pet the dog.

'For God's sake, Billy! Hurry up!' Chizzie yelled, mopping sweat from his brow.

Billy heard him, waved, and ran to the causeway, where he skipped over the glistening grey stones with the dog bobbing in his arms.

As Billy and Chizzie ran up towards the car park, Chizzie turned and saw the big man grab one of the boys who'd patted the dog. The man pulled him off his feet. But, wise beyond his years, the little chap sank his teeth into first one hand and then the other and broke the big man's grip before running off to join his little pals – a victory in the field for regular toothbrushing and vitamin D. Chizzie found himself smiling as he got back into the car.

'It's whimpering,' Billy announced. 'It needs a wee.'

'Quickly, then,' said Chizzie, looking in the rear-view mirror as Billy got out with the dog.

The dog took up the correct stance, but nothing happened – then a menacing shape appeared in the rear-view mirror. It was the big man, pounding up the path.

'Get in!' yelled Chizzie.

'She's not started yet.'

'Forget it! We go – now!'

Billy hopped back in with the dog, and Chizzie hit the gas. Now the man very probably knew the type of car he drove, and possibly even the registration plate.

'Should've slapped some mud on the number plate,' Chizzie muttered. 'Where are all the plopping pigeons when you need them?'

'Ugly man scared them, probably,' muttered Billy.

Chizzie sped out of the car park, zigzagging slightly as he went, hoping to obscure his registration plate, and then he headed out towards the motorway. But it quickly dawned on him that a motorway is not the place to try and shake off a Maserati. Small country roads were what he needed, so he headed for Stirling and turned off at the first country road.

A few hundred metres down the road, the little dog began to whine again, so they pulled in beside a field gate. Billy took the dog out, and this time – success! – she relieved herself.

'She's gone very quiet now,' Billy remarked.

'Probably traumatised. Whacked and kidnapped – quite an afternoon for the little thing.'

'What kind d'you think she is?'

'Mongrel, I'd say. Bit like Greyfriars Bobby, bit of spaniel, bit of Jack Russell there too, maybe. Who knows? Needs breath freshener, that's for sure.'

'I'll give her some water.' Billy took a bottle and a bowl from his picnic box and poured out some water.

The dog lapped thirstily while Chizzie cast his eye over the panoramic view of Strathmore spread out before him: to the left, his eyes met the wooded slopes of Birnam Hill; while away to the right he could see Dunsinane. *Macbeth* sprang to mind. The cackling of the hoary witches echoed in his head: *Eye of newt and toe of frog... toad in the...* well, maybe not. It occurred to him that he, like Macbeth, was now some kind of outlaw. He was no assassin, but he had just become the getaway driver in a canine kidnapping. He felt bewildered. His mind raced. Whether it was nobler to be a righteous thief or a betraying confessor; that was the question. Chizzie couldn't decide. He leaned back in his seat and sighed, waving a fly away from the open window.

'What now?' he asked, though he knew what Billy's answer would be.

'I'm keepin' her,' came the reply.

'And what if Paw says no?'

'I'm eighteen. I can make my own decisions.'

This was true, but Billy lived with his adopted grandfather, an elderly hill farmer known locally as Paw, and while they generally got on very well, Billy could be very awkward sometimes. As a young child, he had been found wandering in a local forest. He acquired the surname Pung because this was the only word he would utter when asked his name. No one – by the name of Pung or any other name – ever came forward to claim him, so Paw and his late wife took him in and persevered with the rugged lad, despite his habit of running off into the hills now and again, often staying away for several days at a time.

'Eighteen, you say,' said Chizzie. 'You could go to prison, you know.'

'Don't care.'

'Well, you should. And you'll take me with you. A criminal conviction won't look good on my CV, and me a youngish man still, trying to make his way in the teaching profession and quite possibly taking over the family hotel. We can't mention this to my dad, or he'll fire you and I'll get disowned. Neither of us will work in a hotel ever again. Or possibly we'll never work again, period.'

'I can look after her on my own.'

'I don't think you quite realise, Billy: we're going to have to make up a story and tell a pack of lies, and we'll need to stick to it, never deviating. Always exactly the same story. All the time, every day, every little detail. Just one little slip, and we're in the slammer.'

'I can do it.'

'It doesn't frighten you?'

'We done right. I'm no' feart.'

'Well, I am. There's no fool greater than the fool that fools himself. That prospect frightens me, Billy. And another thing frightens me: the man in the Maserati. Who in God's name is he? And where is he now? I can't go back into town; he might be there.' Chizzie glanced at his watch. 'Yolanda's probably close to coming away from the conference centre now, and I can't pick her up.' He groaned and ran his fingers through his hair.

'I thought she was at the hairdresser's?'

'No, hydroponics: a talk about growing plants with no soil, only nutrient solution. It's farming for the future. She wants to grow fruit and veg for Tannadee all year round.'

'No soil?' scoffed Billy. 'Paw calls me a son of the soil. I don't fancy being called a son of nutrient solution. And what about sunshine?'

'She's creating a small hydroelectric plant.'

'A what plant?'

'Hydroelectric. I need to call her now and pick her up somewhere out of town.'

'Won't be happy.'

'She'll understand.'

'I've thought about getting married, but I don't fancy all the argy-bargy. You had fights yet?' Billy asked.

'Nothing serious.'

'Early days.'

'Billy, you're far too young to be thinking about getting married. Mary's certainly a nice girl, though, and I'm sure she'd make you a fine wife someday.'

'They're the same, really, Mary and Yolanda, aren't they?'

Chizzie blinked in surprise but said nothing. Yolanda Bryson and Mary Boone could hardly be more different. Yolanda was trim with shoulder-length auburn hair. Mary was stout with curly blonde hair. But it was clear that whatever Chizzie saw in Yolanda, Billy saw in Mary. Sunflower or cauliflower, what mattered, it seemed to Chizzie, was what people meant to one another. And with that in mind, he phoned his beloved wife. She understood his predicament and arranged to get a lift from a friend whom she'd met in the cafeteria at the conference centre. All that Chizzie needed now was a clear road.

CHAPTER 2

Forty or so miles away as the crow flies, in the village of Tannadee, deep in the Central Highlands, Gordon Weever was learning to dance. As the billionaire owner and president of the Weever Corporation, he was an international titan. He knew this because people told him so – especially his most highly paid employees, and they were clever people; almost as clever as Weever himself.

Though born into a wealthy family, Weever, with almost no help from anybody else, had blessed the world with his own brand of hotels and exclusive leisure resorts. But there was more to his greatness than the sum of his businesses. There were other subtle indications of his innate superiority: recently, for example, he had acquired, quite naturally, the habit of slipping his right hand inside the breast of his sports jacket – just like Napoleon.

Now, in his mid-sixties, Weever's fascination with making money had been overtaken by a fascination with his Scottish ancestry, and his sights were set on becoming the greatest, most wonderful chief of his clan ever. Armed with his six-foot-two-inch frame and a new toupee fit to rival any bumper harvest, he was currently based at his new, exclusive hideaway resort in the heart of the Scottish Highlands, close to his clan's historic seat near Tannadee.

9

Like many a controversial figure, Weever knew that everywhere you go there are negative persons who have nothing better to do than to try and thwart you at every opportunity. What you don't expect, though, is opposition from within your own family. Regrettably, that was just what had happened. His beloved daughter Yolanda – so lovely, so athletic, so smart, so seemingly set against him – had gone and married a local man by the name of Chizzie Bryson, who seemed to have persuaded her that the great Gordon Weever would be the worst clan chief imaginable. Wounding comments like those nevertheless bounced off Weever nearly every day; nothing new there, he hardly noticed them – with one exception: those from his daughter. He noticed them all right, and they stung. He was her daddy after all.

Undeflected, though, Weever pressed on. If he was to become chief of Clan McShellach – and not just any old chief, but the greatest and most beloved clan chief ever to walk the face of the earth – he had to become a fine exponent of Scottish country dancing. He had already attempted two dances, namely Strip the Willow, which proved very exhausting, and the Dashing White Sergeant, which initially left him dizzy. Now, with some trepidation, he was about to tackle the Gay Gordons. Before he'd even taken a step, though, there was a problem: the name.

'I'm not gay,' he whined to his instructor, Ms Florence McTaggart. 'But people will sure think I am. They'll think all Gordons are gay or end up gay. But Gordon Weever is certainly not gay. We need to change that name – maybe something like the Jolly Gordons, the Mighty Gordons; something… anything – anything but gay. I don't want gay.'

His dancing instructor was unmoved. She glared at him. She had the look of a woman who had her own thumbscrews. 'The Gay Gordons refers to the Gordon Highlanders,' she informed him, 'a very famous regiment.'

Gordon Weever, bullying billionaire though he was, was reluctant to push his luck. He had hired her because she had a record of success with even the most unpromising material, including Highland lairds and royal personages. Sturdy but light on her feet, Ms Florence McTaggart had never yet failed, and Gordon Weever, though in a class of his own, was going to succeed in at least three traditional dances whether he liked it or not. Weever had absolutely refused to dance in dancing pumps and, having put up a fight, he was now dancing in dancing pumps. She was a persuasive woman, was Ms Florence McTaggart. He had referred to her as 'an oven-ready buffalo' and believed that of all the bad decisions he'd ever made, this was shaping up to be one of the worst.

'A man of my build does not do Strip the Willow,' he had pleaded.

'It's exactly what you should be doing,' she'd retorted. 'It's your signature dance. "McShellach" means "Son of the Willow".'

'What? That can't be right. I'm not a willow – look at me, I'm not willowy. Do you see willow? I'm an oak type of guy; a Scots pine; a redwood. I am no weeping willow!'

'Not all willows are weeping. There's hundreds of species of willow. Willow is ubiquitous,' she said, before adding, in a softer, calculated tone, 'promiscuous, you might even say. The Casanova of trees.'

It had the desired effect: Weever brightened.

'I used to be in forestry,' continued Florence, 'and I know my willows. One of the toughest trees in the world is a willow: the dwarf willow, about an inch high and lives on mountaintops in Scotland. The highest tree in Britain. No tree higher.'

'A dwarf?!'

'Tough as they come. And cricket bats – they're willow. Get hit with a cricket bat and you know all about hardness.'

'Well, yeah, that's more like it. Big hitter, eh?'

'Then there's aspirin – the first safe painkiller. It's from willow.'

'Kills pain. Hits hard, tops the mountains – fantastic. That's a great set of cards. We got the best goddamn tree in the business.'

'Indeed you have. So chin up, son of the mighty willow, and let's get stuck right in.'

So the big man had manned up, and now he was ready to try out his new skills in the company of the local Scottish country dance club. Florence went to greet the dancers as they arrived in the clubhouse foyer. Weever dropped into a chair and sipped a bottle of water.

'Right, we're ready,' declared Florence, marching back into the function suite.

'I need a break,' said Weever.

'Break is in ten minutes,' insisted Florence. 'We keep at it while it's still fresh in the mind.'

'Look, when I signed up for this, I didn't sign up to be twinkletoes. I just wanted to be a cut above the rest, but no Gene Kelly. I need a break.'

'A quitter? Gordon Weever is a quitter? A snivelling, weak-kneed quitter? Man up, big man! We have the wind in our sails; we carry on. Enter!' she bawled at the door, and the dancers entered in a column of eight couples, each person holding their partner's hand shoulder high. The ladies wore flowing white dresses with a blue tartan sash over the left shoulder, and the gentlemen were in blue tartan kilts and white shirts with blue tartan ties.

Weever looked surprised and impressed. He liked good order and a splash of colour.

'The Tannadee Scottish country dancers!' barked Florence, making the whole thing sound like the orderly evacuation of a sinking ship.

Some of the dancers seemed a little overawed by the expensive surroundings and the presence of one so great as Gordon Weever. Others simply smiled politely, one or two acted with military poise, and one rather stiff gentleman carried himself like a puppet on strings.

Florence pointed to a bald dancer with a moustache. 'That man used to be two hundred pounds before I got to him. See him now – pronking like an antelope. Strip the Willow, that's the thing. Made a man of him. And that one there – tall and toothy – his feet were all over the place. In the Canadian Barn Dance, no backside was safe from his flailing feet. Not even the band. Now look at him: his feet can almost sing. And that one wiping his forehead – feet like flippers, he had. Now look at him: fleet as a ferret.'

'Well, a fine zoo you have here, Ms McTaggart.'

'Florence. They're a prize-winning ensemble, Gordon. They're punching well above their weight. And right now, you're weighing well above your punch. But we'll see to that, we'll see to that.'

Suddenly, Weever's head jerked back in alarm. 'Who's

13

that fat guy smiling at everybody? That's not Lord Tulloh, is it?'

'Patrick Tulloh indeed. He moves very well for a man of his age and figure – quite light on his feet. He took up dancing four months ago to immerse himself in Highland culture before he becomes chief of Clan McShellach – your clan. There's your very own chief over there.'

'What?!' yelped Weever. 'But… but that's what I'm doing; he can't do that. *I'm* going to be clan chief!'

'Oh? Well, well, well, looks like you're going to have to fight it out with dear old Patrick, the Lord Tulloh. A good old Highland tradition, that. I look forward to it.'

'The lousy creep. For hundreds of years, nobody's done anything about McShellach things – not even a tartan – then I come along and, hey presto, out they come: out of the woodwork like crawling insects. Slimeballs.'

'If this was hundreds of years ago, you and your rival would prove your fitness for the title of clan chief by your prowess in battle or by stealing another clan's cattle.'

'Well, he's gonna get a fight, that's for sure.'

'And quite a fight it will be, then – he's got the backing of the clan council, I believe.'

'Clan council?'

'Yes – several well-to-do members of your clan have got together, formed a council, and looked into the clan's history. They seem to have concluded that Patrick is their chief. And they're preparing a presentation for the Lord Lyon King of Arms.'

'The Lord what?'

'The Lord Lyon King of Arms; he's the King's officer in charge of heraldry and titles in Scotland.'

'One of them goofy guys in tights?'

'Tights or no tights, to be a clan chief you have to be recognised as such by the Lord Lyon King of Arms.'

'Tulloh's not fit even for consideration. Clan chief? Him? Can you imagine that leading you into battle? I'd slay him in seconds; chop him to pieces.'

Florence laughed. 'Oho – you had better sharpen your broadsword, doughty warrior. Patrick might be more of a warrior than you think.' She looked quickly at her watch, then stepped forward to thank everyone. 'A resplendent turnout as usual, ladies and gentlemen,' she declared. 'Don't they look magnificent, Gordon?'

Weever bit his lip and got to his feet. 'A great honour to welcome you all here today, ladies and gentlemen,' he announced with a professional smile. 'You gentlemen – boy oh boy, do you look great. Really great. But, ladies, ladies, ladies, I must single you out for your—'

'Right, Gordon, we're off!' broke in Florence. 'Take your partners for the Gay Gordons!' She pressed the button on the sound equipment, then in one fluid movement she grabbed Weever's arms and escorted him into the circle of dancers. 'On your toes now, Gordon! Lift those buttocks!' commanded Florence, loud enough for all to hear. 'Two, three, and swivel! Lift those buttocks!'

With his mind on his buttocks and his swivel, Weever nearly disintegrated when a piercing 'Heeeee-yooch!' erupted right behind him. It was the toothy dancer, seemingly possessed. Weever broke free in alarm.

'What's wrong, Gordon?' asked Florence.

'Him – screaming like a demented parrot! Is he some kinda nutter?'

'It's tradition, Gordon. Every now and again you show your delight by cutting loose with a hee-yooch or two.'

'I should've been warned. Nobody told me about the hee-yooch! I thought he was off his head!'

'I thought you'd have known!'

Weever bit his lip and resumed dancing. Then, with the Gay Gordons successfully overcome, there came a livelier dance: the Dashing White Sergeant. With Weever in the mix, however, the Dashing White Sergeant became something more like the Hashing Black-and-Blue Sergeant; a dance in which one takes an alternative path through the steps, administering a crushed toe here, a poke in the eye there, and an occasional elbow in the earhole. Fortunately, the dancers, forewarned, were ready for him and nimbly avoided the worst of the floundering. Strip the Willow, though, proved a dance too far for Weever. Even Florence had to relent in the face of a man flushed, sweating and panting heavily. So, the company now free from the danger of a clumping assassin, gladly demonstrated what could be achieved by ordinary mortals full of enthusiasm and hours of practice.

Everyone then retired to the dining suite for refreshments and chatted cheerfully among themselves while Weever washed his face in the gentlemen's cloakroom. Washed and deodorised, Weever re-joined the dancers and accepted formal introductions in the manner of a royal personage attending a gala night at the theatre. The introduction to Lord Tulloh was very brief; almost non-existent, in fact: a squashed smile and a skim of the hand from Weever, prompting a puzzled, slightly apprehensive look from Lord Tulloh. However, there was one introduction which seemed to provide especial pleasure. She was Erica Heyden, a slim and elegant figure with a small white rose in her neat grey hair.

With all the introductions completed, Weever lost no time. Grabbing a coffee, he went straight for Erica Heyden, edging out the gentlemen conversing with her. 'What a wonderful dancer you are, Erica,' he declared.

But no sooner had he spoken than two loud bangs rent the air. It was Florence McTaggart bringing her hands together. 'Right, everyone!' she yelled. 'Gather round. I want to go over the arrangements for our performance at the Highland Night in Glen Cannich Castle tomorrow.'

Erica excused herself, and left Weever looking daggers at McTaggart. He turned to his general manager, Charlie Fairfoull, who some mistook for Weever's son, so similar did they look, except Fairfoull was genuinely handsome and had his own hair.

'That goddamn McTaggart!' hissed Weever. 'If you stuffed that into a cannon and fired it at North Korea, they'd sue for peace in a day.' As the dancers and McTaggart left, Weever rubbed his aching legs, then closed his eyes for a moment, seemingly in thanksgiving for a safe deliverance. 'Why in the name of heaven did I ever sign up to this? I should have you sacked for getting me into this.'

Fairfoull grinned. 'A clan chief that can't dance the classic Scottish dances is no clan chief at all. Florence said you did rather well for your first attempt in company and coming from her that's high praise indeed.'

'You've no idea what it cost me. God help my feet, my knees, my hips, my head – I'm wrecked. No wonder there's no clan chief right now: they probably all died in a Strip the Willow!'

'Fear not. You can do it, Gordon. The hard part's behind you now. Your body's fully primed.'

'She kept on saying she wanted me loose. Well, I tell you, I nearly cut loose. She's a she-devil. She looks at you with those eyeballs and it's like two nuclear warheads coming straight at you. She's trying to take possession of me. Look at what she's done to that lot – a bunch of hee-yooching nutters.'

'Not all of them – I saw your eyes on the lady with the white rose in her hair.'

Weever chuckled to himself, then drew a deep breath. 'Never come across anything quite like that before. So dainty – so very, very dainty. When she took my arm I thought she was floating. As light as a feather.'

'As light as a flame, perhaps. Maybe too dazzling and hot for you, Gordon. You could get burned.'

'What? You mean I can't handle her?'

'She's not your type, Gordon.'

'More smarts than me? That what you're saying?'

'I know a little about Erica Heyden – or Viggers, as was. She divorced Paul Viggers, the flat-pack furniture tycoon, and he was no pussycat.'

'Paul Viggers… rings a bell.'

'He was the one that put the "FU" in "furniture". Unofficial motto: "Caveat emptor." She cleaned him out.'

Weever rubbed his chin. 'Interesting. Often the worst kind, these ladies – or the best kind, as I see it,' he said with a lascivious grin.

'Now, now, Gordon, you're better than that.'

Weever tapped his nose and gave a wink. 'You bet. What else d'you know about her?'

'Well, I've only met her a couple of times. I met her right here in Tannadee, actually: last week, in the Co-op. I said hello and we spoke briefly.'

'About what?'

'Well, this and that, you know. She's got a cottage up on the hill, a bit beyond the outdoor centre; it's creamy white. In fact, you can see it from here. Look out the window and it's up on your left.'

Weever sprang to his feet and went quickly to the window. 'Does she… does she have a man in her life?' he asked without turning round.

'I have no idea. But if she hasn't, I suspect she's about to get one.'

'You're a very perceptive young man, Charlie. Tell me more.'

'Well, she's divorced, as I said—'

'Interests? Golf? Ponies? Shooting?'

'I dunno. If I remember rightly, she was some kind of academic… a historian? Yes, she lectured in history somewhere.'

'A historian? Brilliant; excellent. Just what I need. I'm hiring her. She's gonna get me my family history and my right to be chief of Clan McShellach. Did you hear McTaggart say that Lord Tulloh, that cringing wimp, is thinking *he* can be chief of Clan McShellach? My clan! *My clan!* The nerve. Well, he's got another think coming. I'll knock him clean out the park.'

'I also heard he's got the backing of the clan council. That'll take some overturning.'

'Stuff the clan council! I'm putting my faith in the people. Let them decide. I'm going on the social media, Charlie. I'll get the clan rising. I'll get me my votes.'

CHAPTER 3

When he'd dropped off Billy and the dog, Chizzie parked in one of Tannadee's little side streets and sat in the car awhile, pondering on what to do about Billy and the kidnapped dog.

Handing the dog in to the police would only cause further problems for Billy and the dog, and in any case, Billy would most likely run off with the dog. Keeping the dog would, however, weigh heavily on Chizzie. Telling Yolanda about it might prove helpful, but on the other hand, it could result in conflict.

And then there was Chizzie's father, Johnny: if he got word of an ill-treated dog, he could go incandescent. It could bring back all the painful memories of a few years ago when Johnny's dog had gone missing and was eventually found dead in a gamekeeper's snare. Since then, the very mention of the word 'gamekeeper' was enough to ignite the man. A former football manager and now a hotelier, Johnny was the kind of guy who could not only light up a room; he could heat up a room. Though only five feet six inches tall and balding, he was stocky and a force by nature.

Chizzie and Yolanda had recently set up home in Johnny's house next to the family hotel, and Johnny wasn't moving out until the annex was refurbished to accommodate him, so holding on to a secret was well-nigh impossible. And, as a newly married part-time teacher and part-time hotelier, Chizzie had a lot to lose, especially in a small place like Tannadee where there was no hiding place for the outlaw.

Despite all the disadvantages of living in a rural community, and in spite of Yolanda's father, Gordon Weever, using his billions and newly built exclusive resort nearby to try and put Chizzie's father out of business, Chizzie and Yolanda had committed to life in Tannadee. The decision was therefore forced upon him. There could be no secret: Yolanda and Johnny must be told. Or must they? Chizzie's head was going one way and his instincts another. What really mattered: slavish obedience to the law, or doing the right thing? He wasn't stealing a dog, after all: he was saving a dog. In his heart, he knew he was doing the right thing. Even now, his heart was heavy recalling the time when his dad's dog went missing and never made it home.

He opened the car door to let in some fresh air, hoping to clear his head. He leaned back, but he couldn't settle, so he sat upright again. To do the right thing by the law or the right thing by the dog? That was the question he turned over and over.

Then in the rear-view mirror, he spied a little Jack Russell terrier approaching the car. There was no owner in sight. He'd seen the dog around the village a couple of times. It passed him by and continued to the end of the lane, where it took an interest in a tiny bluish flower growing out of the stone wall. It sniffed the flower, then sneezed before lifting a leg and squirting onto the wall its own solution to plant nutrition, and then it trotted off round the corner.

Chizzie smiled. 'A dog o' independent mind,' he muttered, paraphrasing Robert Burns. 'That settles it,' he said, slapping the steering wheel. 'The dog wins!' Yolanda and Johnny would be told, and the dog would stay until its welfare was secured. At least, that's what he hoped.

When he got home, Chizzie was surprised to hear Yolanda's laugh coming from the living room. He went straight there and entered, shutting the door immediately on seeing that Candy the budgie was out. Not that the bird was likely to escape while her beak was fixed on uprooting the last few hairs from Johnny's head.

'How did you get here so quickly?' Chizzie asked, pleasantly surprised.

'Vicki's got a brand-new electric car, and she knows the road really well,' explained Yolanda. 'Though I have to say, it's nice to be on terra firma again. You said you had a problem with the car.'

'Well, sort of,' said Chizzie. 'It's a bit complicated, really.'

'I keep telling you it's time to ditch that old thing,' Johnny interrupted. 'Get an electric car like Vicki. It's bad for our image with you rattling about in that old crate.'

'Actually, the car's perfectly fine. I only said the car because the reality is complicated, as I said. I'll explain but let me get a coffee first. How did your conference go?'

'Excellent,' replied Yolanda. 'Can't wait to get started; a lot of form-filling ahead, though.'

'She wants a chunk of my golf course for solar panels,' said Johnny, with the budgie now on his finger.

'You don't have a golf course, Father,' Chizzie reminded

him. 'You have a parcel of ground on which you imagine a golf course.'

'You'll have enough for a nine-holer,' Yolanda assured him. 'That'll be much more manageable.'

Johnny turned and put the budgie back in its cage. 'Well, I suppose you're right,' he said, and sighed.

'Right,' said Chizzie, 'I'm having a coffee. Anyone else?'

Yolanda said yes; Johnny said no. Chizzie picked up the empty mugs and headed for the kitchen.

As he waited for the new coffee machine to produce the goods, Chizzie contemplated the best way of introducing Yolanda and his father to the fact that they were now in the company of a felon.

Then the doorbell rang and Chizzie rushed to answer it. He had a shrewd idea as to who it would be. And indeed it was Paw, Billy's dad. A worried look hung on his craggy, weather-beaten face. `He wanted to know more about the dog and what Billy had got himself into. Chizzie led the way through to the living room and offered him a coffee, which he declined, being focused on the need to get things sorted. While the other three exchanged pleasantries, Chizzie fetched the coffees, then sat down next to Yolanda on the sofa and gave his account of the day's events, emphasising that the thug had been cruel to the dog, had thrown a golf trolley into the river, and had assaulted a young lad.

This did nothing to comfort Paw: he became even more agitated. 'Billy says he'll run away with the dog if we get the police. He doesn't like the law at the best of times, so I know he means it.'

Johnny too was agitated; the painful loss of his own

dog looming large in his mind. 'We have to get the police in,' he advised.

'No!' insisted Paw. 'Billy'll run off.'

'And what's more,' added Chizzie, 'Billy could be charged with stealing a dog.'

'Well, he did, didn't he?' argued Johnny. 'You can't change the facts.'

Yolanda held up a hand to calm things down. 'Maybe the dog was already kidnapped. We don't know who the real owner is, and we don't know if the police would simply return the dog to the thug.'

Chizzie nodded. 'We have a choice. We obey the letter of the law or we do what's right.'

Silence fell. Paw had already made up his mind and looked anxiously at the others. Johnny rubbed his forehead; Yolanda leaned back, looking pensive; and Chizzie, who, like Paw, already had an answer, sat still, willing everyone to make the right decision.

Johnny rubbed his chin, then delivered his verdict. 'You're right, you're right,' he said. 'The dog's the thing. The law can wait; we'll find what's best for that poor dog. How's it doing now?'

Paw brightened with relief. 'The dog and Billy are gettin' on great. Too great, even. He won't give it up easy. Gotta be the right owner done right.'

'I agree,' said Yolanda. 'We need to get things absolutely right. Take some time. At least a couple of days.'

Chizzie was delighted. 'I'll take her to old vet Sandison and he can check her over and scan her microchip, if there is one.'

'Won't that get him into trouble?' asked Yolanda.

'He retired long ago,' said Johnny. 'He knows what's right and he has the right connections.'

Next day, Sandison, the retired vet, phoned to say that the dog's owner was Joseph Casey of 59C Broomhill Crescent in Millburgh. The phone number was a landline number.

Over the kitchen table, Chizzie and Yolanda discussed their plan of action. Yolanda felt that caution was vital: 'Firstly we need to know if Casey is Maserati Man, or perhaps he's the grieving owner of a stolen dog. If the latter, Casey's house could be under surveillance by persons unknown.'

Chizzie nodded. 'Yeah, we're going to have to go political.'

Yolanda's eyebrows shot up. 'You want politicians involved?'

'Not exactly. I refer to Denis Dekker, the chippy. He's putting himself up as a candidate in the Millburgh Council by-election; the area includes the Broomhill estate. We can distribute some leaflets for him. That way, we get direct access to Joseph Casey, while appearing to be perfectly normal.'

Yolanda thought for a second. 'Good thinking, Sherlock.'

'I'll ask Denis to bring his van with the slogan on it. He's got a big sign on the van's roof, saying, "Vote Dekker: the Middle-of-the-Road Candidate." It looks good. We can phone Casey's number a few minutes before we start delivering to make sure he's at home. Then if he's in, we move in.'

'If he's not in?'

'We leaflet Broomhill Court – it's very small.'

'Right, if it's on, I'll take Casey's side of the street – Maserati Man's never seen me.'

'Well… it could be a little dangerous, don't you think?'

'Maybe – a little, perhaps.'

Chizzie weighed the odds. Should he allow Yolanda to take any kind of risk, even if little? Better if he took the risk. On the other hand, he might come face to face with Maserati Man – then what?

'I take Casey's door,' insisted Yolanda. 'Much safer for me than you.'

'Hmm, okay. I'll get on to Denis and get some leaflets.'

'Ask Denis about his policies so we can appear like the real deal.'

'Policies? Denis? He's probably only doing it to get publicity for his chip shops.'

'He's bound to have something to say beyond "Buy more chips."'

'I wouldn't bet on it. He's an Independent, I know that. But more than that I don't know, and frankly, I don't think he knows either. If people ask for policies we can just be vague – you know the sort of thing: "We want to make the world a better place", "Our kids are the future", that kind of thing.'

'Does he have a chance of getting elected?'

'None whatsoever.'

'Good. We can't do any harm, then.'

Chizzie and Yolanda went to the chip shop and offered their services to Denis Dekker, whose delight at gaining two volunteer canvassers was made manifest in the shape of a free fish supper for Chizzie and a vegetarian burger for Yolanda.

'I'm surprised you've never heard of Joe Casey, though,' said Denis. 'One of the infamous Fighting Caseys. The others died some years ago. Joe died only two weeks ago; it was in the papers. He was the only one of them with any sense, but he was well known to the police. I get all the info from the police lads when they come in for their chips. They tell me his daughter, Caitlin, has come up from down south somewhere to sort out Joe's affairs.'

'Why would anyone be desperate to have his dog?' Yolanda asked.

'Breeding, maybe,' answered Denis.

'The dog's a mongrel,' said Chizzie. 'It can't be anything to do with breeding. Unless you like lucky dip.'

Outside in the street, with no one about, Chizzie surmised that Maserati Man might be Caitlin's boyfriend.

Yolanda shrugged. 'Or she might have nothing to do with him.'

'Maybe,' said Chizzie. 'But whatever the case, it's too risky to discuss things on the doorstep. He might be in the house, listening.'

'I'll write a quick note explaining the position,' Yolanda suggested, 'and if she seems likely to be receptive, I'll pass it to her. Then we clear off.'

Chizzie and Yolanda approached Broomhill Crescent in the dark of evening looking sprightly and purposeful, like people charged with ideology and political fervour, while Dekker cruised the streets with his old van. He'd even managed to recruit other canvassers who covered neighbouring streets.

'Probably people who'd been promised free fish and chips for life,' suggested Chizzie.

As agreed, Yolanda took the odd numbers while Chizzie took the even ones, thus allowing Yolanda to knock on Casey's door. For the most part the houses in Broomhill Crescent were small 1950s apartment blocks comprising two flats on the ground floor and two above with a common stairway in the middle. There were fewer houses on the even-numbered side since a large car park occupied the last quarter of it. It meant that Chizzie was able to finish before Yolanda. He crossed the road and assisted Yolanda until they reached Number 59. At first, Chizzie was reassured to note that there was no Maserati around. But then it occurred to him that if you had a Maserati you wouldn't park it in a street like this, where it would almost certainly meet the morning looking like macaroni. Just as Chizzie was about to move off, a Ford Transit van turned slowly into the cul-de-sac. As it drew closer, Chizzie took cover behind a parked van. Yolanda watched sidelong, making as if to count her leaflets.

'The driver of the van's a middle-aged man with a younger man in the passenger seat,' Yolanda whispered before deliberately dropping some leaflets, then attempting to pick them up.

The van turned in the turning bay at the end of the street, then cruised slowly by, causing Chizzie's heart to beat faster. But the occupants of the van didn't seem particularly interested in Yolanda or himself. So maybe they were just lost, or maybe they were just political rivals out to spy on opponents. Then again, maybe they were just very good at surveillance.

The Casey flat was on the upper left. Yolanda looked up.

'Anybody at the window?' Chizzie asked nervously, now counting his own leaflets.

'Nope,' replied Yolanda. 'Onwards and upwards.'

They stepped into the common hallway. Instantly, a gunshot echoed round the concrete walls. Chizzie and Yolanda froze in alarm. But it was only a stiff door bursting open as two elderly ladies emerged and came ambling into the hallway, one with a fur coat on.

As Chizzie's jangled nerves calmed down, he gathered enough of his wits to offer a leaflet. 'Hope we can count on your vote?' he uttered with a nervous laugh.

Yolanda smiled dutifully at the ladies and went to the other flat on the ground floor.

The lady examined the leaflet. 'This is your candidate?' she scoffed incredulously, pointing at Dekker's photo. 'He looks more like one of the toughs that come and go in the flat above me. If he wants my vote, he needs to stop the council dumping all their problem cases on our street.'

'Gone right downhill, it has,' bristled the lady in the fur coat, levelling her eyes at Chizzie, who was clearly to blame.

'I'll just note that down,' said Yolanda, returning and producing a small notebook and pencil.

'And another thing – potholes!' declared the fur-coated lady. 'They're everywhere here. The only thing that can make it along this street in one piece is a kangaroo!' The echoing 'rooo!' carried like a distant wolf baying at the moon.

Chizzie felt his heart thump. The wolf noise might just

excite Maserati Man and bring him running down the stairs, eager to join the pack.

'And while you're at it,' broke in the householder, 'dog doodah!'

Chizzie blinked.

'Poo!' explained the coated woman, again producing an echo like a baying wolf in a cave.

Having now engaged in all the politics he could stand, Chizzie thanked the ladies for their time and led Yolanda off up the stairs. Halfway up, they stopped to calm themselves and focus on the real objective of their visit to this building.

'Are you sure you want to go ahead with this?' Chizzie asked.

Yolanda was in no doubt. 'Of course,' she said. 'I haven't come all this way to back out now.'

Chizzie smiled wryly. 'Well, you've more guts than I have.'

Yolanda kissed him on the cheek. 'Onwards and upwards. *Courage, mon brave.*'

They continued up the stairs, trying to keep the echoing of their footfall low. The footsteps of the fur-coated woman departing below sounded louder than their own, though it was hard not to sound like a horse in such an echoing building.

Chizzie remained at the top of the stairway as Yolanda moved swiftly but quietly to the door with the name 'Casey' on it. She took a deep breath and rang the bell. Chizzie listened carefully. His gaze met a stain on the stair at his feet: it looked like it had once been tea or wine, or – more worryingly – blood.

The door opened, thankfully without a bang. Chizzie watched discreetly from round the corner as Yolanda edged forwards and introduced herself.

A young woman's voice replied pleasantly, 'I'm not a registered voter here.'

'Are you Caitlin Casey?' Yolanda asked.

The young woman's tone changed to alarm as she answered, 'Yes.'

'Then this is for you,' said Yolanda, handing over her note.

The young woman took the note and read it before locking eyes with Yolanda. A smell of tasty stew or boiling soup suffused the air; very homely, but the young woman was anything but welcoming. 'Just who are you?' she asked abruptly. 'Is this some kind of ransom note?'

'No,' Yolanda assured her softly, shaking her head. 'It's just what the note says.'

The young woman hesitated, then snapped, 'You take me for a mug. Well, just clear off or it'll be the worse for you!'

'But—'

'Clear off!' shouted the young woman, before turning back into the flat. 'Alex!' she cried. 'Call the police! The goons are here!' Then she turned to Yolanda. 'Clear off now! Or Alex'll punch your lights out.'

That was it for Yolanda. She turned and walked speedily away. Down the concrete stairs she and Chizzie fled, their clattering feet echoing like a drum roll.

Suddenly a door burst open with a bang and a woman shouted, 'You noisy prats! I'm not voting for you now. Clear off!'

Out on the pavement, Chizzie and Yolanda continued running until finally, halfway up the street, they looked back and were relieved to see they were in the clear.

'What d'you make of it?' Chizzie asked, puffing and leaning on a car. Its alarm screamed into life, and he and Yolanda went speeding off again. Round the corner, they got into their car and drove off.

'The Casey girl sounded as scared as we were,' said Chizzie with the exhilaration that comes from having pulled off a daring deed unscathed.

'Scared with good reason, I'm sure,' replied Yolanda quietly. 'But she'll be in touch.'

'How d'you know?'

'Her eyes.'

CHAPTER 4

As Weever eased himself out of the car, the moonlight sparkled off his belt buckle, his bejewelled skean dhu, and the large brooch that secured the plaid over his shoulder. The aspiring clan chief had spared no item of adornment. In his Highland bonnet he wore a sprig of the local heather; his Jacobite shirt was fashionably open at the neck; his kilt was of the right length; his badger-hair sporran, though large, was not actually in the roadkill bracket; and the woollen socks and brogues completed the ensemble. He clumped powerfully into the hall with log-chopping strides. Charlie Fairfoull walked more discreetly behind him, like a valet. The lights were being dimmed, but up they came again to greet the great man. Sitting next to the great man, Charlie looked impressively Highland, but there was no mistaking who was meant to be the chief.

The evening began with a display of sword-dancing accompanied by loud bagpipes that brought an occasional grimace from the great man. Then came the singing, lots of it – the usual flood of dirges and laments in which Scots love to wallow. In the Scottish psyche, there is no song of victory that can compare with the bliss and sheer pleasure of total disaster. Once the singing had wrought every tear from the audience, a couple of agriculturally orientated comedians attempted to restore some uplift, with results that would produce famine if their husbandry were of equal merit. However, when the Scottish country dancers took the floor to close the show, Weever brightened, looking sharp and keen-eyed, for here, as he had anticipated, was the opportunity to meet Erica Heyden at the buffet supper.

The show over, Weever made his move. 'Looking fantastic, Erica. Tremendous, wonderful, really magnificent,' he purred, wielding a chief-sized plateload of stovies.

Erica smiled graciously. 'Well, thank you, Gordon. But I must say, my magnificence pales into insignificance before your towering luminescence.'

'Why thank you, thank you, so very kind, so very kind. It helps, of course, if you happen to be wearing one of Bonnie Prince Charlie's very own shirts.'

'You mean the real thing?'

'Absolutely.'

'Oh, I wasn't aware that Bonnie Prince Charlie was quite your... your build.'

Weever hesitated for a second. 'Well, you know, of course, if you're judging by paintings, they never show the real guy. Paint the real guy and you're dead meat – out of business. Never work again. If you want to see the real guy, add twenty pounds.'

'Only twenty?'

Weever looked stunned for a moment. Then a smile broke across his face. 'Look, I'm getting into the part. I want to be chief of Clan McShellach; I can be a great chief. I can lead my clan out of the shadows and into the limelight. We can be a great clan and a great brand, like the McDonalds.'

'McShellach Shellfish?'

'Yeah… yeah. Why not? The world's our oyster.'

Erica grimaced.

But Weever was flowing: 'Can you believe there's next to nothing written about Clan McShellach? Can you believe that? Clan McShellach – the great sons of the willow? Well, I'm changing all that. And that's where you come in, Erica. I know there's chiefs in my family history somewhere. There's got to be. I need a historian to find them, and I need the best. I want you. I have a rival, you see.'

'I know – Patrick, the Lord Tulloh.'

'The very one. He thinks it's in the bag. He's got the votes of some self-appointed clan council, but that's not democracy. If they want a vote, they need *all* the votes. And I'm gonna get them. I'm working on it. But there's dirty tricks in play, and most of the votes are going to the wimp Tulloh. I need to swing that around pronto.'

'That could be difficult. You haven't a proven ancestral link to a clan chief. Patrick Tulloh has such a link.'

'I am all the proof you need. Living proof. Look at me – there's "chief" written all over me. What's he got written all over him? "Loser!" He's ridiculous! I must be chief.'

'You need to offer proof to the Lord Lyon King of Arms, and it needs to be more than simply "I look chiefy." You need proof, and you need a PR campaign.'

'Right then; how about you get me the proof and the PR? I want the best.'

Erica laughed. 'Well, I have to say I'm very flattered, Mr Weever.'

'Gordon. Name your price.'

Erica laughed again. 'No price, Gordon. But yes, I

would be very happy to help. Certainly I could do some preliminary work in return for occasional access to your country club. How's that sound?'

'You can have all the access you like, Erica. Come every day if you like; you're absolutely welcome, absolutely. Anytime you like. I am completely disposable to you.'

'That's settled, then.'

He went to kiss her on the lips, but she gave him her cheek.

CHAPTER 5

The following morning, Chizzie and Yolanda were sitting in Johnny's office, discussing the advertising and promotions budget for the hotel. The phone rang, but Johnny let it ring until his recorded voice broke in and invited the caller to leave a message. When the call finished, Johnny replayed it immediately on speaker. The caller was Lord Tulloh desiring to know if Chizzie and Yolanda would accept an invitation to tea at three o'clock that afternoon.

'I think that would be lovely,' said Yolanda cheerfully, the sunlight glowing in her auburn hair.

'Whoa, whoa there,' snapped Johnny. 'He wants something. You don't just phone out of the blue and invite people to tea at short notice unless there's some ulter... ulter... underhand motive.'

Chizzie felt peeved. 'Well, even so, there's no harm in finding out. If you'll pass me the phone, I'll let him know we're coming.'

'No!' barked Johnny. 'No – he can talk the hind legs off a donkey, that man. You'll be on the phone for hours, and I want this budget finalised today, so we press on, get it done, then you phone.'

Just after three o'clock, Chizzie and Yolanda sat down to tea and cakes in Lord Tulloh's small summer house on the highest part of his garden grounds. Lord Tulloh was a rather reserved but genial middle-aged man, average height, with ruddy cheeks and ears and a puffy face. The upper half of his head was covered with woolly grey hair in the cumulo-nimbus style. Also woolly was his knitted cardigan in beige featuring a pattern of different coloured butterflies on the front.

Tulloh explained, 'I have been approached by a body of people from various parts of the world. They want me to be their clan chief – chief of Clan McShellach. The clan's ancestral lines are thin and fragmented, and the line of chief is something of a mystery, but apparently I have the most plausible connection to the clan chiefs of old.'

Chizzie nodded. 'Wonderful.'

'Wonderful but troubling,' continued Tulloh. 'As you know, I have allowed myself to fall before the simplest of foes – gambling and the demon drink – so I have to ask myself, *Am I fit to be a clan chief?*'

'You beat all your foes, Patrick. You're a free man now,' said Yolanda.

'You're never free once you've yielded to those devils.'

'You've done the hard bit. You've believed in yourself. You believed you could do it and you did.'

Chizzie agreed. 'You set yourself free, Patrick – to be clan chief, if that's what you want to be.'

Tulloh sighed. 'I'd love to be clan chief; I just don't think I'm up to it, or even worthy of consideration.'

'You're more than worthy,' advised Yolanda. 'Certainly more worthy than my father.'

'And that's another thing,' continued Tulloh. 'I know your father wants desperately to be clan chief. And despite everything, I really haven't the heart to disappoint him. He so wants it.'

'No, Patrick, no,' insisted Yolanda. 'My father would be the worst clan chief ever. Within six months he'd be a god. Vlad the Impaler, Ivan the Terrible, Attila the Hun – they'd be nothing compared to my father. He craves attention, and he'd bring a whole lot of it to our clan and possibly even the whole nation. None of it complimentary. This is an ego trip for him. In his dreams he's probably leading the charge at Bannockburn. And he won't take kindly to anyone getting in the way.'

'Oh dear. In that case, I withdraw. I do not like confrontation.'

'Most of us don't,' replied Yolanda. 'But we need you. I implore you, Patrick, take the title, for the sake of your clansfolk.'

'Well… maybe. I'll think it over a bit more. There's yet another problem, though: I'm actually rather shy. I used to be very sociable, my diary was full, but with all the gambling and drink, I've lost all my confidence and I like the quiet life now. A chief needs to be outgoing; he needs to be meeting clansfolk, helping them, and above all giving them pride in their own identity, a self-belief – the very self-belief that I have lacked for years.'

Chizzie shook his head. 'Not anymore, Patrick. You've won your battle – and you can do the same for others.'

Yolanda put down her cup. 'Why did you bring us here, particularly to the summer house? Not just for the view, I suspect.'

'You're very shrewd, Yolanda,' replied Tulloh. 'Yes,

I brought you here because with you two here, in the presence of one other, I felt I could make a firm decision on my fitness to become clan chief.'

Chizzie looked about. 'You say, "one other". You mean Donald?'

'No, Donald is away in Spain, tending his mother. He said the decision about the chieftainship was entirely for me to make. We discussed it but he offered no opinion, saying only that he believed I could do it.'

'Then who is the other you speak of?'

'The other is what you see before you and all around you: the terroir, as they say in France.'

'Terroir as in vineyards?'

'The same.'

'You're not planning a distillery?'

Lord Tulloh laughed ironically. 'Oh Lord, no! No, no. That would be the death of me. What I'm trying to say is that everything you see before you is part of our clan. The unique character of the land, the air, the water and the life here – they quietly shape us. The Gaels historically never regarded land as property: what they saw was part of their greater self; part of the family. We're not a big clan and our land has always been rather small – but we knew it, it was our home, it nurtured us, we're part of it and it's part of us. The question for me is: *Am I man enough to embody that greater self and all that it means?* I really don't know. I think… I think I'm just too shy. Your father is so much stronger; maybe I should just give way.'

Yolanda was adamant. 'No, no. No way. You think my father cares about terroir and community? It never enters his head. For him it's all about big-shot chief Gordon

41

Weever. You have every reason to be chief, and my father is one of those reasons.'

Lord Tulloh turned his head towards the sweep of the glen below, then drew in a large breath. Then he closed his eyes and let his breath go. Deep in silent thought, he bowed his head. To Chizzie it was like watching a man undergoing some kind of transformation: nothing visible, no sound, but a lot happening. Finally, Tulloh opened his eyes and turned towards Yolanda and nodded, saying, softly but very resolutely, 'Thank you, Yolanda. I will stand. I will do it. I will offer myself for chief of Clan McShellach.'

'Marvellous!' declared Yolanda.

'Bravo, Patrick! Hail to the chief!' cried Chizzie.

'I'll go and talk reason to my father,' chirped Yolanda.

Tulloh grimaced. 'Then again… maybe I should just think it over a bit more. I'm… I'm just not sure.'

Yolanda answered, with a chastening smile, 'Don't overthink it, Patrick. You go and dust off your sporran.'

Yolanda decided to call on her father that evening, reckoning that a surprise visit would likely see him relatively relaxed and malleable. After a quick phone call to her father, she drove over to his house and met him in the drawing room.

'Hi, Dad, how are you?' she said, going to him and kissing his cheek.

Weever returned the affection but was wary. 'Nice to see you again, Yolanda. Even nicer if this is entirely social.'

'We'll get there, Dad, we'll get there.'

They sat down near the bar. Yolanda declined a drink,

but Weever got himself a whisky and soda. Then he made himself comfortable in a big leather chair and took a sip.

'So, sounds like this is some kind of business meeting. What's the deal?'

'The deal is, please let Patrick Tulloh be chief of our clan.'

Weever nearly choked on his whisky. 'What?!' he gargled, before eyeing Yolanda sternly, his face reddening as he took a deep breath. Then, quietly but angrily, he moaned, 'Always on my case, Yolanda. Always on my case. Always rooting for somebody else. That's not right. Back me for once. I've got blood in this game. And you're my flesh and blood.'

'It's not a game, Dad. Identity and ancestry matter to people.'

'Of course they do. That's the point. It matters to *me*. And the people round here matter to me – we share blood. I want the very best for them, and the best is me, and that's a fact. I am the best there is. It's my duty. I'm called to it.'

'You're hearing your own echo.'

'No. No. I feel it; I feel it too. It's destiny calling.'

'It's fantasy!'

'Why don't you ever back me? All you ever do is shoot me down. It's your mother, isn't it? She's twisted your mind against me.'

'Nothing to do with Mother. Supporting you doesn't always mean agreeing with you. If you make the wrong move, I say so. That's caring, Dad.'

'You never back me.'

'You pick the right battles, I'll back you. But this isn't one of them. Please don't fight Patrick for clan chief. With him as chief, it's good for him, it's good for you and it's good for Clan McShellach.'

'Wrong! You can't fight nature. I am a natural leader. It's in me. It *is* me. I'm a natural winner. It's a no-brainer. What's he? He's a natural loser.'

'Patrick's a winner. He fought gambling and alcohol and he won. In spite of you, I might add. Patrick is a fighter.'

'Fighter? He's a dancer! Imagine him leading the clan into battle – charging in, knocking 'em dead with a Strip the Willow.'

'Patrick fought his demons and won, which is more than can be said for you. Goodbye.' And with that, Yolanda got to her feet and stomped out the door.

Echoing down the hall came her father's angry voice: 'I fought bigger battles and won!'

Yolanda ignored it and wiped a tear from her eye.

CHAPTER 6

The brief exchange at Caitlin Casey's door had proven more productive than Chizzie had expected. Two days after visiting the Casey home, Yolanda received the email she was waiting for, though the sender's identity, GutsyGorilla1001, was not quite the sort of thing she had expected.

'I don't think giving Caitlin Casey your email address was actually a good idea,' said Chizzie.

Yolanda smiled. 'It's an old one I rarely use. Anything new that appears on it will be from her. She needs to be sure she's doing the right thing. She doesn't know if I'm for her or against her. There're nasty people circling around her. She needs time to think things over.'

The message was very brief: it simply gave a mobile phone number and asked Yolanda to phone at four o'clock. At the appointed time, Yolanda put the phone on speaker and made the call with Chizzie at her side.

'Can you meet me today at Glendochy Wood?' Caitlin Casey asked. 'It's five miles north-west of Millburgh.'

'I know it,' said Yolanda. 'What time?'

'Six o'clock?'

Yolanda looked enquiringly at Chizzie, who nodded. 'That's fine, Caitlin.'

'Good. You park in the main car park at the east end,

and I'll park at the old monument on the west side. Then we meet at the top at the ruined tower at six. I'll be in running gear: orange T-shirt and green shorts.'

'Oh, you're a runner? So am I.'

'Well, not so much a runner as a fitness freak.'

'Yeah. Me too. In that case, I'll be running too. Blue top, blue shorts.'

There was a faint chuckle. 'Right, see you there.'

Yolanda was sure this was no trap, but Chizzie wasn't so sure.

'What makes you so sure?' he asked.

'The tone of voice.'

'That's not a lot to go on.'

'It's enough to tip the scales for me.'

'I'm coming with you.'

'Of course you are. I need an escape plan and you're part of it.'

'So much for the tone of voice.'

'I didn't say I was absolutely sure, just confident enough to agree a meeting where I have options. We've been to Glendochy Wood often enough to know the paths in and out. If we take our bikes instead of the car, we can escape along the cycle trail.'

At 5.40, Yolanda and Chizzie were within sight of the meeting place at the top of Glendochy Wood. They carried their bikes into the high bracken growing thickly beneath the trees and laid them down.

As planned, Chizzie jogged towards the meeting place like someone keeping fit. There was no one else around. He listened intently. He heard nothing other than a wood pigeon nearby. If there was someone poking about in the trees, that bird would not be there, he thought. On the other hand, he was there, and the bird was hanging around, so that theory went out the window. Satisfied as much as he could be that there was no imminent threat, Chizzie jogged back to Yolanda. They waited quietly, enjoying the cooing of two wood pigeons and the fresh, almost cucumber-like smell of the still air; a hint of autumn settling in. Then, with five minutes to rendezvous time, Yolanda slipped out of the undergrowth and jogged towards the rendezvous spot. Chizzie watched through the bracken fronds. He saw a figure arrive shortly after Yolanda stopped jogging. The figure wore orange and green. They engaged in conversation.

After a few minutes, Yolanda called to Chizzie and beckoned him to join her and Caitlin. Caitlin likewise called to someone in the direction from which she had come. They all laughed as the four of them came together – neophytes in the world of subterfuge. Yolanda introduced Chizzie to her new acquaintances, Caitlin and Jenna. Caitlin was tall and slim with a broad, friendly face. She wore her dark hair in a ponytail. Jenna, in black T-shirt and black shorts, was smaller and broader with sharper features and close-cropped bleached hair. Jenna recognised Yolanda from her race in the Highland Games a few months earlier, but she did not recognise Chizzie. Caitlin revealed that she was a garden designer and landscaper, while Jenna was a self-employed plumber and gas fitter who also played football for Millburgh Women's Football Club.

Taking a sombre tone, Caitlin explained how the grey dog came to be so important. 'My father lived on the edge of the criminal fraternity,' she said with a sigh. 'He specialised in hiding loot. He's stashed away some kind of loot belonging to thugs by the name of Gorrie – probably drugs or stolen jewellery. My dad was very fit, so he was able to cycle widely and hide things in remote places. He took Peggy, his dog, with him everywhere. He always used to say that if ever he forgot where he'd hidden things, Peggy would know. She would get excited and dig at the spot. With Dad's eyesight failing, Peggy was all the more valuable to him. Unfortunately, I didn't get on with my dad. We had row after row, so I left and went to Glasgow mainly to get away from all the mayhem, but also to learn garden design. Then about a year later, I got a call informing me that my dad, at the age of fifty-six and in the prime of life, had suffered a major brain haemorrhage and lapsed into a coma. He died never having regained consciousness. The thugs he was working for got to him before he went into the coma, but they seem to be short of vital information. They broke into Dad's house. They turned the place over and took the dog and some stuff. You don't really want to be a part of all this, I'm sure, but if you could possibly hold on to Peggy for a few days, I could get myself sorted out without the thugs getting in my way.'

Yolanda looked at Chizzie, who nodded. 'No problem,' said Yolanda. 'We're happy to look after Peggy for however long it takes.'

Caitlin hugged first Yolanda, then Chizzie. 'Thank you. Thank you so much. I'm sorry I frightened you at my door. There was no Alex to punch your lights out. It was all a bluff.'

Yolanda smiled. 'I understand. Nice move.'

Jenna too offered her gratitude: 'Any plumbing you want fixing, you just let me know. Free of charge; on the house – or, better still, *in* the house.'

'That's very kind of you,' said Yolanda. 'Can you tell us anything else about the thugs, the Gorries?'

Caitlin obliged. 'The Gorrie brothers and their sidekick Ally Muirhead are petty burglars and drug dealers. Dean Gorrie's the hitman: big guy with a small crocodile tattoo on his neck. Greg Gorrie's slightly older and more sophisticated, if you can say that about a criminal. They fall out a lot and don't speak to each other for a while. When they fall out, they communicate through Ally Muirhead. Last time they were jailed they'd more or less shopped each other.'

CHAPTER 7

'You're in the news!' declared Johnny Bryson the next day as he entered the living room carrying two newspapers. 'In the *Perthshire Advertiser* and *The Courier*.'

'Me?' asked Chizzie.

'The dog. There are ads in Lost and Found.' Johnny raised one of the papers close to his face and adjusted his reading glasses. 'Says here, "Medium-size grey dog with longish hair. Spaniel/terrier cross. Six years old. Answers to Peggy. Much-loved family pet. Lost in Perth. One hundred pounds reward."'

'Who's the contact?'

'A box number. No ad in the *Millburgh Express*, though, so seems like they don't quite know where to look.'

'Well, that's a relief.'

'Not really. Bruce Sandison, the vet, saw the ads and phoned a few minutes ago. He says you'll need to hand the dog over to the police now.'

Chizzie shook his head. 'No. No way. She won't be safe if the thugs get her. That's not on.'

'Well, Bruce insists. It's the law.'

'The law, the law. The law's a secondary consideration here. We're talking about the dog's welfare. I'm going over to see Billy now; he'll need to know about the ad.'

Chizzie found Billy chopping some logs. He laid down his axe when he saw Chizzie.

'How you doin'?' he called.

'I'm fine, Billy. How are you?'

'Fine.'

'And Peggy? How's she doing?'

'She's fine too. She's round here somewhere.' Billy turned his head towards the small barn and called, 'Peggy! Peggy!'

A short-haired, brownish dog came trotting out of the barn.

'Who's that?' asked Chizzie.

'It's Peggy,' replied Billy proudly.

'Uh? What happened?' exclaimed Chizzie.

'She's had a haircut – and a hair dye.'

'Who did that?'

'Me.'

'Dyed her with what?'

'It's called henna. Mary Boone gave me it a while back. She said I'd suit brown hair – good camouflage. Paw said there's an advert in the papers. The bad guys are after Peggy.'

Chizzie blew out his lips. 'Well, you sure fooled me… maybe… yeah, maybe henna's actually a good thing.'

'Brilliant. Got everybody fooled. Bet if you put Peggy in front of a mirror, she'd think she was somebody else.'

'We'll need to be careful all the same. No more walks in public places. Use the Weever estate – the golf course.'

'The Weever man doesn't like me.'

'Yolanda will see to that, don't worry.'

'I was goin' to take Peggy for a walk when I'm through choppin'.'

'Okay, I'll help you stack and then we'll all go for a walk with Yolanda. I must get back to the hotel first, though. You're on bar lunches, that right?'

'Yeah.'

'Right – phone when you're ready. See you in a bit.'

Chizzie and Billy met Yolanda at the main gate of the Weever estate, where they let Peggy off the lead. As they passed the main house, now named McShellach House, the zipping sound of a hastily opened window drew the attention of the walking party. The man at the first-storey window was Gordon Weever in pyjamas.

'Hold it, Yolanda!' he shouted. 'What's going on?'

'Good morning, Father. I'm exercising my right to roam.'

'You roam where you like, but the others – they clear off.'

'They do nothing of the kind. I will continue walking with my dear husband and my very good friends Billy and Peggy.'

Weever pointed at Chizzie. '*He* is not allowed on Weever property – you know that. And your so-called "friends" are not welcome either.'

'Are you coming down to evict us in your pyjamas? Why are you in pyjamas anyway? Are you sick?'

'Me? Sick? Hah! Never better. I was up late last night doing deals in three continents; more than most twenty-year-olds could do in a week. Now turn around or I call security.'

As Weever spoke, Florence McTaggart came striding up the drive.

Yolanda smiled and addressed her father. 'Your dancing teacher has arrived. Better get yourself dressed quickly.'

Weever looked aghast, then slammed the window shut and pulled the curtains closed.

Yolanda turned towards the advancing dancing instructor. 'He's slept in, Florence! Might need a little coaxing.'

'Is he ill?'

'Perfectly healthy! Never better!'

'Right, thanks, Yolanda,' replied Florence. 'I'll see to him!' And she strode with menacing purpose towards the Weever door.

Billy furrowed his brow. 'Why is your dad always so angry?'

'A whole bunch of reasons, Billy,' said Yolanda. 'Basically, when he's here he misses the hurly-burly, and when he's in the hurly-burly, he misses here.'

'And he doesn't like me,' added Chizzie. 'He won't accept that Yolanda and I are married. He's banned me from his property.'

'A sad man,' said Billy.

Yolanda laughed. 'Sad only for as long as he wants to be. He's like a caterpillar emerging as a butterfly but taking a helluva long time in doing it. Come on, let's just walk and enjoy ourselves.'

Though Chizzie enjoyed the soft feel of grass under his feet, he couldn't shake off the slight feeling of apprehension that sprang from Weever's dislike – possibly even hatred – of him. It seemed Gordon Weever would never accept the fact that Yolanda was now Mrs Bryson, the wife of a humble part-time teacher and hotelier.

They'd passed two of the new golf greens, ambling along in their own little worlds, when Billy suddenly called out, 'Look! A man! Crawled out the trees and then back in again.'

Chizzie laughed. 'Maybe the guy's birdwatching. Though it's an unusual approach, it must be said.'

'Could be something's up,' said Yolanda. 'Let's go see.'

Billy and Peggy were first to arrive at the man, who wasn't exactly birdwatching – he was lying on his back, sprawled out in the long grass beneath a tree, seemingly unconscious.

'He's breathing,' Billy declared, leaning into the man's face.

The man had long, fluffy black hair and a pale, gaunt face, and wore a black T-shirt, denim jeans, and red trainers. Suddenly, the man's eyes flicked open. 'Ah, Coleridge!' he cried. ''Tis thine own sweet face!'

'Uh?' gulped Billy.

Yolanda leaned over the man. 'What happened, sir? Are you all right?'

'Oh, fairest one! Thy face is very heaven!'

'Who are you?' asked Yolanda.

'William Wordsworth – delighted to meet you.'

'It's Tommy Neptune!' yelled Billy, suddenly electrified. 'It's Tommy Neptune, lead singer of The Luvvin' Vulcans.' Now mesmerised by the presence of his idol, Billy purred. 'What a guy! Tommy Neptune. He's magic – "Gasman's Rock"; that's a great track. I love it! Man, oh man, Tommy Neptune, Tommy Neptune.'

Yolanda and Chizzie eyed one another, then Yolanda spoke to the man again.

'Have you been taking any substances, Mr Neptune?'

There was no reply.

Chizzie tried a different tack: 'Mr Wordsworth, have you been taking any substances?'

'Indeed, sir. I am a man of substance,' declared the seemingly resurrected poet.

'What substance exactly, Mr Wordsworth?'

'I have sipped of the sylvan nectar in the greenwood, my good sir.'

'A bit more than sylvan nectar, I think,' muttered Yolanda.

'Tommy Neptune,' purred Billy.

Mr Neptune, aka Wordsworth, offered further information: 'The trees of the greenwood are my friends where'er I go,' he said dreamily.

'Well, I know where you're going right now,' said Yolanda. 'We're going to put you in your golf buggy and then we'll see a doctor.'

Chizzie and Yolanda each took an arm over a shoulder, while Billy shouldered the man's feet.

Neptune, aka Wordsworth, now seemed to form the impression that more than mere human hands were at work. He was seemingly being transported in more than just physical format. 'Halloo, sweet sprites,' he declared. 'I rise through the ether: aloft I float; up, up, free of care, where the air is rare.' And, thus aloft, Neptune, aka Wordsworth, departed the long grass while reciting a revised version of his greatest work: '*I wandered lonely as a daffodil, that floats o'er hill and dale, When all at once I saw a host... a host... a host of... ehm... ehm...*'

Having got Neptune, aka Wordsworth, and his gear

into the cart, they headed for the car park. The great poet, seemingly still in a state of spiritual transport or daffodil-induced turmoil, sat quietly between Chizzie and Yolanda while Billy and Peggy ran happily behind the buggy. Passing the main house, they came upon Florence again, who this time was facing off two security men.

'What's up?' asked Yolanda.

'We have to remove this woman,' replied one of the men, turning to Florence. 'Come along now, madam,' said the man, reaching out.

But Florence was not for moving and glared menacingly. 'Touch me, my boy, and I'll kick your goolies so hard they'll hear the throbbing in Tannadee!'

This information, together with Yolanda's intervention, saw the security men back off.

Florence wasn't entirely subdued, though. She called up to the curtained window, 'I'll be back, you wimp! You're not ruining my reputation.' And with those words resounding off Weever's bedroom walls, she turned and strode towards the gate.

CHAPTER 8

By early afternoon, Tommy Neptune was in the Oxdale cottage hospital, kept in for observation, and Gordon Weever was in his office, attending to business. A security guard stood at his door, following an earlier scare when Florence had come to the gates armed with a bunch of flowers containing a note with the message:

Reminder: your next dance class is at 10.30am tomorrow, Monday 8th. No reply will be deemed confirmation.

However, a more uplifting call came Weever's way soon after. It came from another lady: Erica Heyden. When she arrived, the welcome she received was effusive; in part, no doubt, a reaction to the trauma he'd suffered earlier in the day on the appearance of Florence McTaggart. Weever, now looking fully fit and feeling quite wonderful, ushered Erica into the drawing room. He sat at one end of the sofa with Erica seated at the other end.

'Very nice coffee you serve, Gordon, thank you,' Erica remarked with a smile.

'My own blend – only the best for the best.'

'Well, let me show you what I've got for you.'

Weever beamed. Erica drew a thin grey folder from her

dark blue leather bag. Weever licked his lips and brushed away cake crumbs from the surrounding area.

She removed two sheets of paper from the folder and told him, 'I spent yesterday evening and this morning in touch with former colleagues and friends, and this is what we've come up with so far in your family history.'

Weever rubbed his hands together eagerly and slid closer to Erica. 'Exciting,' he whimpered.

'I got as far back as the Vikings.'

'Oh, awesome. I knew it: strong, smart, tough – I knew it!'

'I've written up a record here.' She made to pass the sheet of paper to him.

'No, no, please, you read it out – read it out.' To hear one's mighty Viking ancestry being read out in the sweet and melodious voice of a wonderful and charming lady – sheer bliss for Weever.

Erica straightened up and began. 'The first record of a meeting between a McShellach and a Viking appears to have taken place in the eighth century when Kenneth McShellach of McShellach, then chief of the clan, sought to strengthen his position by marrying his daughter Matilda to a Viking lord. First, she tried to marry Ketill Flatnose, a Norse King of the Isles renowned chiefly for pioneering the headbutt as a negotiating tool. Unsurprisingly, he turned her down flat. Subsequently she tried Harald No-Hair, without success. There then followed a brief dalliance with Gronald Amberhead. Finally, having exhausted all other possibilities, she ended up with one Magnus Yellowlegs, son of Thorvald the Unheavy. Whether they had issue or not is unknown;

there are no further records. In fact, there appears to be no further record whatsoever.'

For a moment Weever was dumbstruck, before whining, 'None? None at all? I was hoping for an explorer, a pioneer, an Indian fighter, something like that.'

'Be not dismayed, though, Gordon; history is probably not quite what you think it is. You see, the historical record is never complete. History is in fact like casting a net upon the waters: the big fish get caught and the little ones slip away. The little histories never see the light of day, and the whole picture becomes skewed and dull: a colourless, two-dimensional thing. But that's where creative historians like myself come in. We are the colourists. We bring life to the dull and dusty. For years I toiled in dark archives and sifted through two-dimensional tracts, hour after hour, day after day. Then one day I just walked away from it all and got involved in the cut and thrust of commerce. But now I yearn to make history something that everyone can enjoy. I want to revitalise it. History has died in the schools and it's almost extinct in the universities. To reverse this trend we need colour, we need light, and I propose to start by painting you into history, Gordon.'

'Oh, excellent, excellent. Not only a chief, but a pioneer – though don't go mentioning Magnus Yellowlegs, will you?'

'Worry not, Gordon – there is no Magnus Yellowlegs. I made him up. I made up all of the names bar one – can you guess which one?'

'Uh… Harald No-Hair?'

'Ketill Flatnose – he was real. At least, that's what history claims.'

'The headbanger? He butted people?'

Erica shrugged. 'Who knows? He was either well designed for it, or just well-practised. But that's beside the point. The point is, I have demonstrated how easy it is to get people to swallow anything, even the most fantastic of confections. And intelligence is no proof against fakery. You, if I may say so, are proof of that. We can make it work for us.'

'Whoa, whoa, whoa. No, no, no. Wait a minute. Fakery? No, no – no fakery here! I want the truth, only the truth. I don't want some smart dude popping up down the line and pulling me apart, making me look like some kinda sick, lying, good-for-nothin' dope. I bend rules, Erica, I don't break 'em – that way, there's always a route out.'

'You have a route, Gordon. History is not truth. History, as everyone knows, is written by winners, and it comes in five guises: proven, probable, plausible, possible and propaganda. We will operate in the probable and plausible areas. We will never provide certainty but, on the other hand, no one will ever be able to prove us wrong.'

'Probable, plausible – whatever, it's fakery. That's what you're really talking.'

'Isn't life just so much fakery? Without suspension of disbelief, where is joy and excitement? And religions, Gordon: what are they – fact or fiction? They can't all be right. And why should history be only for dullards? It wasn't always so. Have you heard of Herodotus?'

'Herod the King? He fought Moses.'

'No, I'm talking about Herodotus – an ancient Greek renowned as the Father of History but also known as the

Father of Lies. He believed colour was just as important as the facts in history. Dead history is no history; it's just dead. Herodotus knew that, so he didn't allow dull facts to get in the way of a good story. We can do that for you and your clan. We can make you whatever you want to be; you can be clan chief, the best chief there's ever been, a big guy, a hero, a leader of men defying all the dullards and pedagogues.'

'What-agogs?'

'And when it comes to painting a colourful picture, you, as a McShellach, have the very distinct advantage of having no historical significance whatsoever.'

'Uh… that's… that's a good thing?'

'It's a wonderful thing, Gordon. No one knows anything about your clan. You're a blank canvas. We can paint you however we wish. And, of course, it's not really about you: it's about the little people.'

'Leprechauns?'

'No – the ordinary people; your ordinary clansfolk.'

'Of course, of course.'

'They need a hero, someone to believe in – a great man who can make his clan one of the greats, like the MacDonalds and the Campbells. You can give them a dream come true.'

Weever drew in a deep breath, then let it out.

'And you'll be the better for it too, Gordon. And history will be the better. It's win-win-win!'

Weever thought for a moment, then smiled. 'Who knew history could be such a wonderful thing?'

'But don't get too carried away, Gordon. The world may be at your feet, but you have the Lord Lyon King of Arms looking over your shoulder.'

'Him again?' groaned Weever. 'Is there nobody higher than him? Like, maybe the Lyon King of Arms and Legs?' he said sarcastically.

'He's the top man.'

'So, I have to impress this doddery old fool in tights? Well, no. No way. I won't bow to him. It's none of his business. This is clan business. I'm not having a fancy-pants telling me I'm not good enough. I'm plenty good enough. I'll go ahead without him. He can shove his tights!'

'Good. That's the kind of talk that makes a great chief. That'll go a long way to winning the clan vote.'

'Oh, be in no doubt, Erica. I will win any vote. Come hell or high water, I will win.'

'That's it then, Gordon. Positive attitude. We can turn things any way we like.'

'Of course we can. With you on my PR team, how can I lose?'

CHAPTER 9

While Chizzie was busy greeting guests arriving for dinner at the Tannadee Hotel, a man was moving casually among the cars in the hotel car park, as if taking time to have a smoke before going inside. He appeared to have a fascination for number plates.

Stamping out his cigarette, the man moved away and wandered into the garden. At the end of the garden path, he quickened his step and made his way to the rear of the hotel, where he took a special interest in Chizzie's old Volvo parked in front of the garage. He took out his phone and scrolled through a file, checking the number plate. Then, looking rather pleased with himself, he looked about before taking a little torch from his jacket. He walked over to the garage window and shone his torch inside. He then looked about again before quickly taking the path to the garden shed where, again using his torch, he looked through the window of the shed. As he stepped back, the kitchen door burst open, and the man bolted for cover behind a small rhododendron bush. He squatted low as Billy Pung emptied a small bucket into a large bin. As soon as Billy closed the kitchen door, the man got up and moved quickly round to the front of the hotel and into his parked car, where he straightened his tie, combed his hair, wiped his shoes with a cloth, then lit up a cigarette and sat back.

Some minutes later, the man got out of his car and went into the hotel. At the reception desk, he rang the bell. Chizzie left his office to attend to him.

'Good afternoon,' said the man. 'I was passing through the area, and seeing how impressive it is, I thought it might be a fine location for my hillwalking group to spend one of our long weekends this season, so I've called in to see if you'd be able to accommodate a group of, say, eight people?'

'When did you have in mind?'

'No date for definite yet; we're just drawing up our list at the moment. I just called in to see if it's possible; if you have the capacity.'

'Well, we have fourteen rooms, so it is possible. If you give us plenty of notice we will do our best to welcome you,' Chizzie enthused.

'And do you accommodate dogs? Some of our party like to bring their dogs.'

'We have two rooms where we're happy to receive dogs.'

'And if we have more than two dogs, is there other accommodation for dogs, like a kennel, say?'

'Nothing like that, no, but again, if you give us plenty of notice, we might be able to arrange something.'

'Right, that's very helpful. Oh, and could I possibly have a look at the rooms for dogs? You know what some owners are like – treat the dogs better than humans.'

'Both rooms are occupied at the moment, I'm afraid.'

'Are they on the ground floor?'

'Yes. In the west wing, with views over the garden.'

'Excellent. I'll be in touch. Thank you.'

'You're very welcome. Hope to see you soon.'

As soon as the man left, Billy emerged from the dining room. 'Who's that guy?' he asked.

'I don't know. Why?'

'He's a funny guy. He was behind a bush in the back garden. I thought he was having a dump, so I took a look after he left, but there was nothing. He went to his car and then he came here. I hid in the pergola and got a photo of him on my phone.'

'Ah, I didn't know you had a phone.'

'Doesn't work here. But everybody else has got one, so I got one. Takes photos; even videos.'

'Let's have a look, then.'

Billy showed Chizzie the photo.

'That's the man, right enough,' said Chizzie.

'D'you think he's a spy?'

Chizzie rubbed his chin. 'Could be, could be. He seemed very keen to know where we accommodate dogs.'

A knowing look passed between them.

'You know what, Billy…'

'We've been rumbled.'

'They're coming for us.'

CHAPTER 10

After dinner, Charlie Fairfoull was summoned to Weever's drawing room, and once he was seated and sipping a single malt, Weever handed him a printed note.

'It's an email from Erica,' said Weever, 'addressed to us both, but mostly to you. She doesn't think much of what you said on the phone.'

'I'm not entirely surprised, but she's wrong, whatever she says. You can't just go making up history to suit yourself.'

'Well, read her note and think again.'

Fairfoull took the note and read:

As you will know by now, Charlie and I have different views on the way forward, and while I appreciate his concerns, I nevertheless maintain that they are unfounded. However, rather than make an argument in emotionally charged dialogue, I sometimes find it better to set things out in writing. So, with that in mind, I respectfully ask you to consider what I have set out below.

Starting with the word 'history' – it is exactly what it says: his story, not yours. And it certainly isn't her story. The record of womanhood is as thin as the air we breathe, while men are everywhere – even appearing in 'menopause' and 'menstruation'. So much for a fair record.

Next, Charlie advises that you should refrain from breaking rules because rules have made you great and keep you great. However, there comes a point in greatness when there is one rule for you and another for everyone else – that is the mark of supreme greatness. Royalty has always embraced the fact. The countryside is full of royal bastards, is it not?

Even the history of our great nation isn't beyond rewriting. Consider the Union of the Crowns: Scotland presented England with James VI, and the English named him James I. Thus, the original James I became James the 1/6th, James II became James the 2/6ths (i.e. James III), the original James III became James the Half (3/6ths), James IV became James the 4/6ths (aka 2/3rds), and James V became James the 5/6ths. If that doesn't convince you that rules are for fools, I don't know what will.

And it's not only Scotland that's confused. Did Robin Hood exist? No. Did William Tell shoot at an apple on his son's head? No. Did the Liberty Bell ring out on the day American independence was declared? No. As for the United Kingdom, it was for over seventy years a queendom, and about half of Scotland wanted to end the union. We thus lived in a country that was neither united nor a kingdom.

So, hold thy nerve, dear Gordon. History is what you make it. The writer is as much a part of history as any fact. I urge you: be the chief you want to be. Be bold, be supreme, and make history your own. What people believe is as important as the truth.

Weever puffed out his cheeks and leaned back in his chair. 'So, what d'you think?' he asked.

Fairfoull thought for a moment. 'It's hard to know, really. The trouble with Erica is you never quite know what's true and what isn't.'

'The thing is, Charlie, it doesn't really matter if it's true or not. If two smart guys like us can't tell the difference, she's proved her point.'

'But we smart guys will check the facts, Gordon.'

'Leaving ninety-nine per cent of the people *not* checking. Who checks? Who cares?'

'Not enough, apparently.'

'Absolutely right, so I'm pushing on with Erica. We're not breaking any rules, because they're all broken already.'

'There's one rule, Gordon: integrity. There're people out there who spend their lives slaving over manuscripts in tiny, tiny detail, inching their way to the truth, then along comes somebody like Erica and she just blows them all away.'

'Hey, hey, hey, don't go slating Erica; she's doing a wonderful job looking after me and helping me get what I want, and for no other reason than simply because she likes me. I can tell. She's a trouper, Charlie. A hundred times better than all those creeps in libraries and museums. I'm with Erica. I'm making history – my own history.'

'All by yourself?'

'With Erica's help, of course. She's getting my PR campaign underway as we speak.'

'Oh, she's doing your PR too?'

'She sure is. It may surprise you to know, Charlie, there's still clansmen out there who object to me being their chief.'

'Good heavens! Object to *you*? Who on earth could be so deluded?'

'The word "loser" ring any bells?'

'Vaguely. Gordon, could these perhaps be people you might've trampled on and rubbed into the dust at some point?'

'Could just be, Charlie, could just be.'

'They don't really know you, of course – that's the trouble.'

'People who know me like me – love me, even, some of them; most of them, in fact. But the trouble is, I'm such a truth-lovin' guy, and I tell it like it is, and people just don't like that. They don't like the truth. So they don't deserve the truth. And they ain't gettin' it from me. They're gonna get what they can't deny.'

Next day, it was clear that Erica had things well in hand when she arrived at McShellach House. She exuded energy and wasted no time on small talk or a second cup of coffee. 'First off, we make a video,' she declared. 'We see you in full Highland costume.'

'Great!' said Weever. 'They die at my feet!'

'We see you striding through the heather, fitter than any stag.'

'I shoot a stag – a big one.'

'Of course.'

'Even better: a bear – they'd love that in America and Canada.'

'A stag will suffice, Gordon. It's very Highland. Then we move to the lighter side; the cultural side of Gordon Weever: we see you dancing.'

'Uh… d-dancing?'

'I'll arrange that with Ms McTaggart.'

'No Gay Gordons! That's out.'

'Strip the Willow would be ideal – a display of grace through strength.'

Weever groaned.

'Remember there are lady McShellachs too. And there's no charmer better than a lively dancer.'

'You must be my teacher. I want you.'

'And incur the wrath of Florence McTaggart? More than my life's worth, Gordon. Now, how are you on the bagpipes?'

'Bagpipes? Me?'

'We need to see you play them, on video. It'll be dubbed, of course.'

'It had better be.'

'We see you helping charities: animals—'

'Animals? I've just shot a stag!'

'Selective culling, for the sake of the herd. We see you on a fishing boat—'

'I'll be seasick.'

'Okay, salmon fishing.'

'I'm kind to animals.'

'Okay, no fishing. You're on a large construction site with a hard hat on. Constructive and strong. Then you're conquering a mountaintop – don't worry, you'll be dropped in by helicopter. You're on a big horse—'

'As long as it's stuffed.'

'You're kissing babies like a big-guy politician.'

'No, no: no politics – a sniff of politician and I'm dead. We keep it human.'

'You visit Bannockburn and come over all emotional.'

'Of course.'

'You walk with a royal.'

'The King?'

'A double. No, on second thoughts, there's probably still clansmen out there all too ready to fight for Bonnie Prince Charlie.'

'He's long gone.'

'He's living history, Gordon. We see you weaving Harris tweed, piloting an aircraft—'

'I'm not a pilot.'

'A double. You're a lumberjack—'

'Timber!'

'You're golfing at St Andrews; you're swimming off Aberdeen—'

'What! Swimming off Aberdeen?'

'A double.'

'Sounds like this double could end up clan chief.'

'Don't worry. It'll be neatly done. We use a little of each – we split the screen into segments. And what we see is a busy man in the best of health, full of bounce and vigour.'

'You make me sound like some kind of dog food.'

'It's called PR.'

CHAPTER 11

Chizzie, Yolanda, Billy, and Peggy the dog strolled down the sixth fairway of the golf course. There was no one else to be seen except one greenkeeper working on a distant green. The smell of summer lingered in the newly mown grass. Blue tits fluttered and piped in the trees; occasionally a bumblebee buzzed by. Chizzie and Yolanda walked hand in hand. Peggy turned to Billy and gave a little yelp, prompting Billy to draw a ball from his pocket, then throw it. As Peggy ran to fetch the ball, a volley of shouts burst out from somewhere in the long grass up ahead. Then two men in camouflage jackets could be seen scrambling through the trees away from the fairway.

'That's the man that whacked Peggy!' exclaimed Billy.

'You sure?' asked Chizzie.

'Yeah, I'm sure,' said Billy. 'And the other one, he's the man I thought was having a dump in the garden. And look,' he said, pointing to a low hill, 'another man on top of the hill over there. I'm goin' after them.'

'No!' cried Yolanda. 'Leave him, Billy!'

But before Billy could make a move, a lean figure dressed in black and sporting long black hair and an odd-looking face came prancing out of the trees. When he stopped advancing, he took to prancing around in a circle, imparting information about his current station in life. 'I am the Lord of fire and fury!' he yelled. 'I feast on the souls of the damned! Fire! Fire! Fire!' And with that, he seemed to expire, falling to the ground with unnatural abandon.

'It's Tommy Neptune!' declared Billy.

'Oh God – not again,' whined Chizzie.

They rushed over to the fallen rock star.

'Greetings, earthlings,' said Mr Neptune, now apparently from another planet. An adventurous pattern of make-up clung to his face, the main features of which were a wide rim of mascara around both eyes, and on each cheek a lipstick-red lightning bolt.

'No wonder the Gorries took off!' said Chizzie.

'Right. I'll go and fetch a buggy,' said Yolanda. 'You guys see he doesn't do any more jumping about.'

Billy offered a suggestion: 'Maybe if we hold him upside down and shake the pills out, he'll feel better.'

Chizzie shook his head. 'Nice idea, Billy, but too late. He's away in another universe, and once Mr Weever gets to know about it, that universe will be anything but parallel to here.'

'Aw, that's no fair. He done a good thing,' said Billy.

'Two wrongs don't make a right, Billy. As far as Mr Weever's concerned, Mr Neptune is history.'

'We can get him back to his house,' Billy insisted.

'Okay, but first you need to give him one of your sticky toffees to clamp his jaws together.'

'Anyone want this last potato?' asked Johnny at lunch in the kitchen.

'Not me,' answered Chizzie before draining his cup of tea.

Yolanda smiled. 'On you go, Johnny. You'll do me a favour: I've had more than enough already.'

'Me too,' said Johnny, 'but a shame to waste it.' He reached out, then buttered the potato and chomped it.

Chizzie leaned back in his chair. 'Did you know the Gorries have a third brother?'

'In prison?' asked Johnny.

'No, he's a preacher. He goes round the parks and hostels in Millburgh. "Creepin' Jesus", they call him. Apparently he creeps up on people and tries to convert them.'

'Convert them from what? Solvent to pauper?'

'No. He's not a thief: he got religion and wants everybody else to get it, apparently.'

'Oh, one of those,' said Johnny. '"The end is nigh" type. How d'you know all this?'

'Sven told me. He knew the guy when he slept rough in the park. Maybe we can get him to call his brothers off.'

Johnny scoffed. 'Call them in and mug you, more like.'

'No,' said Yolanda. 'I think you're right, Chizzie: it's worth a try. I got an email from Caitlin. She desperately wants the Gorries to leave her and Peggy alone. She's had enough emotional turmoil with her dad passing. Maybe this other Gorrie can help.'

'Well, leave your wallet at home,' advised Johnny.

'And Caitlin's invited me to join the Millburgh Women's Soccer Club. What d'you think?' asked Yolanda.

'Soccer club?!' roared Johnny, gulping the last of his potato. 'No such thing as a soccer club in this country. We play football! Football! A game played with foot and ball, as opposed to American football and rugby football, played with hands and a manbag! These impostors don't play football; they play handbag! Handbag! And yet we're supposed to give up our word "football" because Americans and fat lads can't tell their feet from their hands! It gets my goat! Absolutely gets my goat! I don't want to hear that awful s-word mentioned ever again in this house!'

Chizzie sprang forward in his chair. The heat coming off his father's red-hot head was almost palpable. 'Okay, okay, Dad, we got the message,' he insisted, waving his hands lightly to calm things down.

Yolanda raised her eyebrows, then smiled. 'Sorry, Johnny. I assure you I will never again utter that word in your presence. I promise.'

Johnny shook his head and sighed. 'Sorry. Sorry I blew up,' he said, 'but it's one of those things that really does get my goat. Horrible, horrible word.'

'It's okay, Dad. We understand. You have a point.'

Later that afternoon, in fine, sunny weather, Chizzie and Sven sat on a bench in Millburgh's Jubilee Park. Like Chizzie, Sven was in his late twenties, but he and Chizzie were very different creatures. Chizzie was local, professional, married, slim build. The sandy-haired Sven, on the other hand, was Danish, muscular, handsome in a puppet-like sort of way, unmarried, and had a somewhat turbulent past. He had come to Scotland originally to make some cash on the Highland Games circuit but had lost his way and turned to drink, which saw him sleeping rough for a while. Having conquered his demons, he now earned a crust as a janitor at Tannadee School and occasionally helped out at the Tannadee Hotel owned by Chizzie and his father.

'Always the way, isn't it?' said Sven. 'If I'd come into the park to feed the ducks or take a stroll, the pastor would be tappin' me on the shoulder within seconds. Now we want the guy, he's nowhere to be seen.'

'Give him another twenty minutes, then we'll try Marlee Park,' said Chizzie.

'This is definitely his favourite. Very poor show today all round, actually,' said Sven, looking about. 'Hardly a soul here. More pigeons and gulls than folk.'

It was true: apart from a woman and a small child feeding the ducks, a few dog walkers, and one man on a bench, the park was pretty lifeless. They sat on a bench by the wall at the edge of the park and waited… and waited. Then, just as Chizzie's legs began to go numb, Sven stood up quickly.

'Mad Dog!'

Chizzie sprang to his feet as fast as his numbed muscles could lift him. 'Where?' he asked, looking about.

Sven pointed to a young man in a red plaid shirt and tattered denim shorts. 'Over there. That's Mad Dog.'

'Him? That's a relief. I thought you meant a dog – a mad dog on the loose.'

'No, him – he's a good guy. Maybe he's seen the pastor. Come on.'

They caught up with the young man. Sven sneaked up behind him before suddenly slapping his big hands over the young man's eyes, shouting, 'Guess who?'

The young man buckled at the knees and yelped.

Sven released his grip, then grabbed the lad in a bear hug. 'Hey, Mad Dog, boy – how are you?'

'Hell, man, I nearly died there,' whined Mad Dog.

Chizzie said nothing but felt for the poor lad as he awaited an introduction.

Typically, though, Sven's mind was focused on only one thing at a time, and he immediately began mining the young man for information. 'We're lookin' for the pastor. D'you know where he is?'

Mad Dog screwed up his unwashed and patchily shaved face and began to look passably thoughtful. 'No,' he said finally.

Before they parted, Sven asked Mad Dog to give him the latest news about the welfare and whereabouts of other comrades; then he gave Mad Dog another hug, slipped him a fiver and sent him on his way. 'I saved Mad Dog's life once. He believed he could crawl along the water lilies in the pond. Wouldn't listen to nobody. He knew he could do it. Wouldn't hear different. So we let him go. He sank like a rock. He was drowning, but folks thought he was clowning. Not me, though: I untangled him and got him out. And the pastor saved him another time when thugs attacked him. I went to step in, but the pastor beat me to it. He swung his arms up in the air and called down the judgement of God upon them in a deep, boomin' voice that could've been God himself. The thugs ran for it. I tell you, I shivered too, and I was yards away!'

'Yeah – amazing what a booming voice can achieve.'

'Sometimes the pastor has black moods, though, and when that happens, steer clear.' Then suddenly, Sven pointed. 'Look! There he is – the pastor! It's him!'

Chizzie swung round to see an older man walking proudly along the path. He wore a dark, heavy overcoat and a brown felt hat perched on flowing grey hair that matched the colour of his thick beard.

'He's not really a pastor,' continued Sven. 'He was a scientist once, but we call him "Pastor" out of respect.'

'Well, let's see what he can do for us.'

'Hold it. He's sittin' down beside that dusty old guy on the bench down there. We can go behind the big bush next to the bench an' see what kinda mood he's in. Come on!'

The pastor offered the dusty old man a bottle of water and he took it, guzzling down nearly all the water in one go.

'That's some thirst you have there,' said the pastor. 'Matched by a thirst for the Lord, I hope?'

'No, it's just my body fluids,' replied the dusty man. 'All to pot right now, my body fluids – mostly vinegar, actually. I'm seventy per cent vinegar, I'd say if asked.'

'Vinegar?' asked the pastor. 'You're seventy per cent vinegar?'

'Yeah. Got it on my chips last night. I said no vinegar, but they put it on anyway. Now I've got vinegar coursing through my veins, to all intents and purposes acting like a body fluid.'

'Well, maybe you're lucky. You've got an unnatural advantage there.'

'Really?'

'An unnatural advantage over all mankind.'

"Because I have my own condiments coursing through my body?

'Exactly. You see, in the event of global warming being

nothing but a scurrilous deception on the part of devious socialists, and the global climate getting closer to freezing your private parts off, you are at an advantage in respect of your freezing point being lower than that of the average punter in the street. When the new Ice Age engulfs us, and day turns to night and there's nothing but darkness for a thousand years, you're laughing.'

'I am?'

'Yes, indeed. And all because of—'

'Vinegar?'

'Exactly.'

'I thought that was it.'

'It's God at work, you see, working in mysterious and wondrous ways. Congratulations. You're marked out.'

'Oh, nice.'

'Yes. When the great Day of Judgement comes and St Peter's sitting at the gates, staring at his chips, and you turn up – suddenly the gloom is lifted; there's rejoicing: there's vinegar. He siphons a little off – strictly through the ether, of course; no pain to you – and he's delighted, absolutely delighted.'

'I expect he would be.'

'And the great Pearly Gates swing majestically open – and you're in! You're in through those mighty Pearly Gates!'

'And all because of vinegar.'

'Exactly. Here, have a pamphlet.'

'Couldn't change some of this water into wine, could you, by any chance?'

'Not today, my friend.'

'Next week, maybe?'

'We'll see.'

'I'll be right here.'

'Peace be with you, brother.'

'Thanks, brother; see you next week. Should I bring some bottles?'

'Bye. Bye, now.' With that, the pastor got to his feet, looked about, and walked away.

Chizzie looked puzzled. 'You really think we ought to have a word? Seems to me like he's not all there.'

'He's complicated.'

When they caught up with the pastor, Sven tapped him on the shoulder, and he swung round.

'Ah, Sven,' he said casually, 'there you are. Nice to see the whole man.'

Sven looked puzzled.

'Next time,' continued the pastor, 'instead of just listening in, how about you join in the conversation?'

'You mean you…?'

'Yes. Next time, find a bush with more foliage. Now, how are you doing, Sven? Looking much better than when I saw you last, I may say. And still a good Christian, I trust?'

Sven looked at the ground. 'Well… right now, Pastor, I really don't know what to believe.'

The pastor tutted, closed his eyes, groaned, then shook his head before turning to Chizzie. 'And you, sir – are you a believer?'

'Ditto,' spluttered Chizzie, caught unawares.

'I beg your pardon?'

'I don't know what to believe either. But I have to say, there's one thing I do know: I don't believe in antifreeze for people.'

The pastor looked at Chizzie sidelong, pondering for a moment. 'You think I duped that man. Well, I grant you that the circumstances were far from ideal. But the important thing is, I have connected where others have failed. Now and again there comes a time in everyone's life when the end justifies the means. I can make that man fit for heaven. That's what matters. Get them through. If he can believe what I have just told him, he's a believer and I can save him. I have that man where he needs to be, though he knows it not. This is my mission. I save the lost, the minds that have gone awry, and so long as there is breath in my body their misfortune will not be their fate.'

'Well… fair enough, sir,' said Chizzie. 'I am not here to praise or argue. My name is Chizzie Bryson, and I have come here to ask for your help in another direction.' He explained how the pastor could intercede and get his brothers to call off their attacks.

'Hah!' replied the pastor with a dry laugh. 'I am the very last person to ask. I am a half-brother, but think of Cain and Abel. My half-brothers have cast me aside. They have thrown me out of their lives. They have brought blows down upon my head and struck me to the ground. They have showered me with the most profane language. But one day, one day, with God's grace I will save them. For now, alas, they are lost to me, and it is beyond my power to help you. I can but wish you well. Pray unto the Lord. Have a pamphlet.' And with that, he spotted a more deserving soul and strode away to save him.

'You sure he's a Gorrie?' asked Chizzie.

'That's what they say,' replied Sven. 'A different mother,

maybe; even a different father, maybe – these people ain't like us: they're more like royalty round here.'

'How about we meet up with Yolanda?' suggested Chizzie.

Sven nodded. It wasn't lunchtime yet but there was clearly nothing to be gained by hanging around in the park. They quickly headed for the cafe where they knew Yolanda was meeting up with Caitlin and Jenna.

Sven knew that a vegan was not something from outer space, but nevertheless he found it difficult to stay within the precincts of the animal-free on the menu. After trying unsuccessfully to persuade the forbearing waitress of the vegan cafe to let him have a sneaky one-off order of egg and chips, he finally settled for, 'Vegan sausage, beans and chips, please – and no vinegar, absolutely no vinegar whatsoever! No vinegar!'

The strength of his opposition to vinegar brought looks from other diners. Yolanda, Caitlin and Jenna looked as baffled and concerned as any other onlooker, so Chizzie recounted the incident in the park. It seemed to allay their fears.

Sven, though, seemed completely unaware of anybody's concern. 'D'you believe in love?' he said, turning to Chizzie.

Chizzie blinked and looked perplexed. 'What? How d'you mean?'

'Like, you think you're madly in love, but you can't really tell if it's real. If it's hot and fast, maybe it won't last. Never do anything between a flash and a bang, as they say. Might be best to take time an' find someone quiet who's nice and caring.'

Chizzie glanced at Yolanda, who seemed as eager as Sven to hear his opinion. Chizzie thought for a moment. 'Well, it's a leap of faith, whatever option you take.'

Yolanda laughed. 'Oh, you chicken, Chizzie.' Then she turned to Sven. 'Sounds like you might be in love, Sven,' she said, teasing.

'I am. At least, I think I am. And I'll tell you exactly who.'

'You don't have to,' said Yolanda.

'It's Caitlin – thing is, though, I know nothing about her. And that's silly, isn't it? There's no reason for it – it's just a feelin'. I mean, I love cheese, and that's a feeling too. Fortunately, it's full of protein an' that, but there's also ice cream, and that's no good at all.'

Everyone gazed as if lost for words.

But the tortured soul was not finished. 'I mean, I'm a good-looking guy, I'm sexy, I got personality, I'm a great catch—'

'Don't hold back, will you, Sven?' said Yolanda.

'Well, that's just it: I *did* hold back. Got lots of inviting looks from pretty girls in my time, but I wasn't ready, and they were – it would never have worked. But now,' he said, flashing his eyes towards Caitlin, 'I think I'm ready.'

Chizzie saw Caitlin blush, and he felt like telling Sven to shut up and save his wooing for a more private occasion.

But Caitlin responded. 'You sound very confused, Sven,' she said quietly.

'You know me already!' declared Sven. 'Would you like to help me get unconfused?'

Chizzie stifled a groan. But Caitlin smiled.

Sven fumbled in his pockets and eventually produced

a phone. Then he pressed a few of its buttons before holding it up to Caitlin. 'Can I have your number in there, please?' he said.

Rather self-consciously, Caitlin obliged.

'Thank you, great,' said Sven, looking very pleased. 'I'll be in touch.'

'That's a very fancy phone you've got there,' Chizzie observed, 'considering how you can't even get a signal in Tannadee.'

'One day, Chizzie. One day. You gotta believe, man. You gotta believe.'

CHAPTER 12

Shortly after seven o'clock, the sun rose over the hills and lit up Glen Shoma. In its early light, three men got out of a Range Rover. They were Gordon Weever, Charlie Fairfoull, and a professional photographer. They were here to video 'iron man' Gordon running swiftly and effortlessly through the glen like any self-respecting clan chief would from time to time, keeping himself fit and checking his boundaries against intruders.

'Looking good,' said the photographer, clutching his camera and admiring the scenery.

They made their way carefully down the heathery hillside to the well-trodden path below.

'None too warm,' complained Weever, turning up the collar on his tracksuit.

Fairfoull, also in a tracksuit, laughed scornfully. 'You need to run up and down a bit, Gordon. Work up a sweat.' He knew very well that a warm-up was about as much as 'iron man' Gordon could muster by way of physical exertion, and Weever knew he knew.

'Cheeky beggar,' growled Weever. 'Let's get this over with as soon as possible. Do we really need to run in vest and shorts? I fake-tanned my legs this morning, but they'll still look white in this goddamn chill.'

'Steam on your breath will make you look like a real

toughie,' quipped the photographer cheerily, before looking smartly away as Weever flashed him a withering look.

'I'm not going far,' insisted Weever. 'A hundred yards and that's it.' He turned to Fairfoull. 'You take over from there and go as far as you like: to hell and back if you want.'

Fairfoull laughed. 'No problem, Gordon. You just run to that sheep pen, and I'll do fading into the distance.'

'The sheep pen!' complained Weever. 'It's over a hundred yards away. I don't need to go that far, surely?'

'Actually, you do, Mr Weever,' said the photographer. 'To get a decent panoramic shot, you'll need to go at least that far. But I'll start with some close-ups. I'll go a little way along the track, and when I say, "Go!", you start running towards me.' He then turned towards Charlie. 'Mr Fairfoull, I'd like you to come with me, and when Mr Weever has passed us, he gives you the cap and you run on until I shout, "Stop." That clear?'

'I've just noticed,' said Fairfoull, 'his socks are different to mine.'

'Does that really matter?' asked Weever impatiently.

'Oh yes, absolutely,' answered the photographer. 'There's people who notice that kind of thing. It'll be all over social media the very same day. You'll need to swap socks.'

Fairfoull grimaced. 'How about we just run without socks?'

'I'm not running without socks!' whined Weever. 'It's freezing up here!'

'Well, I don't fancy swapping socks.'

'You insinuating my feet are insanitary?' snapped Weever.

'Well, we all know your feet give off a bit, Gordon.'

'"Give off a bit"?! What's that supposed to mean?'

'I'll give you *my* socks,' said the photographer.

'What the hell's that gonna do?' Weever asked sharply.

'Uh… yeah… right… nothing,' replied the photographer. 'Bad idea.'

'Tell you what,' said Fairfoull. 'You put my socks over your socks, then give me them back when you're done.'

Weever smiled and, pointing at Fairfoull, turned to the photographer. 'That's what I pay this punk for. He's almost as smart as me.'

'Hey – what's that running towards us?' asked Fairfoull, looking down the track.

They watched as a dark creature came bounding swiftly towards them.

'Jeezuz! It's wolf!' exclaimed Weever.

Fairfoull narrowed his eyes. 'It's a sheepdog, I'd say.'

'Helluva big sheepdog. It's a wolf!' insisted Weever, his voice loaded with apprehension.

'We don't have wolves here,' said the photographer, with an uncertain gulp.

The creature quickly got within twenty yards.

Fairfoull narrowed his eyes. 'It's a sheepdog! Only a sheepdog!'

And a sheepdog it was, but it wasn't exactly man's best friend. With no hesitation, it charged at them, growling and baring its glistening fangs. Drool hung from its mouth like mealtime had arrived. Weever flinched and drew close to Fairfoull. The photographer bunched up closer, clutching his camera. The large, black, shaggy dog looked like a cross between a Border collie and something bigger, maybe a wolfhound. It circled low and menacingly, never taking its eyes off the huddled humans. Then it stopped and lay snarling in front of them.

Fairfoull ventured to make friends. 'Nice boy,' he pleaded, leaning towards the dog.

But the dog was having none of it. It leaped towards him, snapping and growling. Fairfoull recoiled.

'It's mad!' whispered Weever.

The humans eyed each other, looking for ideas.

'I suggest we just back off very slowly,' said Fairfoull finally.

So, very slowly, they retreated, and to their pleasant surprise the dog seemed happy with the move.

'Look!' exclaimed the photographer. 'It's stopped growling! Maybe it's calmed down.'

But, no, he hadn't. When they stopped, the dog snarled and bared its teeth again.

'Jog on to the sheep pen,' said Fairfoull.

'It thinks we're sheep!' declared Weever.

'I think you're right,' agreed Fairfoull. 'It's collecting us. See how it's running from side to side? It's collecting us.'

'I don't want to be collected,' Weever wailed.

Fairfoull offered a note of optimism: 'If we keep on going, we can get to the village down the hill.'

But the dog had other plans. As they came to the sheep pen it wheeled round and blocked their way, snapping and snarling.

'He wants us inside the sheep pen!' yelped Fairfoull.

Weever gasped and groaned. But, employing the better part of valour, they swung into the pen. The dog wanted more, though: it barked and nudged the gate with its nose.

'He wants the gate shut!' said the anguished photographer.

For the sheep on the hill, this was surely a wondrous sight. Here was a day they could only dream of: the day the mighty humans were rounded up and penned, putting an end to their wool-robbing ways and their shocking inability to eat planet-friendly grass. And the retribution didn't stop there: as the humans entered the sheep pen, the dog leaped at the photographer and clamped its teeth on his camera. Then it tugged the camera out of the photographer's hands and ran off with it.

Instinctively the photographer went off in hot pursuit, yelling the all-too-obvious: 'He's got my camera! He's got my camera!'

But Weever and Fairfoull were not people who were going to do anything about that. They saw their chance and they scrambled up the slope. Red in the face, puffing and gasping, they clambered into the Range Rover and slumped into their seats. For several minutes, they just let the whole world go by as they leaned back with their eyes closed, speechless, aching and sweating.

'We…we…' said Weever finally. 'We could've been mincemeat out there. And for what? To get votes. Bloody democracy! No more for me. I don't need votes!'

'Yeah,' agreed Fairfoull, 'you can carry democracy too far. Clan chief and democracy – it's not a good mix. More in the "might is right" category, I'd say.'

'Yeah, sometimes you just gotta think out the box.'

'Out of the ballot box.'

'You bet.'

'The main thing is,' said Fairfoull, 'we're safe now. By the time that dog gets through with the photographer, it'll be well sated. Let's just get out of here.'

Weever froze with sudden realisation. 'I-I don't have the keys. They were in the pocket of my short pants. They're gone! They must've fallen out.'

Fairfoull groaned and thought for a moment. 'Right, nothing else for it: we hoof it over the ridge and down to the village before that mutt gets back.'

Moaning every minute, Weever trundled behind Fairfoull down to the village, where they arrived looking like joggers who'd just stepped out of a hurricane. Few people were about: only a man with two little boys standing at a bus stop. Past the bus stop, Weever decided he could go no further and sat on a low wall.

'You go on and find a phone,' he whispered to Fairfoull. 'There's what looks like the entrance to a park down there. I'll meet you there.'

'Sure,' replied Fairfoull. 'By the way, your lace is undone.'

Weever nodded weakly, and Fairfoull jogged away down the road. Wiping the sweat off his face onto his shirt, Weever got to his feet then turned to put his unlaced foot on the wall. One of the little boys came over to him and said hello. Weever ignored him and bent over to tie his shoelace.

The little boy watched for a moment; then he bawled, 'I can see your willy!'

Instantly the other boy yelled, 'Dad! Dad! A man showed Robert his willy!'

The dad looked around. Weever immediately realised that truth hadn't a chance here; at least not without enormous energy behind it – energy he just didn't have. He did the only thing he could do: he got the hell out of there as fast as his sappy legs could carry him. Off down the road he scuttled, panting, feet flapping, head wobbling, arms flailing. A couple of hundred yards later, he glanced around to see if anything was behind him and, horror of horrors, there was the man running after him. There was definitely no possibility of explaining now. Now that he'd done a runner, he was guilty as hell. Seeing a cyclist, Weever used his initiative and pulled the guy clean off his bike; then he clambered onto it and sped off down the hill and into the park, where he spied a toilet building and headed straight for it. He threw the bicycle into the pond and ran into the toilet.

For over half an hour he remained in the toilet, enduring several rather nasty disturbances to the atmosphere, but stoically he kept quiet and out of sight, venturing from his cubicle only occasionally to peer out of the slit window above the handbasins. Eventually, to Weever's immense relief, Fairfoull looked in and, by offering a large tip, got a taxi to flout the by-laws by entering the park and whisking the pair away.

A few days later, metal detectorists hired by Weever recovered the Range Rover's keys. The photographer, after a week's rehabilitation, was fit enough once more to capture weddings and other special occasions on camera, though never again would he tackle promotional videos in the hills.

The pervert-cum-bicycle-thief was never traced.

CHAPTER 13

Weever was lying, half-dozing, on his recliner in his spacious office when Charlie Fairfoull entered. Weever stirred, then removed the cucumber slices from his eyes and flicked them into the bin.

'Feeling better?' Fairfoull asked, grinning, and seating himself in one of the sumptuous leather armchairs.

'Whajja think?' growled Weever, remaining in the reclined position. 'No more PR for me,' he insisted. 'Forget votes; votes are out. They've rigged it all against me anyway, so I ain't playin' their game. I'm calling the shots now. We take it to them with a two-pronged attack. Prong one: Erica creates history; my very own history. Prong two: Digger and his boys scare the bejeezuz out of old Tulloh until he hits the booze and backs off.'

'Might be best if we try offering the carrot before we hit with the stick,' suggested Fairfoull.

'No offer – we hit with the stick, then we hit with the carrot. I can't stand the man.'

'Well, bit of a problem there actually: Digger isn't available. He's lying low in South America.'

'The law after him again?'

'They seem to have the impression that he played a part in some jewellery heist. However, one of his professional colleagues has suggested a local outfit who can do some heavy lifting for us: the Gorrie brothers. They're currently at liberty.'

'And Digger's mate recommends them?'

'Well, not exactly *recommends*, but they do seem to be adequate for local work.'

'Okay, get them in here and let's see what they're made of.'

When the Gorries arrived at McShellach House, they were like men who'd just undergone some kind of religious experience. The shine in their eyes could have graced the eyes of people who'd been given the winning lottery numbers for next week's EuroMillions. In their wildest dreams they couldn't have expected to receive an invitation to McShellach House. It was nothing short of amazing – no need to prise open a window in the dead of night, or dig a tunnel, or drop in through a skylight. This was tantamount to a trolley dash in a jewellery shop. Everything they wanted was at hand: Peggy the dog would be somewhere near, and they would be surrounded by a wide selection of valuable items; things very much worth the attention of master burglars.

The Gorries smelled strongly of cheap deodorant with a little hint of pig muck, so Weever directed them to Charlie Fairfoull's office, where the Gorries lost no time in surreptitiously scanning the room's contents, forming a mental inventory of everything fit to remove. Weever was nevertheless satisfied: here were professionals, or at least near-professionals. He didn't like them, of course, but he did respect them – except for the smell, but they would no doubt be smart enough to lose that when they were better prepared and going about their professional business.

After a welcoming drink, they got down to business.

Fairfoull explained the situation and the part he expected the Gorries to play in resolving the Lord Tulloh problem. 'We need to frighten or discredit the man in some way,' explained Fairfoull. 'And we're calling upon your expertise and local knowledge to do just that. You come highly recommended, so we take it we can rely on your complete discretion and ability to get results.'

Greg Gorrie smiled and nodded confidently. 'Oh, we'll get results all right, and "discretion" is our byword.'

'We know nothing about this, you understand?' Weever interjected as he stood over the seated Gorries.

Greg Gorrie smiled again. 'Understood – no problem.'

'So, what's the plan?' asked Fairfoull.

'Well,' said Greg, 'we find it most beneficial in these matters to open with a couple of frighteners, soften them up a bit, get them all edgy, and then we administer the coup de grâce.'

'We don't want anything permanent,' said Fairfoull with a note of alarm. 'We just want him back on the booze for a while.'

Greg Gorrie nodded. 'Understood. A fall from grace is what I'm alluding to. We can be very subtle.'

'Yeah,' broke in Dean Gorrie. 'We put a horse's head in a guy's bed once, just like the Mafia.'

Weever and Fairfoull froze for a second, then looked at one another.

'Okay,' said Weever, 'we'll leave the details to you – just rattle his nerves and scare him off.'

'No problem,' replied Greg Gorrie.

'Let me know when you're making the move,' said Fairfoull. 'I want to be there.'

Greg winced. 'Ugh… well, actually, we normally work alone.'

'I want him there,' insisted Weever.

Greg shrugged. 'Okay, yeah, no problem.'

They agreed a fee and shook hands. However, just as Weever was eyeing his hand sanitiser, Greg raised the problem of Peggy the dog.

'Now, I'd like to raise another matter, if I may. We are prepared to reduce our fee for a little help with a problem of our own. We want our dog back. Your daughter's friends have snatched it from us to breed puppies. It's a rare pedigree, you see; worth a bob or two. We loaned it to a dear friend to comfort him while he was very sadly dying, but when he popped his clogs, in comes his cheeky, ungrateful daughter and she grabs the dog and claims it's their family pet. I'm sure your daughter knows nothing of this. To keep it from getting ugly we'd like to sort it out personally with a little help from your good self.'

'There's some right nasty people about,' observed Fairfoull.

'Sure are,' chimed Dean. 'Some right dirty ba… bad people.'

'Okay,' Weever agreed. 'Charlie will get you some refreshments while I fetch some cash for your upfront.'

Charlie provided the drinks, then excused himself for a few minutes. He joined Weever in the adjoining room, where a large screen showed the Gorries inspecting some of the artworks, before hurrying back to their chairs as if startled by some noise.

'Turn up the sound a little,' said Weever.

Charlie obliged and sat down. They watched and listened.

'What did you go mentioning a horse's head for?' said

Greg, as he watched his brother help himself to a couple of cigars from the box on the desk.

'To impress,' replied Dean. 'Like the Mafia.'

'It wasn't even a horse's head we used: it was a sheep's head we bought from the butcher.'

'A horse's head sounds better.'

'Well, a sheep's head is out now; can't get them after mad cow disease.'

'I saw a flattened hedgehog on the road not far away.'

'That won't do; it'll look like a hat.'

'Hat; rat – we can get a rat. Plenty round our place.'

'You're right there – good thinking, Ratman.'

'See, I'm not as thick as you think.'

'You have your moments. Put some poison down and we'll pick the fattest.'

'Easy-peasy. Can't wait to get started. We break in and do old Tulloh over – give him a good hiding!

'That would be criminal.'

'We are criminals.'

'No, Dean: we used to be criminals; now we're law-abiding citizens. We're employees.'

'We're gonna put a dead rat in the guy's bed.'

'Public schoolboys do that all the time. It's a practical joke; a prank.'

'Do that to me, I punch yer lights out.'

'You always see the worst in people. Lighten up. Look on the bright side. We're mixing with a better class of people now. We're networking.'

'Going soft.'

Weever looked concerned. 'They sound like a right pair of liabilities.'

Fairfoull smiled. 'They're exactly what we need, Gordon: good enough to get the job done, but if anything goes wrong, who's going to believe anything they say?'

'Good – let's get back and see them outta here before they start thinking about lifting my stuff.'

'I believe the thinking is well underway.'

Weever and Fairfoull returned to their new employees, and Weever handed a brown envelope to the smiling Greg. 'Right, you get the rest when Tulloh pulls out.'

'No problem,' said Greg. 'Now, what I need from you, if you'll be so kind, is—'

'Charlie'll see to it,' said Weever.

After lunch, at the school, Chizzie went to his classroom to inspect the tank full of pond water obtained earlier in the day by the third-year pupils. The big diving beetle and the other predators had been placed in separate smaller tanks to avoid carnage, and Chizzie was at first pleased just to watch a caddis fly larva shuffle around, carrying a tube of organic matter and grit by way of camouflage. Then a wonderful thing caught his eye: a nymph floated to the surface of the water and gradually its skin peeled open, and something began to emerge. It was a mosquito, a fully adult mosquito. Chizzie waited and watched, enthralled as it slowly prepared itself for flight. Should he kill it? Wonderful though it was, it was an enemy. But maybe it wasn't an enemy; maybe it was a plant-feeding mosquito. On the other hand, it might be a bloodsucker. Even so, a wonderful thing in its own right.

Chizzie swithered. Then a movement beyond the window caught his eye. He looked up and saw a small

97

boat speeding across the loch. It landed on the shore near the cottage where Billy and Paw lived. Two men leaped out of the boat and ran towards the cottage. Minutes later they came running back again; one of them clutching something in a large bag. They clambered back in the boat and sped off across the loch.

'The Gorries!' gasped Chizzie, his heart sinking. He drew back from the window. He had to get to the cottage right away and check things out, but just as he turned, he saw Paw running down to the loch shore, waving his fist and shouting at the men in the boat, who by now were well away. It had to be the Gorries, and they'd got Peggy. Chizzie ran to the door and out of the school and headed for Paw's place.

He found Paw very distraught, putting on his cap and jacket.

'They've got the dog,' wailed Paw. 'I phoned Tunnock at the police station but he's not there. Billy'll go nuts!'

'He will, but we can't phone the police, Paw. Very soon, you'll get a call saying they'll kill Peggy if you get the police involved, and Caitlin will certainly get a call telling her the same. Once she's had that call, Caitlin will call Yolanda.'

And sure enough, not long after, the call came. Yolanda agreed to meet Caitlin at the Millburgh football ground in the evening, where the Millburgh Women's Football Team would be training. Chizzie was surprised but pleased to be invited too.

On the way to Millburgh, Chizzie reflected on the theft of Peggy. 'I'm surprised your father's not raving about his speedboat being pinched by the Gorries.'

'Yeah, very unusual for him. He didn't even sound perturbed. Mellowing with age, maybe. One can always hope.'

Chizzie shook his head. 'Not even reporting it to PC Tunnock.'

'He wouldn't want that kind of publicity.'

'We have to get Peggy back.'

'Dear old Father suggests we just get another one from the local pound.'

Chizzie groaned, then changed the subject. He warned Yolanda not to expect too much of the Millburgh ground's facilities. On the one occasion he'd used the club's changing facilities for a cross-country running event several years ago, he'd come away with a party of fleas.

It was a very pleasant surprise, therefore, for both to find that the club's rickety old pavilion had been replaced by a new community sports hub and Millburgh FC had almost exclusive use of the changing facilities beside the grass pitch.

Caitlin and Jenna had already changed and were out on the pitch. They came running over when they saw Chizzie and Yolanda arrive. Yolanda was directed to the away dressing room since this was the one used by the women's football club. Chizzie was advised to use the changing facilities in the main building, since the men's football club used the home dressing room, and it had a reputation for what Jenna called 'life-threatening sanitary arrangements'.

With a wide experience of dressing rooms, Chizzie felt confident that he could cope with anything Millburgh FC could throw at him, but best to check first. 'What sort of arrangements exactly?' he asked.

'Jockstraps falling on your head when you open the door,' said Jenna.

Chizzie grimaced.

'And the standing shorts,' added Caitlin.

'Standing shorts?'

'Yes,' replied Caitlin. 'A pair of horrible shorts that stood upright all by themselves, supported by nothing more than years of wear and no washing. They were apparently some kind of lucky totem for the club.'

Jenna scoffed. 'So lucky, in fact, that the club were twice relegated before the women's club burned the shorts and turned their luck around – one division up, at least.'

'And the bombing jockstraps ceased after we presented the boys with a jockstrap in a rat trap. That seemed to have a profound psychological effect,' said Caitlin with a giggle.

'Nevertheless,' advised Jenna, 'you really should change elsewhere.'

Chizzie took her advice.

After completing the fitness and skills training, the women played a seven-a-side match with a rolling turnover of players, including Chizzie, who was surprised to see how good some of the players were, notably Jenna, and indeed Yolanda. *They're better than I am*, thought Chizzie.

Showered and changed, the four of them found a quiet corner in the cafeteria. Over coffee and a round of tomato and cheese sandwiches, they turned their thoughts to the daunting dilemma of rescuing Peggy themselves or getting the police involved. Jenna strongly favoured acting on their own.

Yolanda agreed. 'If we press the Gorries they could

turn very nasty, with consequences for Peggy. Best they know nothing.'

Caitlin reluctantly agreed. Chizzie was in two minds: an encounter with the Gorries could come down simply to a crude contest of brute strength, and in those circumstances the three ladies might be more of a liability than a help. Jenna apparently read Chizzie's mind and reassured him that she could take care of herself and that the other two were good runners – certainly better than the Gorries. Chizzie didn't press the matter; the women were clearly resolved and ready to deal with the Gorries in their own way.

The first part of the plan was surveillance. Jenna and Caitlin were going to watch the Gorries' farmhouse from a safe distance as often as they could; then they would follow the Gorries discreetly and seek an opportunity to retrieve Peggy.

'I'm reasonably happy with the surveillance,' said Yolanda, 'but not about following the car.'

Jenna remained silent.

Yolanda took the hint. 'Okay, but first let Chizzie and me check out the Gorries' place and see if we can find Peggy and maybe get her back. It's a bit safer than tailing the Gorries to God knows where.'

Caitlin nodded. Jenna hesitated for a moment; then her pride gave way to cold reason.

CHAPTER 14

Erica strode breezily up to the doorway of McShellach House. 'Cry very heaven and gadzooks, good sir!' she called. 'Prepare thyself to enter the royal court of His Majesty King James VI of Scotland!'

Weever's smile shrank to a quizzical look. 'Ugh?'

Erica laughed. 'A vervel, good sir. I'll explain inside.'

Once they were seated comfortably and refreshed in the drawing room, Erica reached into her document case. 'I have here a vervel. It's a ring used for tethering a hawk. In days of yore, hunting with hawks was a popular pastime for royalty and noble gentlemen.' She held up a silver ring about two inches in diameter and then pointed to the inscription on it. 'This one,' she said, 'is made of high-quality silver, and thy forefather's name is writ large upon it. See there – it says, "John McShellach". I had that engraved on it. I know a restorer who likes a little joke now and again. He's engraved it and aged it nicely for you. It's worth a few hundred pounds, probably, but I inherited it and it's no use to me. So, we shall put it to good use in your cause. You'll bury it in a field near the royal hunting palace at Falkland. And when it's found, it will associate your line with royalty, since the only Highlander likely to be hawking with the King would be a clan chief.'

'What if it's never found?'

'It will be found – I happen to know that metal detectorists plan to survey a particular field tomorrow. They've already found valuable artefacts in a neighbouring field. This will be a nice little gift for them; a little thank-you gift for their unwitting help in promoting your cause.'

That night, under the half moon and starlit sky, Erica's car drew into a lay-by within sight of Falkland Palace. A few minutes later, Gordon Weever stepped out of the car wearing a camouflage outfit.

Erica, in the driver's seat, wished him good luck and gave a final instruction: 'You go straight ahead, beyond the ploughed field and into the next one; the one with the molehills in it. Carry on up the slope to the corner and you'll find an area where hairy pigs have been rooting and turning over the soil. Use the trowel I've given you to disturb some of the soil further and place the vervel in the ground, then cover it up loosely. It won't be the first time hairy pigs have uncovered something interesting.'

'It's very dark,' Weever whined.

'Not too dark; your eyes will adjust – there's enough moonlight.'

'The clouds are passing over the moon.'

'They're few and far between. Just get your big-boy pants on and go. You'll see well enough.'

Weever looked anxiously about, then shuffled across the road before attempting to get over the wire fence by grabbing hold of a fence post and inserting his left foot into the wire mesh while applying his other foot to the top of the fence. In theory, this would provide the perfect platform to see him launch into the field. In fact, he fell headfirst onto the ground; his left leg remaining where it was in the mesh and his trousers issuing an alarming ripping noise.

Erica dashed across the road and helped to extricate the cursing Weever. Relaunched, Weever skulked away across the field and into the darkness, crunching through the crisp, silvery stubble. It was very dark and very quiet, but he felt a thousand eyes upon him: never before had he seen so many stars. The sky was absolutely stuffed with them, and all seemed to have an eye on him. It was as if they'd all come out specially to watch him commit some devious act. But in that respect, it was nothing he hadn't done before, so he carried on.

He came to a stone dyke, a section of which seemed partially demolished. To avoid loosening any stones, he made to hop through the gap. Unfortunately, as he hopped, his left foot caught on a stone and he tumbled towards the ground, arms flailing. Shock enough, but an even bigger shock came when his right hand slapped against something soft and clammy. And a further shock hit him when the soft and clammy thing leaped up and took off, revealing the vague outline of a woman lying on her back.

Weever scrambled quickly onto his knees. 'Ugh! What's this? What's going on?' he whimpered.

'You filthy beast!' screamed the woman, now on her knees. 'None of your creepy business!' And she slapped him on the face.

They got to their feet simultaneously.

'You filthy beast!' repeated the young woman.

Weever could barely comprehend what had happened. 'Were you… were you…?'

'Yes, we were! And I'm a grown woman so perfectly entitled to, you filthy beast!'

'Will you stop calling me filthy beast?! I don't care what the hell you do with yourself. Only, I'd say this: I'd be looking for a new boyfriend if I were you. That jerk didn't waste any time getting the hell out of here and leaving you behind.'

'You don't understand. You're not the first private dick my father has sprung on us. Leave us alone, you beast!'

'I'm not a private detective. I don't know what on earth you're talking about.'

'Well, just who are you, then?'

Weever stammered, 'You don't... you don't need to know. It's a private matter. I'm not spying on anybody. I'm not hurting anybody. I'm—'

'Poaching.'

'No, no. I'm just here to... I'm here to... you see, my ancestors are from round here and I just... I just want to experience... you know, what they felt here.'

'Apart from my fiancé's bum?'

'I want the atmosphere, the feeling. I'm sounding crazy, maybe, but that's it; it's...' He threw his arms wide and swung his head towards the heavens. 'It's... it's—'

'The stars!'

'That's it! Yes.'

'The timeless stars.'

'Yeah. The timeless stars.'

'I get it. I get it. I know. My Clive's like that; he says the stars are the only things humans haven't ever changed. He spends a lot of time looking up at the sky and going speechless. I'm always having to bring him round and get him back onto solid ground. That was Clive who ran off. Sorry I called you a beast, but it's all just getting to me; to me and to Clive – he's a nervous wreck. We just want to get married – at least, I do. Clive wants to as well, really, but he's got an awful lot on his mind: he wants to join the priesthood, but he can't do that *and* marry me. An' my dad's got it in for him – he hates Catholics. He's sent private detectives spying on us. Twice he even phoned the cops, and they nearly caught Clive in the bushes. Believe me, when the big, hairy hand of the law grabs your privates in the dark, you don't hang about. So, you understand now – it's not the first time he's been grabbed by the bobbies. Poor Clive. I'm trying to break him in, but it's so difficult, so difficult.'

'Break him in?'

'Into the real world. He's had a very sheltered upbringing. It's his mum, you see; she wants him in the priesthood. His father wants him to be a plumber because that's where the money is these days. I mean, really, does he look like a plumber?'

'Well, I didn't see all that much of him really, except something that frankly looked a bit like a ballcock. So, I'd have to say go with the plumber,' Weever advised with an apologetic smile.

But the young woman was not for smiling. 'Oh, he'd be wasted. He's got so much more to offer; so much more. That's why I bring him out to the great outdoors: to get him invigorated, pump fresh air into him, give him… you know… more puff. If we had a baby, nobody could stop us getting married.'

Weever remained speechless.

'On top of that,' continued the young lady, 'I'm the farmer's daughter here. One day I'll inherit all this – it's a good living, and on top of all that, we have folk with metal detectors finding treasure here and we get a cut, so who needs plumbing or the priesthood? I've got his future ready for him right here – all ready and waiting for him. I aim to build him up. If I can raise pigs, I can make a man of Clive. I have a feeding plan.'

Weever stepped back to gather his wits. Rubbing his top lip, he pondered the situation, while the young lady gathered up some of her belongings. He admired the young lady's ambition, but he found his feelings straying towards Clive. In a rare bout of empathy for his fellow man, he muttered, 'The poor devil. First, he's raised like some delicate plant; then he grows up and gets treated like a horse, and not just any old horse – a stud horse. Then when he's done with that, he's on pig rations and bodybuilding. No wonder he took off – probably to the nearest monastery.' He thought hard, but for once he had no advice to give. He was no marriage counsellor; in fact, he was a veteran of three failed marriages. All he could offer was a sigh and a smile. He stepped forward and hugged the girl. 'Look, I have to go now,' he told her, almost apologetically. 'If you're okay, I'll be off.'

'I'm fine; I know my way, even when it's pitch black. Thank you for listening – I just needed to get it all out. Wish my dad was like you. You're a very nice man, actually.'

Weever gulped. 'Well, nobody's ever called me that before.'

She kissed him on the cheek.

'Well, okay, then. Goodbye,' Weever said warmly,

before looking up at the sky to be sure that it really was a half moon and not a full moon.

He moved off in the direction of the ploughed field, which he soon found by stumbling into it and falling flat on his face. He got up, made a cursory attempt to clean himself, then lumbered through the furrows as a cloud passed over the thin, silvery moon. At last, he came to another stone dyke, which he clambered over before dropping onto boggy ground covered mostly with rushes. He squelched through the rushes and continued up the gentle slope. Then he tripped over a molehill and landed on his knees and hands, which immediately were caked with sloppy mud. He was sodden and he was cold but, at last, he was in the right field; and after a couple of deep breaths, he continued and arrived at the uprooted area.

Now, where to put the vervel? Floundering about in the darkness, Weever couldn't make up his mind. With a sense of panic rising, he finally took out his trowel, turned over some loose soil, placed the vervel under it, and then covered it with soil and bits of sod to make it look like part of the general upheaval. He'd done all he could. It was time to get back over the fields.

Then suddenly, something pale and barely visible loomed, and with a slight yelp it turned and ran away. A ghost? A llama, maybe? Or a donkey? Or maybe… maybe it was just poor bloody Clive running round in circles? An owl hooted; something screamed. This was no time for delay. Weever hurried to the dyke and clambered over it in seconds. Then, staggering across the ploughed field as fast as he could, he hurried back towards the road.

As Weever hove into view, Erica got out of the car and rushed to help him over the fence.

'That's absolutely the last goddamn field I ever set foot in! Absolutely the bloody last!' Weever gasped as he plunged into the passenger seat. 'This is somebody else's job. No way I'm cut out for that kind of experience ever again.'

CHAPTER 15

Next morning, Chizzie, Yolanda and Billy arrived in the woodland car park not far from the Gorries' farmhouse. There was no one else about, which pleased Chizzie. He turned the car so that it pointed towards the exit to be sure of a fast getaway if that should be required.

Leaving the car without a word, they walked swiftly along the forest track. They were lightly attired, ready for a quick escape. When they came level with Gorrie territory, they broke off the path and scrambled through the undergrowth before climbing over a fence into the first of the Gorries' fields. They continued beside the little stream that ran between two little hillocks. Following the stream for about a quarter of a mile, they came upon the Gorries' outbuildings, as fine a picture of neglect and decay as any scrap merchant ever clapped eyes on. Rusted machinery lay in pools of long grass, while the dilapidated carcases of wooden and metal buildings dominated the site, except for a fine-looking farmhouse discernible about a hundred yards away. They moved up to the nearest of the outbuildings, making sure not to bump against anything in case the whole lot came crashing down. Flaps of corrugated iron squeaked in the breeze, causing Chizzie to look about nervously. At the end of the building, he peered round the side and cast his eye over the scene. There was no one around.

110

'Right,' said Yolanda, 'you see that little old caravan down there? I'll look in there and into what's left of the wooden barn beyond it.'

Chizzie agreed. 'Be careful, though,' he cautioned, 'and meet back here in ten minutes.'

Yolanda nodded and hurried away.

Chizzie turned to Billy. 'Right, we go for the big shed straight ahead.'

'There's pigs in there,' said Billy. 'I can smell 'em. We need to be real calm, real calm.'

Chizzie nodded. 'Okay, let's go.'

They ran up to the open doorway of the big shed – the door was off its runners and stood separately inside, propped at an angle against the wall.

'You go down the right, Billy, and have a look among the bales and the wee hut thing at the far end. I'll go along the left side and look in the alcove and the stores.'

The pigs appeared to relax as Billy ambled towards them; then he stopped suddenly. 'Somebody's comin',' he hissed.

The pigs froze. Chizzie darted over to the door propped against the wall and slid in behind it, crouching and slashing through the clinging, dusty cobwebs that festooned the space. Billy, meanwhile, had climbed on top of a stack of rectangular straw bales and lain down. A tough-looking man entered the barn with a younger man who was probably in his late teens. The older man was in fact the very man who'd whacked Peggy in Perth: it was Dean Gorrie. He wore a leather jacket and leather boots; the young man wore a green boiler suit that was still shiny-new. Chizzie remained absolutely still and listened.

'Take that shovel!' ordered the Gorrie man. 'An' put it in the wheelbarrow.'

There was a clunk.

'Now get the wheelbarrow over to the pigs.'

They moved off and Chizzie could no longer make out what was being said, but in between scraping and shovelling noises it was clear that the young lad receiving instruction on how to clean out pig pens. A few minutes later, their voices became distinct again as they crossed to the bales of straw near to where Billy was hiding.

A shadow appeared in the doorway. It was Greg Gorrie. He entered wearing a wax jacket and green wellies. 'Aha, Luke Dungwalker!' he cried, addressing the young lad. 'How's it going? Finished yet?'

The young lad eyed him nervously.

'One bale to each pen,' said Dean Gorrie. 'Cut the string with the knife I gave you. Now, any questions?'

The lad pointed to a large crate down the far end of the barn. 'What's in that little hut down there? Sounds like there's something moving.'

'Oho! You don't wanna know that,' said Greg Gorrie with a menacing smile. 'That, my boy, is Sharky the boar. Steer clear, or he'll have your leg off. We keep him just to get rid of human remains. So, be careful, watch what you're doing – he's got a taste for human flesh, and he's got teeth three inches long and they're bloody sharp.'

'Worst of all, though,' said Dean Gorrie, lowering his voice, 'if there's a bloody awful smell comin' off him, he's got the hots for you, so I'd keep out of reach if was you.'

The young lad's lips crumpled.

Greg Gorrie rubbed his hands together. 'But on the

bright side, lad, you're all set. You are now a member of the Honourable Company of Gentlemen Shit-Shovellers. So, pick up your symbols of office and get started. Dean'll be back soon to see how you're getting on. Don't let him down,' he said ominously.

When the Gorries had gone, Chizzie peered round the door and watched as the neophyte pigman entered the first pen and began shovelling up the soiled straw. The pigs slowly gathered around him; one even ventured to sniff his wellies, triggering what looked like a panic attack in the lad, who jolted backwards, almost falling over. Regaining his balance, he swung his shovel at the pigs with a scream of 'Get lost! Leave me alone!' He was almost crying, pleading. 'Go away!' he screamed and took another swipe with his shovel.

Chizzie winced.

Then suddenly Billy came rushing out of hiding. 'You! You!' he shouted, as he ran up to the lad. 'You can't do that!'

The lad recoiled, then braced himself, holding his shovel like a weapon. 'Who… who are you?' he asked.

'You hit the pigs!' Billy replied. 'You can't do that.'

'Who are you?' repeated the lad.

'Never you mind,' replied Billy.

'Bloody hell!' hissed Chizzie. Disaster loomed. He slid out from behind the door. 'Hold it! Hold it!' he shouted, staggering to his feet. 'Agricultural Inspectorate! Stay where you are!'

Billy and the young man stood dumbstruck as Chizzie strode quickly towards them with all the assuredness of a man who knew that you can get away with anything so

113

long as you say it with conviction and authority. The trick is to first trick yourself. Believe, and they too will believe.

A desperate belief overcame Chizzie. Exuding a commanding presence that surprised even himself, the new Chizzie advanced towards the young farmworker. 'On behalf of His Majesty's Inspectorate of Agriculture, Food and Fisheries,' declared Chizzie, directing his gaze at the lad, 'I hereby hold you in breach of the Animal Welfare Scotland Act 2003 and I order you to desist immediately. How say you?'

The young lad whitened. 'Eh? Uh, what?'

Chizzie continued imperiously, 'I am obliged to inform you that anything you say may be recorded and used in evidence against you.'

The young lad, now utterly bewildered, spluttered, 'Eh? But... but I didn't... who are you again?'

'His Majesty's Inspector Wilson, and this is Cadet Inspector—'

'Dangerfield,' Billy informed him.

'Inspectors?' croaked the young man.

'HM Inspectorate of Agriculture, Food and Fisheries.'

'Can I see your ID?' whined the lad nervously.

Chizzie eyed him sternly. 'I beg your pardon?'

'Uh... nothing. I-I'm a bit confused.'

'They all say that,' snapped Billy. ''Specially the guilty ones.'

The lad blinked. 'You look awfully young for an inspec—'

'He's a vegan,' said Chizzie quickly. 'Part of an experiment in genetically modified superfoods.'

'A human guinea pig,' Billy was quick to add.

114

Chizzie nodded. 'And looking good on it too, so far, don't you think?'

'Uh… yeah, yeah,' replied the lad, with little conviction.

Chizzie regained his gravitas. 'I have to inform you that this building is under surveillance by webcam and your cooperation or obstruction is being recorded.'

The young man gulped and took a quick look at the rafters.

'Now, how many animals are under your care?' Chizzie demanded.

'Eh? Uh, I don't know.'

Chizzie drew back in mock astonishment. 'You don't know?'

'I-I just started today. I don't want to be here. They sent me here… I think… I think I'm going to… going to faint.'

The lad turned very pale, and his legs gave way. Chizzie and Billy grabbed him quickly by the armpits. They helped him over to a pile of loose straw and laid him down, and Chizzie opened the lad's collar, then raised his legs until they were almost vertical. Now it was Chizzie's turn to feel faint; with a possible casualty on his hands and the arrival of criminals possibly imminent, he began to perspire.

'How're you feeling, sir? Better now?' he asked, with more than a hint of desperation.

The lad nodded and took a deep breath. 'Yeah. Yeah. I need to get up,' he whined. 'It's draughty and… and smelly down here. I'm okay. I'm okay now.'

'Excellent. Grab hold, Billy – Mr Dangerfield.'

They helped the lad to his feet.

'Good news, sir, good news,' said Chizzie. 'We won't be taking any action against you on this occasion.'

The lad sighed and grinned weakly. 'Oh... oh, that's a relief. Thank you, thank you.' His look of relief was matched twice over by the expression on Chizzie's face.

'Right, just one more question,' Chizzie said hurriedly. 'Are there any pet animals on this site – dogs, cats, that kind of thing?'

The lad, now with colour returning to his cheeks, was eager to help. 'Yes, yes: two cats – one called Bugsy and the other... the other...'

'Yes. Right. Two cats – any small dogs?'

'No... Oh, wait – hang on! Yes. I saw a small dog in the back of a car – Maggie, or Peggy; something like that. They took it into the house.'

Chizzie's face lit up and Billy smiled.

'Birds?' asked Chizzie, trying to maintain an official face.

'Well, yeah, some – some wild birds about. Don't know what kind, though.'

'Excellent, sir. You've been very helpful. Thank you for that. We're going to let you get back to your work now. Check the doorway, Bill – uh, Mr Dangerfield.'

Billy ran to the doorway.

Chizzie patted the young man on the shoulder. 'Good luck to you, sir, and remember: the webcam's still watching you.'

Billy came running back. 'The tough guy's coming!' he said hurriedly.

Chizzie froze for a moment, then thought hard.

'Behind the door!' advised Billy.

'Good thinking, Dangerfield,' said Chizzie. 'When Gorrie goes to the bales, we leave.'

'I'm coming too,' insisted the lad. 'I don't want to be here anymore.'

Chizzie shook his head. 'No, no, you must stay here and—'

'No, no, he'll bawl at me or hit me – he's dangerous. I haven't cleaned any pens; there's no work done. I don't feel safe.'

Chizzie's mind raced. 'He'll search all over the place if you're not here.'

'No way I'm staying,' the lad insisted.

'Right, come with us, then,' agreed Chizzie.

They filed in behind the propped door, crouching and creeping backwards: Chizzie first, then the lad, and finally Billy.

Moments later, Dean Gorrie entered the barn. A few steps in, he stopped, looked about, then called out, 'Jamie! Jamie!'

'That's me,' whispered the lad.

There followed a minute of silence.

'Take a peek, Mr Dangerfield, and see what's happening,' said Chizzie.

Billy carefully peered round the door. 'He's down the far end, walking about, looking into things. I think we should go now.'

'No. Wait until he's gone in beside the bales.'

'I think… I think I'm going to sneeze,' Jamie announced, screwing up his face.

Billy immediately turned and slapped his hand against Jamie's mouth, causing a reversal of pressure, and Chizzie caught the fart full in the face.

'Oh God, I'm sorry about that,' Jamie whined.

'It's okay,' replied Chizzie, with a tortured smile. 'It's no worse than anything else I'm breathing in here.'

'Actually,' said Jamie, beginning to tremble, 'I think… I think I'm going to be claustrophobic.'

'Going to be? Or currently are?' asked Chizzie nervously.

'I am,' replied the lad shakily. 'I'm going… I'm going to panic.'

'Think about something nice,' whispered Chizzie. 'I'll help you find a job, how's that? A nice job. What d'you like doing?'

'Making soup,' said Jamie, sounding a bit wobbly.

'Anything else? Not much chance of carving out a career in soup.'

'Heinz did okay,' Billy remarked.

'And Campbell,' said Jamie.

'Well, it's a bit crowded, then,' Chizzie whispered. 'How about something else?'

'Baking – I quite like that,' Jamie replied.

'Perfect,' said Chizzie. 'There're possibilities there. I have friends in the baking world. Give me your phone number later and I'll find you something – enough to keep your benefits coming at least.'

The young man seemed almost reinflated; a broad smile crossed his face. 'Thank you, thank you. My mum'll be over the moon. Sorry I swung at the pigs. I was just a bit dizzy; I didn't know what—'

'It's okay, we'll let it go,' said Chizzie. 'Now, a word to the wise: don't tell the employment people you met agricultural inspectors. They know nothing about us, and we need to keep it that way. Just tell them you got a better job offer. That shows initiative; they like that.'

Jamie turned and smiled; gratitude gleaming in his eyes even in the half-light. 'Great. Who would've thought my career in baking would take off in a pig shed?'

Billy grinned. 'We spend a lot of time in pig sheds, cowsheds, sheep sheds... And we help a lot of people into—'

'Yeah, we're a broad church,' Chizzie broke in. 'How are things out there, Bill – Mr Dangerfield?'

Billy peered out again. 'He's going into the bales now!'

'Right, we're outta here! Go!' hissed Chizzie.

They scrambled out from behind the door, and without looking back they ran out towards the first shed.

'Go and find Yolanda,' said Chizzie.

'I'm here,' came a voice from behind a rusty barrel. 'What on earth's going on?'

'We'll tell you shortly. Let's just get the hell outta here.'

On the way back to the car, the lad cleaned his wellies in the stream and Chizzie recounted the pig shed experience to Yolanda, as one agricultural inspector to another. The pretence was maintained until finally Jamie was dropped off near his home in Perth. Chizzie ensured that the lad never saw the registration plate, lest he succumb to interrogation.

They knew now that Peggy was held prisoner in the farmhouse, and they knew too that they would be back. They would enter the house.

CHAPTER 16

'Absolutely never again!' insisted Weever. 'No more running through fields and mountains for me. I'm still getting nightmares.'

Erica smiled. 'Well, we'll arrange something less taxing when you feel better.'

'If it lifts my pulse more than two beats, it's out.'

'Let's just wait a bit till we feel renewed. For now, we turn our attention to augmenting the historical record. And I am pleased to inform you that we have wheels in motion. We have a student who will pluck the McShellach clan from near non-existence into colourful prominence.'

'What's that mean exactly?'

'We lay a trail of evidence, the student gathers it, and then he writes it up for us.'

'How much?'

'Not a penny. We have the perfect young man for our purposes. He's a history honours student and an anarchist who wants to go straight into politics.'

'You're kidding me, right?'

'No.'

'Sounds like he wants to go into a mental institution.'

'That may be, but he's just the fellow we need. He's clever, but he is not wise.'

'He'll go far in politics.'

'He's spent so much time on his student politics, he's left himself virtually no time to write his honours thesis or revise. He's desperate and down. He needs to present an outstanding thesis. We ride to the rescue by practically writing the thesis for him. Not literally, of course: we simply stick his nose in the scent, and he hunts out our tasty morsels.'

'Where'd you get this guy?'

'One of my former colleagues at the university offered him up for mutual benefit. The young man is my colleague's nephew, and his mother is at her wits' end; she's pressing my colleague to get the young man through his degree. So, we'll see that he gets through, thus pleasing his mother, who in turn pleases my colleague, and – most important of all – the young man validates your claim to be clan chief. It's a win-win-win-win.'

'What if someone follows up and checks it out?'

'It's an honours thesis; no historian is going to read it beyond a few worn-out examiners. Besides, we're in the plausible and possible parts of the spectrum.'

'Awesome! Wonderful! Happiness, happiness, happiness!'

'All we need now is an expert forger.'

'No problem. I'll contact Digger.'

'Who's Digger?'

'My fixer. Lying low for now, but he'll know the best in the business.'

'Excellent. Once the forger's on board, I'll give him genuine period paper which I've liberated from dusty archives, along with samples of period script and type. He then puts it all together and the rest is history.'

'You know, I never used to like history, but I've rather changed my mind now.'

'I think you'll like it even more when you see this.' She took a sheet of A4 paper from her document case and handed it to him. 'This is where we show the Lord Lyon King of Arms that you are descended from the bastard son of a clan chief.'

'What?! *Bastard* son? You mean… you mean *I'm* some kind of a bastard?'

'Not that it will be entirely new to your ears, I'm sure. On this occasion, however, there is some justification. And, being of bastard stock, you are of course in very exalted company. In the company of half the landed gentry and nobility, no less. When you're rich and powerful you have the opportunity to put it about a bit, as you may already know.'

'What's that mean?'

'How many children do you have?'

'Three: two sons; one daughter.'

'And that's it?'

'Yes,' he replied sternly, but with just a hint of doubt.

'Fortunately for us, some of the great houses have not been quite so honourable as your good self, and in their shadow we have an excellent opportunity to present impressive credentials. As you will see, the document in your hand shows that Clan Chief Alasdair John McShellach of McShellach arguably raised the low-born son of one of your ancestors as his own and made him clan chief.'

'For real?'

Erica smiled and paused a moment. 'You tell me.'

'Go on.'

'You see, the chief was desperate for a male heir; so desperate that, when his wife gave birth to yet another stillborn, he arranged to swap his dead child for your ancestor's baby boy born two days earlier.'

'You mean he took my ancestor's baby in exchange for a dead one?'

'These were harsh and desperate times, Gordon, and your relatives, with five other children, could not afford another mouth to feed. So, the swap was in everyone's best interests: the chief needed to prove he could sire a viable heir, your relatives escaped further poverty, and the child enjoyed a standard of living beyond the dreams of most. Inevitably, there were rumours that the boy was in fact the chief's very own bastard son, so in that regard you are in right royal company. As you can imagine though, not everyone was happy. The clan chief had a brother, who now was denied the chance to become clan chief. He contested the succession, and you hold the very document presenting the brother's case.'

'The real thing?'

'The draft we submit to the forger.'

Weever gazed at the draft document and looked impressed. 'Well, this, I must say, would convince me, even just by looking at it.'

'Fortunately, the action did not succeed.'

'Ugh. The Lord Lyon guy killed it?'

'It never went that far. Money changed hands; debts got settled.' She reached into her document case and took out a thin foolscap-size box. 'You'll find two blank pages of paper from the period in this box. They're for the forger.'

'So that's the real McCoy,' purred Weever, 'ye genuine oldie worldie paper.'

'Indeedie. Saved from obscurity.'

Weever made to pull out the blank pages.

'No, don't touch! Your greasy fingers'll foul the forger's ink.'

'Greasy fingers!' growled Weever, his face reddening rapidly.

'Sorry, oils. I meant oils. We all have nice oils in our skin, Gordon. They keep it healthy,' she said reassuringly. 'A sign of rude health, but not good for ye oldie paper about to receive ye oldie ink.'

Calming down but still a bit red round the collar, Weever focused on the draft document. It was upside down, but Erica said nothing, she looked away. Moments later, with a self-conscious glance at Erica, he turned the draft document right way up and saw:

A full Submiffion
of
Arguments concerning the Birth of
Ranald Alasdair McShellach
The Intreague thereof detected
whereunto is annexed
being fet forth with the way and manner of doing it.
Defcribing the place wherein the true Mother was delivered
with the particular door and paffages through which the
child was convey'd
to the
CHIEF'S BEDCHAMBER

'Have you checked this?' exclaimed Weever. 'It's full of typos!'

'That's the way they wrote in those times.'

'What?! "Paffages"? "Submiffion"? No wonder they wore tights.'

Erica smiled. 'Actually, Gordon, what you see as an "f" is how they sometimes wrote the letter "s". So, if you want to be authentic, that's how you write it.'

'Impoffible!'

'But true.'

'Well, I hope the King of Armf paffef it okay if he feef it.'

'I'm fure he'd be impreffed, Gordon, but it won't go that far.'

'You really think people will believe it?'

'Certainly they will. There is royal precedent for the very same thing.'

'Really?'

'Really. In 1688, no less than King James VII and II was widely believed to have pulled off a similar ploy after he and his wife, Mary of Modena, seemingly failed to produce a son who could perpetuate their dynasty. A son was raised, nonetheless. It was claimed by the King's opponents that the royal baby was actually illegitimate; a changeling born in a nearby convent before being smuggled into St James's Palace in a warming pan carried by the gentleman of the bedchamber. So, dear Gordon, we are in highly exalted company.'

'Jeezuz! And I thought I was devious.'

Three days later, Weever was in the drawing room at McShellach House. He had great news for Erica. News that had him swollen with pride. If pride was a gas like hydrogen he would've been off his feet and floating round the room, elevated to a feeling of even higher greatness. When Erica finally arrived, he wasted no time in greeting her with a kiss on the cheek, and then triumphantly he announced, 'It's official! I am a great-great-great-great-bastard! I have the proof to hand!'

'If it's what I think it is, it's "great bastard" a dozen times over.'

'It is indeed. See what you think.'

He took a sheet of yellowish paper from a cardboard folder and handed it to her. She leaned back in the comfy armchair and scrutinised it carefully. Weever sat in the armchair next to hers, watching her eagerly like a puppy waiting for a ball to chase.

A few minutes later, Erica chuckled. 'Your forger fellow is to be congratulated – excellent work, and so quick! We'll deposit the document in the private letters of Lord Kinntoul at Letterknowe.'

'The forger found it very easy, apparently. He asked a few questions, but we told him it was a prop for a film we're making. He thought that was nice.'

'Well, let the cameras roll, Gordon. I have two more props for him. When he's worked his magic on them, we'll insert them into one of the unclassified boxes in the archives of Duncrieffe Castle.' She opened her document case and took out a sheet of A4 paper. 'I have here two further proofs of your standing as a descendant of the McShellach chiefs. Many of the parish records have been digitised and they're almost impossible to alter, so we need to create a trail that leaves a few open ends. Fortunately, I've found two of your forebears who vanished – only God knows where – in the wilds of North America.'

'The Alamo?'

'Earlier.'

'Indian fighters?'

'Maybe. Who knows? Maybe they just fell into a bog. The important thing is, there is no record of death. I have two documents dated before your ancestors left for North America. Firstly, look at this one.' She handed him a sheet of paper. 'It's a letter extolling your ancestor's kindness when he met a captain of the Buffs Regiment. A perfect example of the officer's handwriting.'

Weever perused the document:

Rannoch, 8th October 1753

Esteemed and Noble Sir,

I am given to understand that you are well acquainted with the Estimable Clan Chief John Baan McShellach. I therefore, by your renowned Graciousnefse, take the Liberty of Requesting that you Present on my behalf the enclosed Letter addrefsed to Clan Chief McShellach. The Letter Exprefses my sincere Gratitude for the merciful Kindnesse shewn by the Chief to my patrole on 28th September last. But for the Chief's Generosity I fear great Suffering would have Befallen my men that day in Glen Lyon when there Came on so dreadfull a Storm as had very near been the Destruction of them all. The Fury of the Storm not abating, with some difficulty they Continued in their Wet Cloths all day. The Poor Men had already Endured great Fateagues and indeed were almost in Total Want of Necefsaries. Yet

127

as Noon pafsed, Fortune turned for the Troops as they came upon Chief John Baan McShellach and a Party of his Men taking Refuge in a Rock Shelter. These God-fearing people gave of their humble Provisions of Biskitt and Mutton, such that the Patrole was raised Mightily in Spirit. And with their Cloths dried at the fire the Soldiers were again enabled to Face the Violent Tempest and return to Barracks with Chearfullnefs and Patience. Praise be to God and His merciful Servants.

I am obliged by your Afsistance, Sir.
Yours very sincerely and respectfully,
Captain Hewett,
The Regiment of Buffs,
Commanding in the District of Rannoch

'Oh yes, yes, marvellous, very believable – generosity is a thing I'm known for. It comes right down the line. That's me to a T.'

'It's not real, Gordon.'

'It's realer than you think. I'm the kind of guy that would give his last… whatsit… biscuit and mutton to anybody in trouble. I feed families all over the world. I put bread and mutton on their tables. Better than that, in fact: I put all kinds of goodies on tables. And everybody should know that. Yeah, great letter, that – very nice letter; very nice.'

'Well, perhaps you'll like this one too.' She handed him another sheet of paper. 'This is a note written by none other than the great Samuel Johnson extolling another ancestor's prowess in the art of dancing. The letter was written to the local clan chief in Raasay following a seemingly raucous ceilidh which Messrs Johnson and Boswell greatly enjoyed in the year 1773. Ignore the introductory stuff, and read the second paragraph,' she said.

Weever began reading:

Glorious as the Sun were the brave and flying feet of Clan Chief Rory Bain McShellach. The wings of Fortune never saw a finer dancer than the McShellach that day. Veritably, I imagined I was among the Gods of Antiquity in the presence of such poise, such swiftsure command of the sweet verdure over which he did move like a whispering Phantom. The Graces and the God Apollo, in the zenith of all their glory, could not have surpassed such elegant exposition.

Weever raised his head and looked thoughtful.

'So, there we have it,' said Erica. 'Your ancestors as clan chiefs were not only gracious and generous; they were men of culture and athletic prowess, with none other than the famous Samuel Johnson vouching for the fact.'

'How real is this?'

'Eminently plausible. We teeter on the rim of reality. And in the absence of anything to the contrary, you are heir apparent to the chieftainship of Clan McShellach.'

CHAPTER 17

'A raid on the Gorries' house?' said Jenna, raising an eyebrow. 'You really think that's safer than ambushing them in the open air? Well, I have to say, I don't agree. I think it's best we get ourselves to a place where we can call to Peggy, and she'll come running; then we hightail it.'

'They have a Maserati,' Yolanda reminded her.

'We can fix that.'

There seemed to be no persuading Jenna, so Yolanda and Chizzie reluctantly agreed to help her and Caitlin put their plan into action. To ensure an early start, Chizzie and Yolanda spent the following night with friends in Perth.

As the early morning mist cleared, Caitlin phoned. 'The Gorries are on the move, heading towards Perth. I think they have Peggy on board.' There was nervousness in her voice.

Yolanda reassured her. 'Right, we're on our way. Stay in touch. Let us know everything we need to know.'

On the outskirts of Perth, as traffic delays caused by roadworks drew frustration from Chizzie and Yolanda, Caitlin called to say that she and Jenna were on the motorway approaching the Craigend junction. Shortly after, as Chizzie steered the car towards the motorway, Caitlin was in touch again.

'We've passed Broxden roundabout and we're heading towards Stirling. No, no – wait a minute… we're turning off towards the Old Crieff Road.'

When Chizzie and Yolanda arrived at the Old Crieff Road turn-off, Caitlin informed them that the Gorries had got out of their car with Peggy on a lead and were entering the grounds of little Ruthven Church.

After that, there were no further calls. Chizzie said nothing but began to fear the worst. A look of similar concern was in Yolanda's eyes. Passing Ruthven Church, they saw a big blue Maserati in the parking bay at the gate. They continued past the church until they came to a four-way road junction, several hundred yards away, and then turned around to assess the situation. Chizzie brought out his binoculars and scanned the small stone-built Ruthven Church, set among fields and surrounded by stone walls. Locally it was known as 'the Ruthven chapel'. It had two graveyards: one in front of the church and a smaller one at the rear. Parked alongside the church wall was their friends' car. Cautiously, Chizzie drove towards the church and found that their friends' car was parked on a strip of mown grass; placed there, presumably, for visitors to the church and the graves. Chizzie reversed his car onto the grassy strip.

After quietly closing the car doors, they hurried along by the stone wall until they came to a small ironwork gate, which they opened carefully and then passed into the main graveyard. They continued beside a high stone wall until they came to an arch spanning the path to the church, and beyond it, the smaller graveyard. Peering round the archway, Chizzie saw two figures moving about only a short distance beyond the church – both were men, one with a small dog on a lead. A few seconds' more observation and it was obvious that the two men were indeed the Gorries. There was no sign of Caitlin and Jenna. The church door was open.

'Let's go into the church,' Yolanda suggested. 'Maybe we can get a fuller view of what's happening.'

Chizzie nodded, and in they went. An information board by the door informed them that Ruthven Church was founded in the seventeenth century and extended in the mid nineteenth century to create the current T-shape. The far door of the church was wide open and the Gorries' voices were audible, so Chizzie and Yolanda crept to the door and listened.

Dean Gorrie apparently had urgent business. 'I need a pee,' he said loudly, looking around.

'Well, see if there's a toilet in the church. If not, don't go and—'

'I know, I know. What d'you think I am?'

'I know what you are.'

Chizzie gulped. Being in a church offered no guarantee that Dean Gorrie would refrain from punching a person's lights out. 'He's coming in!' Chizzie whispered tersely. 'Hide in the pews.' Quickly, he and Yolanda got into the sixth row of pews and lay down.

Dean entered with a heavy, loping stride. He stopped at the pulpit, looked into it and, for a moment or two, seemed to think things over. Then, having thought, he proceeded to the other door and left the building. Chizzie heard him yell, 'No toilet!'

'Let's listen in again,' suggested Yolanda, getting to her feet.

They took up their positions again at the door; this time daring to take a look. Greg was walking slowly among the graves with Peggy on a lead.

'Not there!' he shouted at Dean. 'Find somewhere out the way.'

Dean grumbled and walked to the shaded side of the church.

'Not on the chapel, you dummy!'

'Since when did you believe in God?' Dean yelled back.

'You never know. I don't want any bolts of lightning hitting the place. It might upset the dog.'

'Hey – dog, God; same thing back to front.'

'Very smart. You should walk with a full tank more often.'

'No kiddin'; I'm really burstin'. I'm goin' behind that big stone.'

'That's somebody's grave, that is.'

'Who cares? The flowers could use a sprinkle.'

Greg shook his head and carried on walking with Peggy.

Suddenly a woman's voice cut the air. 'Oi, you!' she bawled, standing next to the church. 'You foul beast! Stop that! Stop that, you disgusting devil!'

Shocked, Dean instinctively swung away and pulled at his zip fly.

The woman – grey-haired, smartly dressed, and carrying a bunch of flowers – marched up to Dean. She was livid. 'You foul brute!' she yelled. 'Get out of here before I call the police!'

But Dean, now fully restored to normality, had advice for her. 'You call the police, lady, and I'll burn your chapel down and smash all the gravestones. So dump yer flowers and clear off.'

Greg came running up, apologising profusely. 'I'm so very sorry, madam, so sorry. Please accept our heartfelt apologies and condolences on your loss. My brother's mentally handicapped and doesn't quite know what's—'

'Whajja mean, "mentally handicapped"?!' bellowed Dean. 'I'm not mentally handicapped.'

'So handicapped he doesn't even know it,' countered Greg. 'Kicked in the head by a horse when he was three. Our mother died young, and we grew up in an orphanage. We got this dog from the rescue centre to try and socialise him – my brother, that is, not the dog. Please forgive him in the name of Our Lord Jesus Christ.' He bowed his head and recited something like a bit of the Lord's Prayer, ending with 'forgive us as we forgive our trespassers'.

Dean looked on like some kind of zoo exhibit brought in for breeding purposes but with absolutely no idea what was going on. The woman took a deep breath, eyed Dean sternly, shook her head, bit her lip, then walked away to place her flowers beside a grave. She then left, never once looking back towards the Gorries, who then started arguing.

'You're not tellin' people I'm mentally handicapped!' Dean roared.

'Actually, you *are* mentally handicapped! Who else would go and pee on a gravestone?'

'Aw, shut up, will ya? Just shut it!'

'What you cryin' for?'

'I'm not cryin'. It's just, my eyes are waterin'. My foreskin's stuck in my effin' zip. It's absolute agony. I need

134

to… I need to get it out, but it's not comin' out. If I pull it, it could be nasty, an' if I pull the zip down it'll run over it, and that'll be nasty too. Aw, God!'

'I'll call the fire brigade.'

'I was hopin' it would just slide out. But it won't shift.'

'Well, you can't walk about with it stuck in there forever. You'll need a new pair of trousers someday. I'll pull the zip for you. It'll be quick. You just look up at the clouds and listen to the birds. I'll give you fair warning, you brace yourself, then I pull – all done in seconds.'

Dean thought for a moment. 'Okay,' he said, and looked up at the sky.

Greg bent over and, without any warning, immediately yanked the zip.

Dean shot backwards with a horrible roar, clutching his crotch, almost dancing. 'Ooyah! Ooyah! Ooyah!' he bawled insistently, like no one had heard him the first time. 'Ye didn't give me time to get ready, ya bastard!' he wailed.

'I did you a favour,' replied Greg airily. 'And not just one. I got the old lady off yer back as well, you ungrateful mutt.'

'Whajja mean, "mutt"? I'm fed-up o' your crap. Mentally handicapped; mutt – anymore an' I'll wallop you, I'm tellin' you.'

'You just try it, Deano, you big brontosaurus.'

'Right! Right, I will!' Dean stepped brazenly up to Greg and swung a right hook.

Greg avoided it simply by stepping backwards with a smile. 'Punch, punch, punch; that's all you think about,' said Greg, laughing. 'You'd punch yer own head if I didn't keep you right.'

'I'm warnin' you.'

'Wow, I'm shakin'. In any case, dear brother, who got your prong out yer zip? I haven't heard any thanks yet. I look forward to a bunch of flowers – and not from here.'

This seemed to strike a chord, causing Dean to think for a moment. 'Okay,' he agreed. 'Okay. I don't punch you, and that's thanks.'

'You just can't bring yourself to say, "Thank you", can you?'

'You were rough with my dinger.'

'Tough love, bruv. You're a free man now. And if you want to make something of it, start doing something useful. Look for signs of digging.'

'In a graveyard?'

'Small area; fairly fresh. Start over in the far corner like I told you.'

'Told me?'

'Okay. I'm asking.'

'Right, that's better. I'm looking.'

To get a better view of what was going on, Chizzie and Yolanda went upstairs, past the peeling paintwork and the sections of wall where the plaster had fallen off. Cautiously they looked through the upstairs window. To their horror, they saw Caitlin and Jenna crouching behind a large gravestone in the smaller graveyard where the Gorries were roaming.

Chizzie's jaw dropped. 'What on earth are Caitlin and Jenna thinking?' he groaned.

'Probably hoping to leap out and grab Peggy,' suggested Yolanda, raising her eyebrows.

Chizzie shook his head. 'It's Caitlin and Jenna that'll

get grabbed. They need to get out of there. If Peggy gets wind of their scent, she could get excited and the Gorries'll think they're on to their loot.'

They both sighed heavily and tried to think of some way to intervene. Two bumblebees on the windowpane buzzed into life and pinged against the glass several times before buzzing round Chizzie and Yolanda, making it difficult for Chizzie to think properly. He tried to waft them away but succeeded only in making them more of a nuisance as they now buzzed closer to his head.

'Two bees or not two bees, that is the question,' he whispered ominously as he weighed the options.

Yolanda smiled and sang softly, 'All Things Bright and Beautiful'.

And fortunately for all, the bees withdrew and flew back to the window.

Then an idea flashed into Chizzie's mind. 'You go round the outside of the wall and help Caitlin and Jenna get away, and I'll draw the Gorries off. I'm the church minister.'

'What?'

'Watch.' He took off his dark blue jumper and his white shirt and put the shirt on back to front to create a clerical collar before putting the jumper back on.

Yolanda buttoned the collar.

'Now give me a middle parting and your sunglasses.'

Yolanda obliged, kissed him, and wished him luck before dashing away.

Chizzie waited nervously, gradually feeling more and more vulnerable. He cast his mind to the rows of empty pews, and reflected on how, in days gone by, the low ceiling and the thick stone walls would have resonated to the power of more than a hundred sons and daughters of the soil, the sound of their voices flowing through the windows into the pure country air and over the fields. Now the only sound that remained was the faint buzzing of confused bees. Chizzie peered out and eventually saw Yolanda wave from behind the far wall. Time for the minister to step up. He opened the window, let the bees fly free; then the Reverend Chizzie Bryson, minister of this parish, did speak these words: 'You two men! Leave this place at once, or I call the police! Get thee hence!'

The Gorries responded in accordance with their normal custom and practice: a fixed smile from Carl and two fingers from Dean.

This uncharitable response silenced the Reverend Chizzie for a moment. Then he saw Caitlin and Jenna scurrying towards the wall. He had to ensure the Gorries didn't see them. He took a deep breath and shouted, 'I said begone, and… and mend thy ways!' It was the best he could think of there and then.

Dean turned and gave Chizzie a studied look, as if trying to place his face. Greg simply ignored him, not even bothering to turn round. Dean, though, now looked aroused: like a bull who'd just seen a red cape; almost snorting with rage. It looked ominously like he might soon be heading back into the church again. 'Time for a tactical withdrawal', thought Chizzie. But then, a miracle: the actual, real minister of the parish came striding along the path, heading towards the Gorries. With a quick look heavenward that was almost a thank-you, Chizzie turned and dashed down the stairs in time to hear Dean Gorrie welcome the good man of the cloth.

'Aw Christ, not another one!' he bawled.

'I beg your pardon?' replied the minister indignantly.

'There's ministers poppin' out o' the woodwork all over the place!' explained Dean.

'I beg your pardon! There's but one minister here, and that is me.'

Dean moved towards the minister. 'You're an impostor, you are! You're fuzz, right?'

The minister eyed Dean like he was confronting an escaped lunatic or a hallucinating drug addict. 'I've had a complaint about your behaviour,' he informed Dean calmly, 'and I'm directing you to leave now, or I will call the police.'

Greg held up a placating hand. 'Wait a minute. Wait a minute,' he said. 'Hold on. Hold on. If you're a minister, answer me this: who wrote "The Lord Is My Shepherd"?'

'It was David.'

Dean, quick as a flash, was in with the follow-up question: 'Yeah, but David who? Answer me that!'

Greg stepped forward. 'Excuse my brother; he's… he's—'

'I'm not bloody mentally handicapped again! I'm not havin' that! No way!'

'All right, all right, calm down,' said Greg. 'So, who's the other minister, then?'

The minister looked perplexed. 'What other minister?' he asked.

'The one in the church right now,' said Greg.

'There is no other minister. As I said, I'm the minister here.'

'So, who was—?'

'Some creep's followed us!' bawled Dean. 'I told you we was bein' followed. He wants our stuff! He thinks it's here.'

'What stuff?' asked the minister.

'Never mind,' growled Dean. 'I'm gonna get that creep!' Glaring at the window where Chizzie had been, he strode swiftly towards the church.

Chizzie swung round and ran to the far door and out onto the path. His back-to-front shirt restricted his arm movements and breathing, but he reached the little gate through which he'd come and sprinted to the cars. Yolanda had the engine running. Chizzie opened the passenger door and swung onto the seat. Careful to avoid spinning the wheels on the turf, Yolanda got the car onto the road, followed by Caitlin and Jenna in their Ford Fiesta.

'Quick as you can, Yolanda,' said Chizzie nervously. 'They'll come after us in their Maserati.'

'No they won't,' replied Yolanda. 'We let their tyres down.'

CHAPTER 18

It was one of those days when Gordon Weever felt what he called 'frisky'. In the passenger seat, with Erica driving, he had time to look out of the corner of his eye and survey her as a woman as opposed to a confidante and consultant. He leaned back in his seat to get a better look. She was a prize catch. If she'd been a fish, thought Weever, what would she be? He wasn't good at fish; his range was limited: salmon and trout he knew, but little else. Erica was certainly no trout, but what could she be? He'd fished for marlin once and caught only seasickness. He'd seen nice, colourful fish on TV, but they were all frightened looking. He switched his attention to land animals; here again though, the range was somewhat limited. The two animals he saw in people most often were the sheep and the hyena, and Erica was neither. Birds were no help – no swallow, no eagle. A big fly hit the windscreen. Insects? A butterfly, perhaps – no, Erica was no flapping butterfly. Then something swept past the windscreen.

'What was that?' he asked excitedly. 'That blue flash?'

'A damselfly,' replied Erica.

Weever smiled, for a damselfly was the very thing. Erica was a damselfly. A dashing jewel of a woman. A high-flyer. They had so much in common, he and she, he mused, and here was an opportunity to catch her off guard while her attention was focused on the road. She took great care with her driving – that, presumably, was why she didn't let him drive her anywhere. She would not surrender herself to the more confident driving style he favoured. To try a line or await an even better opportunity; that was Weever's dilemma. He turned his head and gazed vacantly out of the side window as his mind churned. When his eyes slyly returned to Erica once more, he was somewhat chilled by a mental picture of the female spider that eats the male immediately after copulating. He didn't feel quite so frisky now.

'Nice bit of country out here,' he remarked.

Erica agreed and kept her eyes on the road.

Weever, calling on all his experience of women, took this to mean *Keep your paws off*. She was a smart cookie, and seemingly very experienced in the field of men as well as history. Certainly, she held the respect of her ex-colleagues, and she'd more than held her own in business. The frisky feeling returned as he eyed her slender shoulders surreptitiously once more.

But perhaps Erica could sense something. 'Like some music?' she asked, simultaneously pressing a button on the dashboard.

The Gay Gordons flew out of four speakers; seemingly all of them strapped to Weever's head. He shuffled uneasily in his seat. Was this her way of containing him, or was it some kind of attempt to condition him into thinking country dance music was a wonderful thing? He tholed it for a minute or two, with increasing torment. Then, on the cusp of shouting, 'Shut the bloody thing off', he heard the sweetest of words.

'We're here,' said Erica, turning into a driveway.

As she parked the car at the front of Duncrieffe Castle, Erica reminded Weever of his instructions. They were very simple: ask the archivist to show him round the castle. Should that not be possible, he should distract the archivist with his undoubted charms while Erica inserted her forged document into some archival material.

They got out of the car and crunched over the gravel towards the door of the castle.

Weever looked up. 'What's that up there?' he asked.

'It's the famous flying turret of Duncrieffe Castle,' Erica replied.

'Looks like it's about to fall on top of us.'

'That's the point. If we were attacking, they could pour boiling oil over us from there. Lucky we're only here for the archives.'

A thin, prim, middle-aged woman met them at the door and introduced herself as Ms Drummond, the castle archivist, before inviting them in and showing them to the room containing the castle's archives. While Erica set to work on the private papers she'd requested, Weever set to work on removing the archivist.

'Wonderful castle you have here,' he observed. 'Pity it's not open to the public, a jewel like this; it's a national treasure, really. You're so lucky here.'

'We're open from May through to August,' Ms Drummond replied in a crisp formal tone, her head jerking very slightly as if she were maintaining tight control of herself.

'Well, I just wish I was here earlier. I'm kicking myself now. I just didn't know this great castle existed, and now it seems I've missed out.'

She hesitated, pursing her lips slightly. 'Perhaps I could show you round later.'

Weever sighed and shook his head ruefully. 'It's the time factor. I leave for New York City tonight. Could you… would it be possible to show me round now?' he almost pleaded. 'I could tell all my folks in America all about this wonderful place and the fantastic hospitality – second to none anywhere in the world. I do so love Scotland.'

With Erica confirming that she needed no further assistance from Ms Drummond, Weever's tour of the castle began with a visit to the great kitchen. They were working their way up. Leaving behind the highly polished and very uninteresting pots and pans, they journeyed to the ballroom, the library, the great dining room, and by the time they had reached the principal bedchamber they had come to know one another a tiny bit more intimately. As they entered, Ms Drummond eyed Weever with what seemed like a seductive smile. It aroused his interest. She told of Queen Victoria's visit, but he was not envisaging Queen Victoria in the big four-poster bed; he was envisaging himself in there with Ms Drummond. And they were making whoopee in a bed that had once held the Queen of England – indeed, the Queen of the United Kingdom, or was it the United Queendom at the time? Never mind the details; here was a right royal opportunity to get a once-in-a-lifetime experience! He would never be this young again. If he was to go for it, it had to be now.

He strolled round the bed, imagining himself a king, the royal supreme, caring not a jot for what anyone thought. Free as a king, he could do whatever he liked. He glanced at his queen on the other side of the bed. She too was lost in imaginings. What they could get up to knew no bounds. In his mind's eye he saw them, king and queen, freed of all care. They let rip. Cavorting in the candlelight, they shed all encumbering attire, and he romps round the bed, opening and shutting the curtains, exhibiting a variety of poses: some Greek, some Roman, some Viking, some even borrowed from the animal kingdom. And she's not idle either. She's pole-dancing on one of the uprights. Now all fired up, they start swinging from the crossbars of the bed. Wild and free as monkeys in the Congo, higher and higher they swing, until finally they loop the loop and launch into the air, clasping each other in mid-flight. Conjoined in ecstasy, they free-fall, plunging into downy, consummate bliss. Such is the sport of kings – and even the sport of clan chiefs! It was there for the taking. He knew it, and she knew it. His pulse quickened. His breathing increased. He glanced again at Ms Drummond. Her eyes met his; she knew what he was thinking. He knew she knew; he smiled; she smiled. She was thin and pale – big questions: would she conk out? Would he conk out? Would the four-poster bed conk out? Conked out and clobbered by a four-poster bed, then carted off to A&E on a stretcher, his image would be in shreds. *And Erica's not far away.* What if she caught them in flagrante? What would she say? Who knows? She might even join in! She's a feisty gal. Three in a four-poster – that would be a right royal experience and no mistake. Chance of a lifetime! His lips trembled as he eyed Ms Drummond sideways. She cocked her head and eyed him with a passion he could feel. They knew the way ahead; they knew the ins and outs; they thought about the ins and outs.

But they thought too much; they tarried too long. And in that cool, musty air, heavy with history, their dreams felt the press as reality rolled in, and the urgings of the present got crushed to rubble. They were to play no part. The life of that room lay firmly in the past.

As Weever waved goodbye from the car, he reflected on where he had just been in body and in spirit, and quickly he concluded that boundless power has the capacity to unhinge even the savviest of minds. On the bright side, though, a good result overall. Bold thoughts may have lost out in one room, but they'd triumphed in another. And who knows? The young student might see to Ms Drummond very soon. Or maybe the gamekeeper – they're always up for that sort of thing.

CHAPTER 19

Chizzie peered round the Gorries' garden shed.

'Any sign of Peggy?' Yolanda asked softly.

'Don't see her anywhere. Just two Gorries and one other man.'

'Okay, Plan C: we go into the house – front door.'

Chizzie thought for a moment. 'I still think that's just too risky.'

'Not half as risky as sneaking through the back door.'

'What if it's locked?'

'We come back here and wait.'

Quickly and quietly, they made their way along the side of the house to the front door.

Chizzie paused. 'It could be alarmed.'

'In which case, we scarper back to the shed again and await our opportunity.'

'You're enjoying this, aren't you?'

'Can't deny it. Aren't you?'

Chizzie shook his head. 'Not at all. It could all get a bit… well, dangerous, not to put too fine a point on it.'

'We just have to be careful and make sure we have a way out.'

They approached the front door. Yolanda put her hand on the handle and turned it very slowly. The door eased open with a faint creak. She pushed, and the door opened further. She put her head round the door and listened for a moment. Then, satisfied it was safe, she slipped inside. Chizzie followed, looking anxiously about.

'Okay,' said Yolanda. 'You go to the kitchen and keep an eye on them. I'll search the ground floor. Any problem, give me a shout. Code word: "Zorro".'

'Okay.

They made their way towards the kitchen, listening intently for any sound. The door to the living room was open, so Yolanda discreetly looked inside, then entered. The kitchen door was open too, so Chizzie entered and crossed to the window. Carefully, he peered round the curtain.

'Christ, they're coming!' he yelped as he saw the Gorrie brothers heading towards the house. He dashed out of the kitchen and swung into the dining room, shouting, 'Pancho! Pancho!'

Yolanda froze at first, and then dashed out of the living room to meet Chizzie. 'What's up?' she asked.

'The Gorries! They're coming!'

'Agh! Right, head for the front door!'

'No. No, we can't, we can't – one of them's heading round to the front.'

They froze; then they heard the back door open.

'Right, into the living room,' said Yolanda. 'There's a big sofa; we can hide behind that till it's clear.'

They crawled in between the sofa and the wall.

Chizzie muttered, 'I'm beginning to feel a bit like a hobbit these days, with all the tight spaces I'm squeezing into.'

'By the way, the code word is "Zorro",' whispered

Yolanda. 'You shouting "Pancho" confused me for a second.'

'Zorro, right, got it. A little panicky moment there. Seeing the Gorries coming all of a sudden, bit of a shock, especially in view of the fact that I'm crawling through their house. It's unnerving.'

'Okay, quiet, just listen.'

They waited several minutes in almost total silence; only the old grandfather clock made a sound with its soporific slow ticking. Then suddenly the clock bonged and Chizzie nearly shot into the air. They waited some more.

Then finally Yolanda whispered, 'I'm going to take a look out the window.'

She made to move, but Chizzie tugged her back. 'Hang on – voices.'

The voices grew louder: the Gorries were approaching. Chizzie and Yolanda eyed one another, listening intently. Then the door opened and the Gorries entered the room.

'I hate that bloody dog,' whined Dean Gorrie, slumping onto the sofa. 'I really do. I could roast it and eat the bloody thing. That's all it's good for: meat.'

'If you treat it well,' said Greg, 'it'll come round. The way you treat it, it's not going to help us. Treat it nice. Then when you're done with it, you can eat it.'

'Be like chicken, I bet.'

'Everything's like chicken these days.'

'You're making my belly rumble.'

'Right, we're going to have to widen our search,' said Greg. 'I got this map from Casey's place; it's pretty new so there might be some marks on it showin' the chapel we're after. I looked already, but maybe I missed something.'

Greg seated himself next to his brother on the sofa. Chizzie could hear the sound of paper rustling.

'You scour the left side,' said Greg, 'I'll scour the right.'

Suddenly a loud and lengthy burp erupted, and Greg let out a yell.

'Aw, come on, man! That is effin' gross!'

'*You* don't burp, of course.'

'Not like that, I don't: not like there's some kinda alien coming outta your guts!'

'It's natural.'

'It's disgusting!' complained Greg.

'Ten pounds, you owe.'

'What?'

'You used the f-word. You said we put ten pounds in the kitty every time we say the f-word.'

'I did not say the f-word, I said, "effin'",' insisted Greg. 'It's an e-word.'

'You said the f-word.'

'Didn't.'

'Did.'

'Didn't.'

'Did.'

'Didn't.'

'Did.'

'Aw, eff off!'

'Thirty pounds.'

'Never mind thirty pounds. Focus on this: if we're going into property development, we need a bit of class and we need to watch our language and control our effin' gases. Flaring off in living rooms is not going to charm anybody. I need to open a window now.' Moaning, Greg got up and opened a window. Then something outside caught his eye. 'Christ almighty! Look! Look at this! Look! Ally's let his mutt out the van.'

'He says it's a sniffer dog; better'n that bloody Peggy thing we've got.'

'It's not a sniffer dog. It's a failed sniffer dog. It's useless. It trained as a police sniffer dog but failed miserably.'

'Ally's sure he can train it.'

'Ally's an idiot. That dog's uncontrollable. Look! There! Look, look, look, it's after him. He's running for his life! He's heading for the apple tree! He's climbing up! What a prat! I knew it – I knew this would happen. The thing's a maniac.'

Dean Gorrie sounded mystified. 'He told me that dog was almost human.'

'How would he know?! It's a werewolf, like himself. Pair of identical twins, those two. Oh my God! Now look – the branch's snapped. It's going for his backside! Serves him ri… oh, nice, nice touch, nice touch with the left hook there. Beauty! Wow! Got to hand it to him, he's a bloody good mover. Aw, Christ almighty, no, no, not there! Now he's in the effin' fishpond. Get outta there, you balloon!'

'Forty quid!'

'That's it. Yeah, yeah, outta there – outta there! Good man, he's getting out the other side now. Aw God, no – no, he's slipped. He's slithering. He's down. He's up. He's down again. He's hit his head on something. It's a gnome. He's clean out – knocked out by a gnome! No, wait, no. No, no, he's getting up, he's getting up, good man! Well done! He's up; up and running. What a guy! What a guy! Thick as planks, but, boy, he has got guts.'

'Yeah, an' it sounds like they're gonna be all over our garden if he doesn't speed up.'

'He's quicker than you'll ever be.'

'I don't need to be quick; I'd knock that thing straight on the head. Punch its lights out.'

Dean rose off the sofa; managing to do so without burping or worse. A feat much appreciated by Chizzie and Yolanda.

'Hey, he's coming this way,' shouted Greg. 'Yeah, yeah, that's it, Ally boy, this way, this way, make for the door! The door! Yeah. That's it! Faster, you clown, faster!'

'He'll be full of water!'

Greg swung his attention to Dean. 'Right, what's on your sandwich?'

'My sandwich?'

'Quickly.'

'Uh… boiled ham.'

'Right, give it me.'

'What? That's my lunch.'

'You can have mine.'

'What's on yours?'

'Cheese and pickle.'

'I don't like pickle.'

'I'm not discussing the menu. Give me the bloody sandwich!'

'But what about my lunch?'

'Ally will be a lunch if you don't hurry up. Give me the meat! I'll hang it out the window. You run to the door and let Ally in. Hurry! Go!'

Chizzie saw Dean's shadow pass quickly as Greg began shouting out the window.

'Here boy! Here boy! Not you, you fool! The dog – the dog! Run to the door! I'll draw the mutt off. Here boy; here boy – choke on this, you mad bastard!'

There followed a sound of terrible growling which quickly subsided. Greg then left the room quickly.

'Right, let's go,' said Chizzie.

They headed for the door, then Yolanda turned back. 'I want to see the map they were looking at.' She quickly examined the open map. 'Ordnance Survey map 58,' she said quietly. 'No marks on it. Okay, let's go.'

They hurried to the door, then listened.

Yolanda ventured to peek into the hallway. 'Okay, we're clear.'

'Hold on,' said Chizzie, listening intently. 'I thought I heard barking.'

'Where?'

'Shoosh.'

They listened, and moments later, they heard distant barking.

'Sounds like it's upstairs,' said Chizzie.

They eyed each other. Should they risk it? Should they come back another day? Would they *get* another day? Yolanda motioned with her head, and they dashed towards the stairs, then quickly ascended. Treading softly along the upper floor, they listened carefully. Then, as they came to a door, they heard whimpering.

Chizzie opened the door slowly. Through the little gap he saw a greyish, brown dog in a travel cage near the window. 'Peggy!' he whispered, before leaning further in to look round the door. 'Only her,' he added, and in they went.

As they approached her, Peggy whimpered and drew back in the cage, clearly frightened.

Chizzie knelt and spoke to her very gently, holding out his hand for her to sniff. 'It's us, Peggy. Remember us? Nice people?'

Suddenly she recognised them and began yelping excitedly.

'Shoosh! Shoosh! Shoosh! Easy, girl,' Chizzie said soothingly as he pulled the bolt to open the cage door.

Peggy squealed with delight and wagged her tail as Yolanda picked her up.

'Right,' said Chizzie, 'let's get downstairs.'

They hurried out of the room and along to the end of the corridor, where Yolanda halted. Chizzie continued softly to the bottom of the stairs to check that all was clear. As he edged round the corner, however, he saw Greg Gorrie stride out of the kitchen and into the living room. A few seconds later, Dean Gorrie came out of the kitchen and went into the living room. Then Greg Gorrie made the reverse journey. Then Dean Gorrie came out and headed towards Chizzie. His heart thumping, Chizzie flattened himself against the stair wall, partly hidden behind the big rubber plant at the foot of the stairs. Fortunately, Dean Gorrie went straight past and continued to what proved to be the downstairs toilet. The situation was clearly too busy for a safe getaway, so the three aspiring escapees went quickly back up to the bedroom.

'Right, classic escape time,' said Yolanda. 'We knot the bed sheet and the duvet cover together and abseil out of here.'

Chizzie agreed. He removed the bedding while Yolanda comforted Peggy.

'Someone very perfumed has been in this bed,' Chizzie observed.

'Let's not dwell on that,' Yolanda replied, opening the window. 'Just knot them together.'

'Between the vapours in here and all the gases elsewhere, they're not exactly fighting climate change, are they?' Chizzie observed. Having secured the knotted bedding to the bedpost, Chizzie dropped it out the window. 'Doesn't go all the way down but it's close enough.'

Yolanda held out her hand. 'Right, give me your trouser belt. I'll put it round my hips and secure Peggy inside my jacket. You pass her to me when I'm outside and ready to go down. I'll throw your belt up to you when I'm down.'

The plan worked well until Yolanda tried throwing the belt back up to Chizzie. It proved too difficult, so Yolanda tied the belt to the bedding and Chizzie pulled it up. Suddenly he heard the door handle move; then he saw a bunch of flowers entering. Quickly he clambered out the window, grabbed hold of the bedding, and slid down it.

As he reached the ground, an old lady's head leaned out of the window. 'Are you on the run?' she enquired sweetly.

'No,' said Chizzie.

'Just practising,' said Yolanda.

'Good luck,' replied the lady. 'My lips are sealed. I won't grass.'

When they were clear of the farm, Chizzie asked anxiously, 'Did a bus go by when I was dropping out the window?'

'Yes,' replied Yolanda with a chuckle, 'so let's just hope

your young farm lad wasn't on it, watching the agricultural inspector escaping from a bedroom window with his trousers round his ankles. Very unprofessional even for the agricultural industry.'

CHAPTER 20

Weever and Erica Heyden sat waiting for the student to arrive in Weever's office. He was fifteen minutes late.

Weever shook his head. 'No wonder this bonehead is a total loser,' he moaned. 'If he can't even tell the time or get himself to a meeting on time, he's a complete waste of space. Why are we meeting him anyway? I don't want to meet him. All I want is he follows the trail we laid and he writes up his report and gets the hell outta my life. I can't stand bums!'

Erica sipped the last of her coffee. 'Let's just see how far he's got,' she advised. 'If he's got what we need, I can write up his thesis for him and he'll be out of your life forever.'

'So much for education; never trusted it in the first place. Seen too many clever idiots.'

Erica went to the window. 'The rain's gone off now and it's getting quite hot out there; I can feel it through the window.'

'That'll be his excuse – couldn't prance his way through the sunbeams. If he's not here in—'

'Oh – I do believe this is him now.'

'Right, no more meetings. We say everything we need to say here today, and that's it.'

A minute later there came a clattering noise from the

hallway, followed by an anguished cry, then a comforting female voice. Shortly after that, Weever's console speaker buzzed and the lady with the comforting voice informed him that Stanfield, the student, had arrived.

'Code five,' Weever replied. Then, responding to Erica's quizzical look, he added, 'The bonehead waits five minutes.'

Five minutes later, Stanfield entered the office carrying a dirty reddish daysack. His long, sweat-laden hair hung heavily in rope-like clumps. The sweat from his armpits had got beyond the armpits. He shuffled towards the vacant chair in front of Weever's big desk. Then he sat down heavily, releasing a wave of defeated deodorant that broke upon Weever's nostrils, causing him to go almost cross-eyed. For a moment Weever thought he'd been blinded. Worse followed, as a taste note reminiscent of boiled cabbage rose from Stanfield's scruffy trainers. Altogether it was an experience Weever would never have wished to meet in his worst nightmares, let alone straight in the face. He leaned back as far as he could in his chair. Stanfield laid his dirty rucksack on the pale beige carpet before offering a muttered apology for his lateness. Erica expressed concern about Stanfield's wetness and offered sympathy along with a tissue. Weever, too, was concerned about Stanfield's wetness: the sweat dripping onto his carpet like battery acid.

'I fell over in your hallway,' Stanfield explained. 'Heatstroke, I think. I knocked over the hatstand and it hit me on the head.'

Weever looked pleased. 'The hatstand okay?' he asked.

Stanfield nodded and rubbed his head. 'You haven't got any aspirins, have you?'

'No,' Weever replied instantly.

'Coffee?' asked Stanfield.

'We're just out,' answered Weever.

'A hairdryer?'

Weever glared. Stanfield's eyes trained on Weever's toupee; then with a slight nod he looked away and sneezed, prompting Weever to recoil and get off his chair and walk swiftly over to a window, which he opened wide. As Weever returned to his chair, Stanfield sneezed again, violently, twice.

'The draught,' croaked Stanfield. 'It's the draught; it's making me sneeze.'

'Right, outside!' yelped Weever, and he led the way out of the room, into the hall, and out the door.

Erica promptly followed. By the time Stanfield had shuffled outside, Weever and Erica were seated close together on the patio with one chair remaining to be occupied by Stanfield – that chair being about eight feet away and downwind from Weever and Erica. The chairs had recently been rained on. Erica and Weever had had the wit to wipe their chairs with handkerchiefs before sitting down, but Stanfield seemed not to notice, failed to wipe, and within seconds he was on his feet again, examining his chair for water, but too late, of course: the water was now largely embedded in his trousers and seemingly it wasn't going anywhere fast, as the dark blue patch on the seat of his jeans testified. This surprised Weever to some extent, as he'd expected the ample grime already inhabiting the jeans to render them fully waterproof. Though being proved wrong was, on this occasion, very pleasing.

'Right, sit down,' said Weever, pointedly looking at his watch, 'and tell me how you got on.'

Stanfield gave a feeble cough. 'Well,' he began, 'I've done really awesome, even if I say so myself. First off, I discovered a note from none other than the famous Dr Samuel Johnson – you know, the great English dictionary guy who thought Scots were dumb as horses 'cause they ate oats? You've heard of the guy, right?' he asked, responding to Weever's blank look.

Weever nodded with pursed lips.

'A really cool thing, that,' continued Stanfield, now talking down to the big fat guy of limited intellect. 'He mentions your ancestor as a clan chief. Got really big impact, that. And that's not all – I am able to report the discovery of a very rare artefact: a vervel with your ancestor's name on it. It's complicated, but don't worry; just know that it's great support for your case. Even if I say so myself, I'm putting together a real top-notch case for you. Really top-notch.'

'That it?' said Weever curtly.

The sharpness took Stanfield by surprise. 'Ugh!' was all he could muster, along with a pained grimace.

'Well, keep at it,' advised Weever. 'And I have to say, next time you go anywhere, wash first. You stink, man, and it bothers me that you're going into places, representing me. Apart from the fact that you're a health hazard, I sell high-end toiletries branded with my name on them, and I don't want my name hauled through the kind of mud that you carry around with you. You understand?'

Erica leaned forward, raising a placating hand. 'Easy, easy, Gordon. I'm sure this is an unfortunate one-off and Mr Stanfield will be tidier next time. Won't you, Mr Stanfield?'

Stanfield looked affronted. Then he stared, stiffened, and looked defiant. 'Well, no, actually,' came his reply. 'I won't. I can't afford toiletries. My mum sent me stuff and I sprayed some on this morning out of courtesy. And frankly, I don't feel well. I don't agree with all that guff. There's a bloody climate emergency on; climate change threatens the planet. All these chemicals folk slap on themselves; they're polluting the rivers and the sea and blowing holes in the ozone layer. It's Armageddon. And it's big corporations like yours, Mr Weever, and capitalist crooks, that're destroying the whole planet, and it can't go on. It just can't go on. I'm doing my bit. And if you don't like it, I can assure you, you'll get used to it after a while. I might stink to you, but personally, I don't notice it anymore. It's natural, see. Nature's got a way of dealing with your own personal ecosystem. You adapt. It's like if you give up sugar: after a little while, you don't notice there's no sugar in your coffee. It's all—'

'Get the hell outta here!' roared Weever. 'You talk climate change – the only goddamn climate that needs changing is the one you carry around with you! Now get out!'

Stanfield suddenly looked dazed and began to sway. His eyes drooped, and then, spinning almost 360 degrees, he fell out of his chair and clattered to the ground. And as if that wasn't drama enough, out of the blue came Tommy Neptune, rushing up like a caveman with his eyes on a fallen musk ox.

'Neptune!' wailed Weever. 'What the… what're you doing here?'

161

'Feelin' magic, so I get the idea I'll come along while the goin"s good. But then – holy moly – I see this guy hit the floor. I got him, though, I got him. Stand back. I was a paramedic once – got fired for enthusiasm; went at it too vigorous, they said. Crazy, crazy people.' To see why he'd been fired wasn't difficult. Pouncing on Stanfield, he set to work. 'I got a pulse! I got a pulse!' he declared. 'But breathing's shallow!' And with that, Neptune plunged furiously into CPR. 'Bouncy, bouncy, bouncy!' He yelled. 'Got to imagine you're on a galloping camel! Bouncy, bouncy, bouncy!' he continued fervently with all the attack of a heavy metal band.

Stanfield stirred and groaned.

'Try the kiss of life, and you don't survive,' muttered Weever. 'Up to you, though.'

'He's comin' round, he's comin' round,' Neptune forecasted.

Stanfield's eyes flickered, then opened. Then they almost leaped out of their sockets. 'Tommy Neptune!' he spluttered. 'What the…?'

'Take it easy, man, take it easy, bro,' counselled Neptune. 'You nearly was a goner there, man. How you feelin' now?'

'Tommy Neptune – wow! Saved by Tommy Neptune! Wow! It's really you. I thought… I thought for a minute I'd gone to heaven.'

'Yeah, their refuse dump,' muttered Weever.

'It's really you!' exclaimed Stanfield, still amazed.

'Sure is, kiddo. In person.'

'Wait till my partner hears about this.'

Neptune offered his hand to Stanfield, who grabbed

it and rose to his feet, seemingly in even better condition than he was in before. Weever, not unreasonably, sensed something of the drama queen about Stanfield.

'Right, let's see if you can walk a bit,' said Neptune, throwing his left arm round the student and supporting him.

'You're a brave man,' said Weever. 'No way I'd touch him with that smell.'

'What smell?' asked Neptune.

'Never mind,' said Weever. 'But if the Grim Reaper had breath like that, he wouldn't need a scythe.'

Erica broke in. 'I really think we ought to get you off to A&E, Mr Stanfield, don't you think? Get you looked over?'

Stanfield shook his head. 'I'm okay, I'm okay – I just felt a bit faint; I haven't eaten since yesterday. But meeting you, Tommy – wowee; man, oh man; I feel so much better, so much better.'

'Ain't eaten since yesterday?' said Neptune. 'Soon put that right, man.' He turned to Weever. 'I'm takin' this guy straight to my place and I want ten turkey legs sent over.'

'I'm a vegan. No meat – not unless it's roadkill.'

Neptune turned to Weever. 'You got roadkill?'

'Certainly not!'

Neptune turned to Stanfield. 'Okay, man, so whajja eatin' these days besides roadkill? Lettuce? Carrots? Peas?'

'Beans an' tofu, mostly.'

'Right,' said Neptune, placing his order with Weever. 'Huge plate of beans, an' all the toffee you got.'

'Hold it!' Weever hissed angrily. 'You're an hour early; you shouldn't even be here yet.' He tapped his watch pointedly. 'But no matter – I'm tellin' you now: your accommodation here is terminated.'

'Fabulous! Fire away! Knock 'em dead! Serious things, termites. I had termites in Texas once – serious thing, man; homewreckers. Go get 'em, man. But first, I gotta get this guy recovered. Let's walk, bro.' Neptune moved off, supporting a cheerful-looking student.

'Walking with Tommy Neptune,' marvelled Stanfield. 'Somebody take a photo.'

'Later, man,' advised Neptune. 'Right now, you just keep on walkin''

And off they went, arm in arm; one with his own climate and one with his own universe.

'I have to get rid of that creep Neptune,' groaned Weever. 'Trouble is, if I throw him out like he deserves, next thing you know, it's all over the tabloids, full front-page spread: "Bully Weever Throws Music Genius in Gutter". Like, who's gonna take my side? Nobody! I gotta get him out under a smokescreen.' Weever froze – a thought had just occurred. 'Yeah, that's it! Fire! We burn him out!'

'What?! Fire?' exclaimed Erica. 'You can't do that.'

'Not for real: we sound the fire alarm, he runs out, and we don't let him back in for technical reasons – the fire alarm needs replacing, that sort of thing. We find him alternative accommodation miles away. We're looking after the guy. His safety is our top priority. We palm him off to somebody else… Lord Tulloh, that's where he goes. Lordy boy's advertising a luxury suite for rent – just the place for Neptune.'

Erica shook her head and shrugged. Not her problem. Weever phoned his concierge and ordered him to set the fire alarm off in Redwood Cottage; the cottage currently serving as home sweet home to Mr Neptune. A few minutes later, the alarm duly went off.

Weever shot to his feet. 'Right, Operation Lockout! Let's go!' He stomped towards Redwood Cottage like a grizzly after a moose.

Erica followed close behind, unable to conceal her smile.

However, two sobering surprises hit Weever when he arrived at the cottage: firstly, there was no sign of Neptune; secondly, the nameplate on the door that should have borne the words 'Redwood Cottage' was now covered with a cardboard nameplate bearing the words 'Daffodil Cottage' scrawled upon it, and should anyone be in any doubt as to what a daffodil looked like, there was a little, colourful drawing there to help.

'Where's Neptune?' Weever asked the concierge, who stood at the cottage door.

'Still inside,' came the reply.

Growling, Weever went to the window and knocked hard on it. 'Fire! Fire!' he shouted.

Seconds later, the window opened, and Neptune peered out, wearing headphones.

'Fire!' yelled Weever. 'Get out! Now!'

Neptune stared past Weever for several seconds, then lifted the headphones off his ears.

'Fire!' repeated Weever. 'You need to get out! Now!'

Neptune paused, then sprang into life again. 'No fire here, man,' he observed. 'No smoke. False alarm, man.' He closed the window and disappeared.

'The cheeky moron!' hissed Weever. 'Right – smoke. He wants smoke; we'll give him smoke. We'll smoke him out like the rat he is.' He turned to the concierge. 'Light a small fire round the back.'

'Whoa! Whoa there!' cried Erica. 'If you're lighting a fire, keep it in a metal bin and bring an extinguisher.'

'We got a metal bin handy?' Weever asked.

'No metal bin,' replied the concierge, 'but we do have a metal wheelbarrow.'

'Right, get it,' said Weever.

A few minutes later the concierge returned, pushing a wheelbarrow containing a heap of newspapers and some fresh twigs. The wheelbarrow was soon ablaze, and the smoke worked its way round to the front of the cottage, where Weever, holding a handkerchief to his nose, knocked sharply on the window again. But this time he got no response. Weever kept knocking, but no one answered.

'He can't smell smoke with that living dungheap in there with him! Kill the fire!' shouted Weever. Then he ordered Erica to stand by the window while he went to the door and banged on it.

Minutes later, a frantic concierge came running round the corner. 'The fire's out of control!' he yelled. 'I used the extinguisher, but the spray came out so strong it blew the burning papers out of the wheelbarrow and the wind caught them, and now they're rolling into the trees. It's spreading! It's spreading!'

The window flew open and Neptune leaned out. 'Fire's round the back, man. Get the fire brigade. Action stations!' And with that, he shut the window and was gone.

'No fire brigade!' insisted Weever. 'I don't want this

hitting the press.' He rushed round to the rear of the cottage and found Neptune and Stanfield already there.

'Yee-hah!' whooped Neptune, whipping off his trousers with all the aplomb of a man who'd done it many a time on stage.

Stanfield followed suit. Taking their trousers by the ankles, they pounded the flames with them.

'Gee, I love this stuff; I just love it, man,' chirped Neptune. 'I love the smell of it, I love the feel of it – it's wonderful!'

'So why're you putting it out?' asked Stanfield.

'It's rogue, man, it's rogue – it's in the wrong place; outta control. Gives fire a bad name.' Neptune went at it with all the vigour to be expected of a man who for more than two decades had taken to smashing guitars on stage and throwing TVs out of hotel windows. He looked up and saw Weever standing idly by. 'Come on, Gordie,' he shouted. 'Get yer pants off an' get whumpin'!'

Little did he know that if Gordon was going to be whumpin' anything, it would be him. Neptune, as far as Weever was concerned, was the root of the fire, and it was only right that he put it out, and preferably acquire in the process some giant blisters in places that would forever keep him from procreating. Pounding away, Neptune and Stanfield were containing the fire. Then Stanfield stopped and took a breather. Spying the idle Weever, he exhorted the great man to action.

'Come and join us! We can win this!'

'All right for you and your crap-filled jeans; you got the flames begging for mercy,' muttered Weever.

Neptune beckoned him. 'Yeah, come on, Gordie! Get

yer breeks aff an' get stuck in!' he yelled, resorting now to his native Glaswegian.

This time the concierge, possibly feeling obliged to do his master's work, responded and took off his trousers and began beating the flames.

Erica turned to Weever and echoed the call. 'Come on, Gordie,' she cried, smiling impishly. 'Get yer breeks aff an' get stuck in.'

Weever gave her a withering look.

'Right, I'm going in!' yelled Erica, and she strode towards the fire.

'No! No!' yelled Weever, remaining rooted to the spot. 'Come back!'

But Erica kept on going, and when she got to the fire she removed her slacks and began beating pockets of fire alongside the others.

Between the four of them, they gradually got all the fires out. Neptune gave a little jig in celebration, then went skipping away, humming a tune, followed by Stanfield. Weever approached the charred brushwood and shook his head, while Erica put on her blackened and partly holed slacks.

'Go after them,' said Erica, 'and thank them. They risked their lives for you.'

That, of course, was not what Weever had in mind. 'When I catch him, I'm kicking him out,' he replied.

'What? The hero of the hour?' asked Erica in mock outrage.

'Hero? He's no hero; he's a round zero. A good-for-nothing.'

'He could've watched you burn your place down.'

'He should've cleared off when I told him.'

'Well, suit yourself, Gordon. I'm off to shower and change.'

'Where have these idiots gone?'

The 'idiots' were currently celebrating their success as naked aeroplanes, wheeling and sweeping over the grassy plains of the eighth fairway.

CHAPTER 21

'I've been thinking,' said Chizzie. 'Maybe we should just abandon the idea of finding the Gorries' loot, whatever it is.'

Yolanda shook her head. 'If we just hand Peggy over to them we're putting her in danger and aiding and abetting criminal activity.'

'We don't know that. We don't know what they're after – it could be a knitting pattern for all we know. No crime has been committed that we know of, apart from the theft of Peggy. Even then they'll argue that Caitlin's dad bequeathed her to their care.'

'Some hope.'

Chizzie sighed. 'If only Peggy would show some affection for Caitlin, it could be very different.'

'Yeah, it would. Caitlin thinks Peggy is imagining that she was abandoned by her, and now she's sulking.'

'Maybe there's reverse psychology at work,' said Chizzie. 'The fact that she sulks and goes on sit-down strike shows that she cares. She doesn't just ignore Caitlin. She's taking the trouble to put out a message.'

'Maybe we need to stage a little accident or something – you know, like maybe Caitlin falls near Peggy and calls for help. Peggy to the rescue; all is forgiven.'

Chizzie thought for a moment, then agreed that such a ploy might just work.

The following day, the ploy went into action – Chizzie and Yolanda took Peggy for a walk along the golf course. As planned, Caitlin came ambling along in the opposite direction. Yolanda let Peggy off the lead, and Caitlin duly fell over with a yell. Unfortunately, Peggy just stared. Then her head turned quickly, and she barked furiously, as out of the trees burst Tommy Neptune, naked from the waist up. He came streaking across the fairway like some wild Caledonian warrior rushing at Hadrian's Wall. He got to Caitlin and pounced on her and put her into the recovery position before she could even utter a word.

'A pulse! A pulse!' he yelled, his voice echoing among the trees. 'I have a pulse!'

Chizzie and Yolanda rushed up and pulled Neptune off.

Two security men ran towards them, shouting, 'Hold him! Hold him right there!'

'What's going on?' asked Caitlin, alarmed and rising onto her elbows.

'You tell me,' replied a bewildered Chizzie.

'My, my, my, you're the quickest success I ever had!' exclaimed Neptune, equally bewildered. 'I thought Stanfield was quick, but this beats him. I have the Midas touch. I'm a true healer, man. I'm possessed with special powers!'

'Right, Mr Neptune,' said one of the security men, 'we're taking you inside now.' He and his colleague each took an arm of the rock star. Then, turning to Chizzie, the security man added, 'We're under orders from Mr Neptune 'imself to keep him on the wagon. That right, sir?'

'Yessir!' replied Neptune, attempting a salute. 'Onwards

and upwards, brave boys!' And as they escorted him away, Neptune burst into song – his own version of 'Auld Lang Syne': '*Should old acquaitance be forgot and somethin', somethin'... an' here's a leg o' mine an'... an'... Happy New Year everybody!*'

In the silence that followed, it became clear that the real casualty had been overlooked: poor little Peggy. She stood shivering, alternating between whimpering and feeble barking. Clearly she was in the grip of emotional turmoil. Caitlin leaped up and ran towards Peggy, but the little dog drew back. Only when Yolanda went to Peggy and stroked her did she calm down. Caitlin wept.

Yolanda consoled her. 'We'll get this sorted out. We will.'

After lunch, a new plan took shape. 'Yes,' said Chizzie. 'Among all the other things she's done, Florence McTaggart was once a dog whisperer. Let's see if she'll take Peggy.'

Chizzie rang the McTaggarts' doorbell. Gladys McTaggart, Florence's younger sister, half-opened the door and peered round it.

'Hi, Gladys, how are you?' said Chizzie brightly.

'Fine,' came the sullen reply.

'Is Florence in?'

'No.'

'Will she be long?'

'No.'

'Hello!' hailed a voice from behind. The very person, Florence McTaggart, came striding up the path, perspiring slightly and carrying what looked like a heavily laden rucksack. Greetings exchanged, Florence led the way into the living room and dumped her rucksack down on a table with a thump.

'Been shopping?' Chizzie asked.

'Nope,' said Florence. 'Keeping fit.' She put her hand in the rucksack and pulled out a brick, and then another, and another, and finally a fourth. 'When I'm pressed for time, this is what I do. And I feel great. I used to manage six bricks, but age is catching up.'

Suddenly the dining room door flew open, and Gladys bounded into the room. 'It's time! It's time!' she announced, almost squealing, while wringing her hands one moment and biting her nails the next. 'It's time! It's time!'

Florence winced, then turned to Chizzie. 'Please excuse us a minute.'

She turned and went into the dining room with Gladys, but she failed to close the door properly and it stood ajar. Through the gap Chizzie could see Gladys clutching a large bag of crisps in one hand, while her other hand shovelled heaps of crisps into her swirling mouth.

'Ten seconds left!' declared Florence.

Gladys revved her jaws even faster; round and round they went, and up and down they went, like some machine designed to reduce trees to pulp in seconds.

'Time up!' declared Florence, snatching the bag of crisps away from Gladys, who vainly tried to grab a handful in extra time.

Gladys moaned, but with her jaws occupied by a volume of crisps that would've kept the average person fed for a week, she could barely utter anything. 'Shocklate at shicksh,' she said.

'Yes, chocolate at six,' confirmed Florence. 'Keep calm.'

'Oo peeshes.'

'Two pieces, yes. Doing very well, Gladys; I'm proud of you.' And Florence kissed her sister's cheek before swiftly locking the bag of crisps away in the cupboard and, aware now that the door had come ajar, returning to the living room. 'Sorry about that,' she said, shrugging her shoulders. 'You shouldn't have been subjected to that awful spectacle. Gladys used to be fifteen stone – she's now twelve and on track for a fairly healthy weight. So, I'm sure you understand. Tough love is getting results. It's dog training, really. We're animals, after all.'

Suddenly the dining room door burst open. It was Gladys again, still masticating. She rushed out of the dining room and headed straight for the stairs. Her technique of ascending the stairs was unusual. Rather than simply stepping up the middle of the carpet, like normal people, Gladys ascended with her feet placed tight against one side of the staircase. Chizzie said nothing; maybe it was some kind of mental condition.

Florence saw the look and sought to explain. 'Our stair carpet is worn down the middle. But the edges are as good as new – so it's a perfectly good carpet up the sides. Using just the sides will save it for another ten years. Besides, it helps with tidy footwork. Now, to what do I owe the pleasure of your visit?'

There was no offer of coffee, no biscuits; Florence was clearly well into financial prudence, so Chizzie got straight to the point. 'We're having problems with Peggy.'

'Caitlin's dog?'

'Yes, and we think you might be able to help.' He outlined the problems.

Florence replied without hesitation. 'Right. Peggy needs her confidence in humans restored. I can fix that, but I need Caitlin and Peggy under my roof for a few days.'

Chizzie smiled. 'Great! Thank you, Florence. You just let me know what you need for all the food and lodgings, and I'll settle up.'

'You'll do no such thing. They will be my guests. Guests do not pay in this household. There's one condition, though: Peggy needs to get along with my dog, Robbie, but that shouldn't be a problem.'

Late the following day, Chizzie received a call from Florence and hurried to her house with Yolanda.

'Definitely someone in the garden,' said Florence, 'and the van took off before I got a good look at it, but it was a dark colour, maybe dark blue.'

Yolanda pursed her lips. 'The Gorries have a dark blue van.'

'Yeah, hundred to one it's them,' said Chizzie. 'Right, we'll take Peggy back.'

'No, you won't, no. We're nearly there. Two more days and we'll have it cracked,' insisted Florence.

Caitlin agreed. 'Peggy and I are getting on really well. And I don't want her being shunted back and forth anymore. It's no wonder the wee thing's so confused. And another thing: there's no way I'm submitting to intimidation from the Gorries. I won't be cowed.'

Florence took Caitlin's arm and squeezed it gently. 'Well said, lass. We'll beat the ba... bandits.'

'You realise they'll be back real soon?' Chizzie warned.

Caitlin nodded.

Chizzie turned to Florence. 'What's Robbie like as a guard dog?'

'He's much more likely to make them a cup of tea than bite them.'

'Right, Yolanda, can your dad provide security for a few days?'

'He could, but he'd want to know what's going on, and there's no telling where that could lead. I'm happy to act as lookout.'

Chizzie thought for a moment, then shook his head. 'No, Yolanda. Far too risky. I'll get in touch with PC Tunnock.'

'Waste of time,' Yolanda replied. 'What can he do? They'll laugh in his face.'

Chizzie pondered for a moment. 'Right, Florence. What d'you say I shack up in the conservatory for a couple of nights?'

Florence shrugged. 'No problem, if you're okay with that. I can give you a camp bed.'

'And Sven too,' said Yolanda.

Chizzie raised his eyebrows. 'I'll ask him, but you never know with Sven: he could get rather too enthusiastic and end up throwing a Gorrie or two out the window.'

'That would be nice,' chirped Florence. 'Sven can have a camp bed too.'

That night, the McTaggarts' conservatory creaked whenever a strong gust of wind blew, occasional showers pattered on the panes, and Sven's snoring was hard to ignore. Through it all, Chizzie lay awake, watching the shadows of branches swaying in the wind and seeing the outlines of human figures every few minutes. In these circumstances it could be quite difficult to detect intruders, let alone get a good night's sleep. The one thing he could do something about was Sven's snoring. He unzipped his sleeping bag and quietly crossed to where Sven lay, then he gently eased Sven onto his left side. Wonderfully, the snoring stopped. Very pleased with his work, Chizzie retired to his camp bed.

An hour or so later, the wind and rain eased off and Chizzie finally fell asleep. At 3.34 Sven began snoring again; not too loudly, but enough to waken Chizzie. There was little wind, and the shadows of the branches weren't moving anymore, but out of the corner of his eye, Chizzie saw something move outside. It was merely a glimpse of a shadow on the blinds, but it looked like the shadow of a man – a big man. The sort of man that was Dean Gorrie. Chizzie needed to investigate. He pulled at the zip on his sleeping bag. It jammed. He pulled again, but still the zip wouldn't move. If only he hadn't zipped it right up to his neck. He had to waken Sven. With a great effort, he was able to push an arm out of his sleeping bag. He then picked up a slipper and threw it towards Sven. It hit Sven square on the face.

'Oh God! Sorry, Sven,' Chizzie whispered. 'There's someone outside.'

But there was no reply other than a muffled snore from under the slipper.

'Sven! Sven!' Chizzie called urgently but softly.

Still there was no reply.

Chizzie groaned and muttered, 'He did say he was a heavy sleeper, but I didn't think he was this bad.'

Chizzie rolled over and tried to get up, but no luck. He rolled over to the couch and, gripping it tightly, he pulled himself upright with his free arm and then hopped over to Sven. He knelt down and shook Sven. Sven slept on. Chizzie slipped his hand under Sven's head and shook it. Still Sven slept on. It occurred to Chizzie that he might've knocked Sven out with the slipper, But, then again, no slipper could be that potent.

'For God's sake, Sven, wake up!' he said, as loudly as he dared into Sven's left ear.

Finally, there was a response: Sven opened his bleary eyes. 'What is it?' he asked.

'I think there's someone moving outside.'

Sven shook his head, drew in breath and opened his eyes wide, and then slowly got out of his sleeping bag. This was a man that once had told Chizzie he was interested in joining fire and rescue. It hadn't escaped Chizzie that by the time Sven woke up, any building that had caught fire would be smouldering dust. 'Let's go see,' said Sven, getting to his feet.

'I can't get out of my sleeping bag,' Chizzie bleated.

Sven inspected the zip; pulled it. Nothing happened. Then he pulled it again with a mighty tug that swung Chizzie almost to the floor. Sven raised him up, gripped both sides of the bag and, with a searing, ripping sound, he burst it clean open. 'Sorry about that,' he said. 'I'll buy you a new one. They're ten quid down at the Co-op.'

'Forget it; we could be under attack.'

'I hope so. I was having a nice dream there – wouldn't want to lose it for nothing.'

Chizzie didn't challenge the logic; there was enough challenge ahead if the shadow should prove to have substance. They went to the door of the conservatory. Chizzie opened it slowly and listened. No sound. So, with slow, careful tread, they proceeded into the dining room.

'Hold it,' Chizzie whispered, raising a hand.

They listened again and heard a rustling sound.

'Could be someone up for a cup of tea,' Sven suggested.

'There's no light on,' replied Chizzie.

Sven pointed to the bottom of the door. 'There is now.'

And indeed there was. A faint yellow glow had appeared under the door. Seconds later, the glow faded away.

'Someone's got a torch,' Sven whispered.

Chizzie gulped. 'The Gorries.'

'Or maybe just a secret midnight tea-drinker,' suggested Sven.

Hoping that Sven's interpretation of events was correct, and that they faced nothing more than a thirsty beverage-seeker, or maybe even Gladys on a secret mission to shovel away more crisps, Chizzie gently opened the door and peered into the hall. He spied the grey outline of a large figure at the bottom of the stairs. His heart jumped. 'There's an awfully big tea-drinker out there,' he informed Sven.

'A Gorrie?'

Chizzie nodded nervously: 'I think so.'

Sven rubbed his hands and loosened up. 'Right, hit the lights, an' let's get 'em,' he hissed.

'Hang on,' whispered Chizzie, wanting to assess the options related to life expectancy.

But Sven was off; he shot past Chizzie into the hall and began fumbling for the light switch. A torch beam swung onto his face. Chizzie ran to the opposite side of the hall where the light switch actually was and flicked it on and then looked around. And there at the bottom of the stairs stood the large, ominous figure of Dean Gorrie.

'Back off if you know what's good for you!' Gorrie barked angrily.

A door opened upstairs, and Greg Gorrie came running down the stairs, failing to observe the side-only rule for preserving the carpet, and thus incurring even greater wrath from the lady of the house, who, close behind him, was hurtling instinctively down one side; a sight which appeared to put fear into the eyes of even Dean Gorrie.

'Keep them there!' yelled Florence. 'I'm calling the police!'

Greg turned to her with an assured, sly grin. 'I wouldn't bother if I were you. By the time they get here, we'll be well gone.'

'No, you won't,' Sven informed him as he stepped towards the Gorries.

'Oh, but we will,' replied Greg Gorrie assuredly. 'But the better option for all of us here tonight is to talk sense and come to an agreement. That way, we all win.'

'You'll come to a sticky end, that's what you'll come to,' declared Florence.

Greg shook his head sadly and, with a smile, offered advice. 'Simmer down,' he said. 'Just think. You've got little to gain and much to lose, Florence.'

Florence reddened. 'Don't you... don't you dare call me Florence! You—'

'As you wish, Miss McTaggart. No problem.'

'And you can get out of my house – now! This instant!' Florence insisted. 'The police know where to find you.'

Greg shook his head again and wagged a finger. 'No, no, no, Miss McTaggart, you don't understand. It's not that simple. You see, if *you* raise the stakes, *we* raise the stakes. You get the police, and my brother and I spend a few months inside renewing old acquaintances. And then when we come out, we will be, unfortunately for you, bent on settling the score. And we will do that with interest, believe me. Now, none of us wants that kind of thing, surely? So, let's just all sit down and talk this out. Ah, Caitlin! Just in time for the peace talks.'

Caitlin, who came down the middle of the staircase but incurred no censure from the householder, came forward, sleepy-eyed in her dressing gown. 'What's going on?' she asked.

Florence answered, 'These vile thugs broke into the house.'

'Are the police on the way?'

'No, they're not,' replied Greg. 'We're sitting down and we're talking things through. Do please join us.'

For a moment there was a confused silence. Sven and Dean glowered at one another like heavyweight boxers at the weigh-in.

Chizzie sized up his chances with Greg and put them at forty-sixty. Sitting down and talking seemed like the best option. 'Okay,' he said tersely. 'Let's sit down and see what they have to say.'

'How about a cup of tea?' Greg asked cheerily, probably as much to assert his dominance as to quench his thirst.

Florence reddened again and fixed Greg with a wildfire glare. Then, without a further word, they sat down: the Gorries took the settee while the others each found a chair, except Sven, who sat cross-legged on the carpet by the door.

'Right,' said Greg. 'Getting straight to the point, we need the dog, and we have every right to it.'

Caitlin bristled. 'You have no right to her whatsoever, you common thief!'

'Now, now, now, hear me out,' Greg answered. 'What you need to know is, your dad owes us – big time. He owes us the dog. We have every right to it.'

Dean chimed in. 'Yeah, we was loyal – we was like that,' he said, thumping a fist to his gall bladder rather than the heart he probably thought he was indicating.

'Your dad betrayed our trust,' insisted Greg.

'My dad owes you nothing.'

'Oh, but he does, Caitlin. We helped him in his hour of need. When he had his first stroke, we were there for him.'

'Yeah, lots of hours we helped him,' added Dean.

'We were there for him when no one else was, and that includes you, Caitlin,' said Greg, fixing his eyes on Caitlin. 'You didn't even know about it. You didn't even want to know him. But we were there.'

'We were there.'

'Yes, because you needed him!' exclaimed Caitlin. 'You bent him your way. You preyed on his addictive nature.'

'He had a choice,' said Greg calmly.

'You had a better choice!' retorted Caitlin.

Greg shook his head. 'Okay, okay, let's all just calm down. Let's just say we're all guilty, or no one's guilty. And the reality is, my brother and I are short of a package, and you can help us get it. We only want what's ours. And we need that dog to find it.'

'My father would not want to have died a criminal. And I'm going to see that he doesn't.'

'Just give us the dog. That's all we ask.'

'No.'

Greg looked hard at Caitlin, then clapped his hands on his knees. 'Right,' he said finally. 'We have tried to be reasonable. You leave us no choice. Goodbye.'

And with that, the Gorries rose and headed for the door. Sven got to his feet quickly and was about to bar the Gorries' departure.

'Let them go,' said Chizzie.

Dean rose to his feet and glared at Sven, who after several seconds' hesitation moved aside and allowed the Gorries to leave.

As if stunned into disbelief, no one spoke until Florence vented her anger. 'Did you ever see such sorry scraps of humanity?!'

'Well, you know, actually,' said Sven, 'I'm feelin' kinda sorry for them. I mean, they're trash, but what the smart one said makes some sense. Let's just give them Peggy, then they get their loot or whatever it is, and we get Peggy back – and everyone's a winner.'

'No, Sven, no,' insisted Caitlin. 'I know my dad. He did not want to die a criminal. He craved redemption; for all his faults he was a God-fearing man, and he loved me. He wanted to clear the dark cloud hanging over our family name. He didn't want me to be a victim of the family infamy. He wrote that in a letter to me just before he died. I

183

want him to have peace, wherever he is. Helping criminals to enjoy their spoils is not what he wanted. But the Gorries are right about one thing: I shouldn't have ignored my dad when he asked for forgiveness. I came to him too late. But it's not too late to find the loot, whatever it is, and dispose of it legally in his name. That's what I want.'

Sven crossed over to Caitlin and hugged her. 'We'll get what you want, Caitlin. We'll find that stuff. We'll see your dad right.'

CHAPTER 22

Weever sat at his desk with a glowering face that matched the gathering thunderclouds. Erica nevertheless managed a smile. She knew Weever's moods by now, and she knew it would be a rare week that went by without some eruption from Weever. Anything could ignite the great man, even a singing bird. Erica sat down opposite him and settled herself before offering a benign expression that hinted at her readiness to play mother.

Weever picked up a letter from the desk and shook it. 'Your pal, the Lord of the Lions or whatever—'

'The Lord Lyon King of Arms?'

'Yeah, him. He's thrown a curveball. Here, read this,' Weever grumbled, handing the letter to Erica. 'He says there's some kinda woman chief – Violet somebody.'

Erica scanned the letter. 'Ah yes,' she said, smiling. 'Dear old Violet Wedderburn. I've heard of her. A centenarian, I believe. Says here that she's the nearest living relative of the last authenticated clan chief of Clan McShellach. The lady herself can't be chief, though. It must be a man.'

'Of course.'

Erica flashed a chiding look at Weever, then continued reading the letter. 'It says here that Violet Wedderburn can appoint an eligible man to be chief. And Lord Tulloh, with the backing of the clan council, has requested to be a candidate. Members of the clan council have spoken with Violet Wedderburn and the Lord Lyon King of Arms, and all are satisfied that she is of sound mind and able to appoint a chief.'

'Who do they think they're kiddin'? Stuff the Lion Lord!'

'The Lord Lyon King of Arms.'

'Yeah. Stuff him! This is for clan members only, not some creep in tights.'

'Well, like it or not, Gordon, you will need to muster all your charm and win the lady over.'

'How much?'

'What?'

'How much will she want?'

Erica gave a wry smile. 'Nothing that you can give, Gordon, beyond a few bits of paper currently awaiting discovery by our super sleuth, Mr Stanfield.'

'Sleuth? Sloth, more like.'

'I'll chase him up.'

'Kick him up the backside. And give him one from me too, the lazy devil.'

When Erica had left, Weever called in his faithful lieutenant, Charlie Fairfoull. 'How come Tulloh's still in the running?' Weever asked petulantly. 'He's supposed to be scared off.'

Fairfoull was apologetic. 'Well, actually, the Gorries screwed up. They took a dead rat into Tulloh's house, but the rat wasn't in fact dead. It burst into life in the big Gorrie's hand, and, white as a ghost, he shot out of the house, setting a new county record for the hundred yards. But worry not: they're going back in – this time with a dead fish.'

'A what?! A dead fish? What's that going to do? Get them back in here; we need something better than a dead fish, for God's sake!'

Later that afternoon, Weever was dozing in his office; his head resting on the back of his sumptuous chair. The spreadsheet that had sent him into the Land of Nod lay open on his desk. A noise woke him up. It was the noise of a man clambering through the window. Weever's eyeballs bulged. Was this a nightmare? No – no, it was real. He was wide awake, and the interloper was real. It was happening.

'Good afternoon,' said the smartly dressed interloper, quickly seating himself opposite Weever.

Weever stuttered into life. 'What the... who the hell are you? What are...?'

'It's me, Gordon – Robert Stanfield.'

'What?!'

'Robert Stanfield the Second.'

'Wha... You? There's two of you?!'

'No, it's the new me – the same, but different. We need to talk. I know what you're up to. I know you sent me on a wild goose chase – or, more exactly, a stuffed goose chase. You're setting up fake records for me to find so you can be clan chief. I didn't want to have to say that, but you forced me. I'm not a fool.'

'What the hell are you talking about? Get your ass outta here! You... you cretin!'

'Your historical records are fakes, Mr Weever. You're a fraud,' Stanfield informed him with confidence. 'Now, you don't want the world to know that, I'm sure. So, we're going to cut a deal.'

Weever looked bewildered. 'Fakes? What fakes?'

'You know what fakes, Gordon. Chasing up your archive pieces, I find it's just all too neat and tidy. You send me here, you send me there, and lo and behold, what do I instantly find? Here a shining record, there a shining record. It's all too neat, Gordon. I've sussed you.'

Weever stiffened. 'You're talking through your trousers, you bozo. Me? Fakes? You kiddin'? I'll sue you for all you've got! Get out now before I get security to throw you out! You cheap, nasty piece of—'

'No, no, no, Gordon, no, let me explain. I'm gettin' out of politics. It's true what they say: politics is just showbiz for ugly people. I want to be with the beautiful people. I've done the giving bit: I've picketed, I've campaigned, I've leafleted and I've harassed, thinking it was all for the good of the blessed poor. Then it dawned on me: being poor isn't a virtue; it's a condition – it doesn't make you a good person. The poor are just capitalists with no money. Give them money and it's "Goodbye, brothers and sisters." Their trade unions serve only their investors – that's to say, their members – like any other company. It's all about self, Gordon, and I want to hitch up with the best. And that's why I went to the considerable trouble of climbing through your window. I won't be stopped. I'm a powerhouse. And it's all thanks to you, Gordon. Through your spirit and charisma, you've got yourself a convert. And no one's more devoted than the converted.' With that he stopped and waited for Weever to react.

Weever remained silent and simply stared, completely motionless.

Stanfield, with a growing look of alarm, leaned forward. 'Are you… are you…?'

Suddenly, Weever raised a hand and, fixing his eyes on Stanfield, he said, 'You know what? For a moment I saw my younger self there – in you.'

'Oh my. My goodness. Thank you, Gordon. No greater honour than to be compared with you, however slightly. Thank you very much; it means so much. You saved me, heart and soul. In a word, salvation, that's what you did for me, Gordon. And I want to repay you.'

'And you can. You have charisma. Needs some work, but I bet with just a few more touches I can make it that you walk into a room and heads will turn. And yes, Stanfield, I'm gonna give you the opportunity of a lifetime. You're hired.'

Stanfield leaped to his feet. 'Oh, Mr Weever, thank you, thank you. You won't ever regret it, I promise.'

'We'll see, we'll see. Sit down. I'm putting you in men's toiletries.'

'Thank you. Very wise if I may say so, Mr Weever.'

'Nobody can know more about stinking and unstinking than you.'

'Yeah, the before and after. The great turnaround, thanks to Weever toiletries. Awesome!'

'You got it, Stanfield. Now go and see Erica about gettin' that thesis written.'

Shortly after, as Weever put away his spreadsheet, the Gorries arrived disguised as tradesmen. Weever drained his whisky glass, buzzed for Fairfoull to join him, then invited the Gorries into his office and got straight to the point.

'You need to up your game, you two – we need Tulloh gone. He's still around; why is that?'

'It's your daughter helping him,' replied Greg Gorrie. 'He'd be long gone but for her. We know how to see him off, though. We'll give him the coup de grâce.'

'Nothing permanent: I don't want—'

'No, no. No worries, Mr Weever, no worries. Just a little blackmail.'

'Oh, right, yeah, good idea, very good. Interesting.'

'We lay on a little private party with certain ladies I know who like taking their clothes off and photographing themselves in intimate poses with men – lords and gentry a speciality.'

Both Weever's and Fairfoull's eyes widened.

'You've done this sort of thing before, I take it?' asked Fairfoull.

Greg was delighted to confirm that not only had he done this sort of thing before; he'd accomplished it with great success every time. He loved the work. He outlined his modus operandi: 'The girls suddenly descend upon Lord Tulloh's house. They're loaded with booze and joints; then, buck naked, they're soon crawling all over His Lordship while one of them captures the happy scene on camera. You get the video and I get a nice slice of lolly for my ladies.'

Weever and Fairfoull took a moment to divest themselves of the scene painted by Gorrie. They were almost jealous of His Lordship.

The Gorries moved quickly and got their team of ladies together. They then informed Weever that it was all kicking off that very evening. Weever and Fairfoull got themselves into position, peering out from behind one of the rhododendron bushes that fringed Lord Tulloh's cottage garden.

'Here they come,' whispered Fairfoull as he eyed a dark-coloured minibus approaching.

'At last,' hissed Weever.

They watched intently as six young ladies in raincoats decanted from the minibus. Some of them carried bottles of champagne, while others carried small shopping bags. Without bothering about the doorbell, they disappeared into the house.

Weever smiled lasciviously. 'Excellent,' he purred. 'I almost wish it was me in there. Lord Tulloh can't say we don't treat him well, even if we are taking him out.'

Fairfoull chuckled. 'It shouldn't take long – the girls get their pictures and then they skedaddle.'

Weever grinned. 'Maybe we should invite them back for coffee.'

'Tempting though it might be, it's worth remembering they could turn their cameras on us. Your reputation is in a good state of repair currently; your youthful indiscretions all but forgotten. We don't want them rising to the surface again – not quite what the clan will be looking for in a clan chief. Best not to risk it.'

'Maybe one day.'

'When you've ordered your blue pills.'

Weever cast him a withering sideways look, then suddenly pointed at something moving on the lawn. 'What the hell's that?' he croaked.

'You mean *who's* that. That's Tommy Neptune. He seems to have lost something.'

'His sanity.'

'No, it's mushrooms – he's picking magic mushrooms.'

Suddenly a wave of loud music broke from the house and swept over the garden. Neptune stopped picking and stood like some wild animal scenting the air. Then, seconds later, he was running over to the door of the house – a party animal who'd got the scent.

'I think they're actually having real fun in there,' complained Fairfoull.

'Get me a rock,' demanded Weever. 'I'll give 'em bloody rock 'n' roll!'

'No, no, wait,' replied Fairfoull. 'With Neptune in the picture, it's even better. Couldn't be better if we'd hired him.'

Neptune looked in at the window and, evidently liking what he saw, he darted inside.

Fairfoull chuckled. 'Light blue touchpaper and retire.'

'No, no,' said Weever. 'We stay. I want to see this right through.'

'Well, let's take a peek.'

'You lead off – I've had enough trouble creeping about in the dark.'

They got to the window and cautiously peered in. Then abruptly the music stopped, and what they saw was nothing like what they had expected. Everyone inside was looking aghast. Neptune stood behind one of the young ladies, hugging her tightly around the waist.

'Jeezuz!' hissed Weever. 'What's that weirdo doin'?'

'It's the Heimlich manoeuvre,' replied Fairfoull. 'The girl's choking!'

Then suddenly the girl lunged forwards and gasped, and everyone cheered, and the girl managed a smile as the others helped her to the sofa. Lord Tulloh brought her a glass of water, while Neptune, the hero of the evening, was thanked and kissed profusely. Then the young ladies gathered round and went into discussion.

'They're getting their coats on – they're pulling out,' squealed Weever.

'What're they thinking?' muttered Fairfoull.

'They can't do that – they haven't got what I need,' wailed Weever. 'I'm not paying for chokers! Go and get them back in there and get the bloody pictures.'

'No, Gordon, best just let it go. It's too late now.'

'Look, look – they're kissing Tulloh! Get a picture; get your phone out.'

Fairfoull pulled out his phone, held it to the window and quickly took a photo; then he drew back and examined the result.

'That's no good,' Weever moaned. 'They're just talking there, and they look like ghosts – you need flash.'

'I can't use flash; they'll see it.'

'Too late now: they're coming out. I'm going to order them back in.'

'No, no – Tulloh's there, waving them off.'

'Get a picture!'

'Not worth it.'

'Did you hear that?'

'Hear what?'

'Neptune – he said something about "my place". He doesn't have a place – his place is my place: it's the cottage. They're going to the cottage! Call security! Get the car up here; we need to head them off!'

Fairfoull took out his walkie-talkie and summoned his car.

When they got to the cottage, Weever's hormones were close to leaping out and hitting someone. 'I'm throwing them out of there!' he roared.

'Let security handle it,' Fairfoull advised calmly.

'No, no, this is personal.' Weever burst into the cottage and strode inside. 'Right, everybody!' he yelled. 'Outta here! Get out! Out! Now!'

A young lady screamed.

'Who are you?' cried another.

'I'm the owner. Now get out, before I kick you all out!'

Neptune, though, was a picture of almost zen-like calmness. 'Ladies,' he began, 'allow me to introduce Mr Weever, my landlord and an international businessperson; a tycoon, no less.'

One young lady was instantly charmed. 'Oooh, hoo, hoo,' she cooed, 'a tycoon. A tycoon, girls! We've never had a tycoon before. What a lovely change. It's politicians with us mostly, and they're all very dull boys, Mr Weever – not like you, I'm sure.'

'Sure, sure, a tycoon has so much more to offer, eh, big boy?' simpered another young lady, fluttering her eyelashes and eyeing Fairfoull seductively. 'And who's your charming friend? Do introduce us.'

'Get outta here. Get out now!' ordered Weever in a voice softened by a flurry of conflicting emotions.

'Oh, tut-tut, now, Mr Weever,' cooed a young lady. 'What's your hurry, you silly, silly man?'

'Yes,' said another. 'The party's just getting started.'

'Just in time for a good time,' said another. 'Do join us, Mr Weever.'

'Get out! Everybody out!' insisted Weever, gathering his wits. 'And that includes you, Neptune.'

A young lady sidled up to Weever and put an arm round him. 'Take a picture, Natalie.'

Weever struggled to free himself, almost throwing the young lady aside. 'Right,' he roared, exasperated, 'everybody out now, or I throw you out!'

An order that was somewhat undermined by a pair of pink panties landing on his head, while another young lady helped herself to his phone.

'You bitch!' roared Weever. 'Give me back my phone!'

'Oh, shocking language, Mr Tycoon! Temper, temper, temper!'

'Tycoon? He's a typhoon now!' chirped a young lady.

'Get my phone, Charlie!' roared Weever.

A young lady, though, had Charlie covered, and was eyeing him from head to foot. 'Ooh, Charlie, Charlie. Such a bonnie prince, Charlie.'

Neptune jumped onto the sofa and waved his arms about. 'Calm down, everybody. Calm down. Change of plan – we're calling it a night.'

'No! No!' yelled the ladies all at once. 'No-ooooh! No-ooooh! No-ooooh!'

'Yes, oh yes,' replied Neptune. 'But what we're going to do is this: you pretty young things are going to come backstage when me and the band gig in Glasgow next month. How's that?'

The young ladies were ecstatic: they screamed and jumped for joy.

'And I'm giving you a signed guitar.' He leaped off the sofa, grabbed one of six guitars propped against the wall, scribbled on it with a felt-tip pen, and then posed for a photo with the young ladies.

Weever quickly brought them all back down to earth. 'And now you clear off as soon as I get my phone back!'

'What phone?' enquired a young lady, completely mystified.

'Give it back,' said Neptune calmly.

With a shake of the head, a young lady complied, and then Neptune escorted the young ladies out to their minibus.

'Right, that creep is next. He's outta here,' hissed Weever.

'You can't, Gordon – he got your phone back. You would never have got it back otherwise, and think what that could mean.'

'Oh, I would've got it back.'

'Oh no, you wouldn't. Not from these girls.'

'His pack took it.'

'Not *his* pack – *your* pack, actually.'

Weever fumed in silence.

Fairfoull smiled wryly. 'Seems that crime doesn't pay.'

'It did for that bloody lot,' insisted Weever.

CHAPTER 23

Chizzie arrived at Lord Tulloh's house to find the owner troubled.

'You see,' Tulloh began, as he and Chizzie ambled round the cottage garden, 'when I received the letter from Violet Wedderburn inviting me to discuss my potential election to the office of clan chief, I said yes, but frankly, the back of my mind kept saying no. Getting involved with a whole lot of people was such a daunting prospect. Then out of the blue – hah! – a party of young ladies descended on me, under the impression that they were at some kind of birthday party; my thirtieth, apparently – times two, if they only knew. And d'you know? There and then, I rediscovered my love of life, my joie de vivre, my mojo, as one of the young ladies would have it. I still don't know what she was talking about. Do you? Never mind. What I can say is, I haven't had so much fun in a long time. It became clear to me that I very much missed meeting people and having fun. Sadly, though, one of the young ladies nearly choked on something, but fortunately a very kind Mr Neptune, who also happened to be looking for a party, intervened and saved her. Then off they went to find the real party, and suddenly, you know what? I missed them. I missed their vitality and their spirit. I am a people person after all, and now I very much want to be clan chief, meeting lots of people. One of the throng again. People who need people are the luckiest people; it's just as they say.'

Tulloh seemed about to burst into song, so Chizzie quickly intervened. 'Excellent, Patrick; you really would make an excellent clan chief. Truly you would!'

'The problem is,' continued Tulloh, 'well, two problems, really: Yolanda's father is still very keen on being clan chief, and the second problem is that Violet Wedderburn wants to interview me at 2.30 tomorrow, like I'm applying for some kind of job. I'll be hopeless at that – I've never done a decent day's work in my life. God forgive me, I'm useless. I have absolutely no idea what to say or do.'

'Just be yourself, Patrick. You, the everyday, natural you, that's all you need. Go to Violet Wedderburn and do yourself and your clan proud.'

'She says I can bring a supporter to the interview. Would… would you be so kind as to do me the honour of being my supporter?'

'I would be the one honoured, Patrick. I would be delighted to be your supporter.'

'Oh, thank you, Chizzie. Thank you so very much. She lives at Fetterwell House in Glenalmond. I'll pick you up at two.'

On the road to Glenalmond in the old Land Rover Defender, streaking along at thirty miles per hour, Chizzie felt he'd be quicker running, but at least Patrick kept his eyes on the road and ignored the beautiful gold and green colours of the glen in the slanting sunshine. Occasionally, an impatient motorist or two would surge past the

Defender with a pointed revving of the engine, but Patrick either failed to notice or was quite unperturbed, bathed as he was in his atmosphere of bonhomie and interview nerves.

Finally, arrival seemed imminent. Glancing at the little sketch map provided by Violet Wedderburn, Chizzie began to see recognisable features up ahead. 'Stop at these gate pillars,' he advised. 'I think this is it.'

And sure enough, when they halted, they saw the words 'Fetterwell House' in freshly painted golden letters on the pillars. Patrick crunched through the gears, got into reverse gear eventually, and then, with the vehicle in second gear, they turned into the drive and proceeded up the mossy drive towards the house. Chizzie got out of the vehicle first and stretched his legs.

Lord Tulloh disembarked with evident reluctance, then looked about cautiously. 'How quiet and eerie this place looks,' he observed.

Then from behind a hedge, a horrendous noise hit the air. It struck Chizzie like the sound of a massed choir of wolves, hyenas and cockatoos having a go at the 'Hallelujah Chorus'. Seconds later, the epicentre of the horrendous noise revealed itself: it was an elderly kilted man playing bagpipes. With a nod of the head, he beckoned the new arrivals to follow, and to the tune of something resembling 'The Hundred Pipers' he led them into the house.

By the time they entered the dining room, the piper had found the tune and both Chizzie and Tulloh had caught the mood and were smiling broadly as they strode in with a fine spring in their steps. To be piped into the house seemed only fitting for a prospective clan chief, thought Chizzie – a fine introduction to engagement with Gaelic culture.

Engaging with Violet Wedderburn, the lady of the house, however, appeared to be an altogether more serious matter. As she sat at the far end of a large dining table, hunched in a tartan shawl, the half-shadow on her face accentuated her sharp, bony features, and she looked all of her many years.

When the bagpipes abruptly fell silent, the atmosphere, as Lord Tulloh had anticipated, took on that of a job interview from an age gone by. Without rising, the old lady seemed about to speak, but a thump and a mighty gasp beat her to it. All heads swung to see the bagpiper slumped against the back of his wooden chair, wheezing slightly and very crimson in the face.

'All right, Roddy?' the old lady enquired.

Roddy nodded but made no sound. Perhaps he'd put everything he had into the bagpipes.

Seemingly satisfied that Roddy would live another day, the old lady introduced herself. 'Good afternoon, gentlemen. I am Violet Wedderburn. Please be seated.'

Chizzie and Tulloh introduced themselves and sat in the chairs indicated to them at the other end of the table.

Wedderburn eyed them sharply, then continued. 'Now, Lord Tulloh, you wish to be chief of Clan McShellach. In God's name, why?'

A little taken aback by the sharp tone and the speed of the interrogation, Lord Tulloh cleared his throat and explained why. 'It's quite simple really. I want to enjoy the company of others and restore self-esteem to a clan that has been so sadly forgotten.'

There was no reply from Violet; instead her attention switched to something outside the window. Then she turned to the deflated piper and announced, 'Welcome party, Roddy. Welcome!'

Roddy groaned, took a deep breath, then, with a grunt, hoisted himself onto his legs, picked up his pipes and shuffled out of the room.

Chizzie wondered who the visitor might be; hoping for the groceries, the fish man or the window cleaner, but thinking it might actually be someone rather more awkward.

The phone rang and Violet excused herself before driving her motorised wheelchair over to the phone by the fireside. She talked into the phone quite freely, possibly confident that her two companions had little or no knowledge of the language she was speaking.

Patrick turned to Chizzie with raised eyebrows and whispered, 'Gaelic?'

Chizzie whispered, 'Probably.' He knew a handful of Gaelic words, and listened out for them purely to see if he could recognise them. He heard '*agus*' several times – that pretty much confirmed it was Gaelic. Then there was 'macaroni'. That sealed it – all the Gaelic speakers Chizzie had ever known were very big on macaroni cheese.

As the phone call ended, an explosion of horrible bagpipe noise arose again in the distance – the visitors were clearly on their way in. Closer and closer the noise came, till Roddy entered at full volume, followed by none other than Gordon Weever and Charlie Fairfoull.

Seeing the others, Weever quickly took the fingers out of his ears and smiled. 'Ah,' he said, 'the Four Horsemen of the Acropolis'; a greeting that left everyone wondering about the man's sanity. There were, after all, only three people in the room; one of whom was a woman and none of whom lived in a Greek temple.

Chizzie quickly concluded that here was a man who cared not a jot about talking sense and cared even less about what people thought of it.

Roddy, meanwhile, staggered to his chair, but in grabbing it, he dropped his pipes with a clatter and crashed to the floor, his face draining from puce to white. Chizzie and Patrick rushed over to him. Patrick loosened Roddy's collar while Chizzie instinctively went to raise the stricken man's ankles. Then he thought better of it: not the best thing to do for a man in a kilt with a lady present – Roddy might be a true Scotsman with nothing below the kilt. But then again, maybe they knew each other well enough and there was nothing there that the lady hadn't seen before, though hardly in the dining room with guests present.

Chizzie and Patrick each took an arm and lifted the sagging piper onto his feet as he muttered defiantly, 'I'm awright, I'm awright – winded, just winded.' They got him into his chair, where he slumped with his head dangling over the back of the chair, his arms and legs spread wide, his pipes sprawled at his feet. It was like the aftermath of a momentous sea battle between a giant starfish and a scrawny octopus.

Violet, though, was unperturbed as she looked upon the piper with affection. 'Would you believe that man was once blow football champion of the Northern Constabulary? And him with only the one lung following his attempt to pipe his way up Vesuvius? Unfortunately for him, Vesuvius blew harder than he did. I've put him in for an MBE in the New Year's Honours List.'

Weever cast his eye over the fallen piper. 'Not quite the welcome I had expected, but it's the thought that counts,' he said in a dismissive tone that suggested the poor man might have died and it wouldn't have mattered.

Nevertheless, Violet Wedderburn introduced herself and motioned for the newcomers to be seated at the table. 'Welcome, Mr Weever, and I presume Mr Fairfoull?' said Violet.

'Ah – you know me?' said Fairfoull, surprised.

'Oh yes,' she replied. 'Please be seated.'

Weever casually pushed his baseball cap a little higher on his head and addressed Lord Tulloh. 'So-oo… you too wish to be chief of Clan McShellach, do you?' he said with a condescending smile.

'I do,' replied Tulloh bravely. 'Yes, I do.'

'But you're not a McShellach.'

'He is,' advised the old lady. 'Now, please be seated.'

Weever remained standing as tall as he could and returned his attention to Patrick. 'I didn't know you were a spiteful man, Patrick.'

'I'm not spiteful. I simply relish the role.'

'Oh, you relish it? Well, well, well. So, it's a council of war you relish, is it?'

'More like brothers in arms, I'd say,' replied Tulloh, getting up and offering his hand. 'All for Clan McShellach.'

Weever ignored the hand. Violet Wedderburn nodded to Roddy, who, now seemingly compos mentis, reached out for a notepad and pen on the sideboard, then scribbled something down.

Weever looked at his watch. 'Am I late or am I early?'

'You're late,' said Violet pointedly.

Weever seemed a little taken aback by the sharpness but, recovering his demeanour, announced, 'That's because I head up an international corporation that covers the planet and puts food on tables and—'

'Yes, Mr Weever, I know what you do. Please be seated.'

Weever and Fairfoull finally sat down as indicated.

'You both know my position,' continued Violet, 'and I thought it best to offer you both the chance to make your claim and counterclaim face to face, man to man.'

'Excellent. Good thinking,' said Weever, brightening at the prospect of beating the living daylights out of Lord Tulloh.

'I'm happy with that,' agreed Tulloh, not quite so brightly.

Suddenly a searing scream cut through the air as a red-and-blue parrot bobbed up and down in a big cage in the far corner.

'Oh, Jocky hates hats indoors,' Violet explained. 'He lived in a barber's shop for over twenty years before I got him. I must ask you to please remove your hat, Mr Weever.'

The parrot issued another knife-sharp screech. Weever flashed it a look almost as piercing as the screech; then, with obvious reluctance, he took off his bright orange baseball cap bearing the words 'Weever International' in blue. However, far from being satisfied with what it saw, the parrot seemed even more agitated, and screeched several decibels louder.

Violet smiled. 'Put your hat on again, please, Mr Weever,' she requested. 'He's even more distressed at the sight of your hair, for some reason. I do apologise, but he has very strong opinions on hairstyles. After twenty years in the business, he's seen them all, and sad to say, yours is not one which meets with his approval. A matter of opinion, simply; nothing more.'

Clearly disgruntled and defiant, Weever did not put his cap back on.

The parrot was not pleased: bobbing up and down, it screeched fiercely again and yelled, 'Follicles!' or something similar.

'My apologies again,' said Violet, 'but the barber he lived with got a bit short-sighted and his language got a bit fruity. I've managed to eliminate most of his more colourful vocabulary, but there are still some words he's rather fond of, and I have to say that "follicles" is likely to be only the prelude to a barrage of words rather inappropriate for use in refined company. So, I really must ask you to put your cap back on very promptly, please, Mr Weever.'

While Weever, clearly angry, put the cap back on his head and flashed another poisonous look at his feathered tormentor, Lord Tulloh, on the other hand, seemed to brighten and gather confidence. After all, if a little ball of feathers could rattle the great man, why not him? Violet nodded again to Roddy the piper, who again scribbled something on his pad. With a flick of the eyebrows, Weever glanced at Fairfoull, then cast his eyes round the room as if assessing the calibre of the lady by the quality of her decor and furnishings. Then he eyed Chizzie and Lord Tulloh with a condescending smile. Weever was re-establishing his dignity following his defeat at the beak of a parrot.

'Now, to the business in hand,' said Violet. 'Mr Weever, why do you want to be chief of Clan McShellach?'

With a little snort and smile, Weever answered condescendingly, 'Well, it's very clear: I'm the best there is. And I can prove it. Put us to the test, man for man, and you will see.'

The old lady turned her head to Tulloh, who in turn looked to her as if in search of guidance. But she offered nothing.

Tulloh turned to Weever. 'Well,' he said, 'what kind of test do you have in mind?'

'You name it; I'll meet it,' replied Weever. 'Any Olympic sport. You name it.'

'Or Highland Games event,' added Violet.

Tulloh thought for a moment, then made his offer. 'In that case, I propose ballroom dancing.'

'What?! Ballroom dancing?' exclaimed Weever, gawping at him like a hot alligator. 'That's not an Olympic sport!'

'Could be soon,' replied Tulloh.

'It ain't today,' snarled Weever.

'Traditional dancing, then. A sword dance – that's part of the Highland Games – or even the Gay Gordons?'

'The Gay Gordons?' yelped Weever. 'God forbid! I say boxing.'

The old lady jolted. 'Oh, I'm not having blood spilled,' she said.

'There won't be any,' advised Weever. 'One punch and he's on the floor – he won't have time to bleed.'

'Very considerate of you, Mr Weever,' said Violet, 'but I have a better idea: football. Soccer, as you Americans would have it.'

'Soccer? That's a team thing; we can't have that – this is about man to man; the Highland way.'

The old lady shook her head. 'Actually, Mr Weever, clansmen have settled their differences with teams in the past; most notably with the Battle of the Clans in Perth in 1396'

Weever turned to Fairfoull. 'That true?'

'I do believe it is,' replied Fairfoull. 'I recall Erica saying something about it once.'

The old lady continued. 'Thirty men from each of two clans fought to the death before King Robert the Third.'

Weever suddenly seemed quite taken with the idea. 'Wow, a Battle of the Clans…'

Violet smiled politely. 'You'll not be fighting to the death, Mr Weever.'

Weever looked robbed. 'Not even—?'

'Not even hitting one another. Football I will agree to, provided the loser accepts the result as final and there will be no further argument. Other than that, I will make my own decision.'

Tulloh shrugged. 'I am happy with you making your own decision, Mrs Wedderburn.'

Weever, eyeing Roddy's notebook, declared, 'You said football. I demand football.'

Tulloh hesitated, then looked at the others one by one, as if seeking advice.

'Are you a man or a mouse?' Weever mocked. 'I do believe my opponent is cowering like a mouse. Clan chief? He's no clan chief!'

'All right, all right – football it is, I agree,' declared Tulloh, sounding like a man cornered.

Weever grimaced from ear to ear and turned to Fairfoull with a look that wouldn't have been out of place on the face of William the Conqueror. 'I'll hire the finest players in the land,' he told his audience, before directing himself particularly to Lord Tulloh whom he informed, 'I'll have your lot beaten within five minutes!'

'Oh no, you won't,' said the old lady. 'You'll get your players locally. They must be currently resident within a ten-mile radius of the Queen Victoria statue in Tannadee. I'll appoint the match officials. The match is to be played within two weeks of today. Any questions?'

Chizzie asked, 'Any particular venue?'

The old lady shrugged. 'Wherever you like, by mutual decision. Let me know when and where.' And with that, Violet Wedderburn closed the meeting.

Roddy grunted and made to gather up his pipes.

'No, no, Roddy, you stay there,' said the lady. 'They'll see themselves out.'

Back in the Land Rover, Chizzie expressed his surprise and concern. 'Football? Why on earth did you agree to football, Patrick?'

'I don't know. I just know I had had enough of Weever's goading, and I came over all defiant. He was taking me for a nobody. I may not be much of a clan chief, he may be right about that, but I'm not nobody: I'm flesh and blood and I will not be mocked and derided. Oh gosh! Here I am getting all worked up again. Let's just go.'

He started the engine, and they sped off much faster than they had come.

CHAPTER 24

Charlie Fairfoull entered Gordon Weever's office. 'I've been in touch with the sports reporter at the *Millburgh Express*. He's sending us a list of the best players in the district.'

Weever nodded approvingly. 'Excellent. But we need to move fast. Buy them all up before Tulloh gets a chance.'

'No problem, Gordon. Lord Tulloh won't even get close.'

While Weever and Fairfoull set about signing all the players recommended to them by the sports reporter, Chizzie was striving to persuade his father to become manager of the Lord Tulloh Football Team. Johnny Bryson was not exactly one of Lord Tulloh's greatest fans and wanted nothing to do with managing his football team. But then, on further reflection, he acknowledged that Weever was even more repellent than Lord Tulloh, and he came to like the idea of wiping the smile off cocky Weever's face.

'One big problem, however,' said Johnny. 'Weever's cash – it's going to swallow up all the best available talent in the area. What kind of dross am I going to be left with? As an ex-professional football manager, I have a reputation to protect. And I need something to work with. I'm a manager, not a magician.'

Chizzie offered some reason for optimism: 'Even the best talent in the district won't be star quality. If they were good, they'd be gone. The gulf between the best and the dross might not be all that big.'

Johnny wasn't entirely convinced. So many questions tumbled over in his head. He sighed heavily, then looked around his office as if calling on the walls for advice. Then he grimaced, then he rubbed his chin, then he drummed his fingers on the desk. Chizzie knew better than to interrupt. Finally, with a big intake of breath, Johnny appeared ready to announce the verdict of the jury clamouring in his head. It was yes – the ayes have it! Johnny Bryson had just become manager of Lord Tulloh FC.

Chizzie jumped off his chair. 'Thanks, Father! You won't regret it. I'll phone Patrick right away; he'll be so pleased.'

'Wait! Wait! Wait a minute – no time to lose. Weever being Weever, he'll be buying up everything as we speak, dross and all. So, get right on it; get the best you can. First off, we need a captain; somebody who knows about tactics and organisation.'

'One of the Muill brothers?'

'The butchers?'

'One's a butcher; the other's a baker. They've played amateur league.'

'Quite a while ago if appearance is anything to go by.'

'They're fitter than they look; they do a lot of jogging.'

'Yeah, I've seen them lumbering along.'

'But good stoppers, Dad: you wouldn't want to run into them.'

'Well, maybe. Football's a simple game essentially: it's

about stoppers and attackers. Right, okay, we go for the Muills, but we'll need a couple of speedsters alongside them.'

'Billy Pung.'

'He plays football?'

'Well, maybe.'

'Okay, doesn't matter – he'll run all day long. That right?'

'Absolutely.'

'Right, all he needs to do is keep getting in the way of the other lot. Now, at this level the ball's going to be mostly in the air, so we need a bit of height; a couple of tall guys: one for goalie; the other up front. Who've we got?'

Chizzie thought hard, but no one suitable sprang immediately to mind. Eventually, he came up with a name from the very fringes of the 'suitable' category – that name was Dave Dalrymple, the maths teacher.

'The hypochondriac runner?!' exclaimed Johnny. 'He wouldn't last five minutes before pulling a muscle or going down with anthrax.'

'He's worth a try – he'll certainly be fitter than most. We can see him at lunchtime; he takes his lunch in his classroom.'

'Not exactly a team player, then.'

'Well, no, not exactly.'

When Chizzie and Johnny arrived at Dalrymple's classroom, they knocked and entered to find the tall, skinny Dalrymple at his desk, munching a plateful of salad while listening to a symphony on the radio. Instantly, Dalrymple looked alarmed and switched off the radio.

Visitors at lunchtime were out of the ordinary and could mean only one thing: trouble. He gulped down the last of his avocado chunks and waited.

'Good afternoon, Dave,' said Chizzie brightly. 'Very sorry to interrupt your lunch, but we thought you might be extremely interested in what we have to say.' He went on to explain the circumstances leading up to the football match.

When Chizzie had finished, Johnny brought on a professional smile. 'So, Dave, how would you like to be our star centre forward?' he asked pleasantly.

'Play football?'

'Yes.'

'Certainly not,' snapped Dalrymple. 'I'm trying to have a child.'

'What's that got to do with it?' Johnny asked.

'I'm not taking a volley in the crotch for anyone,' Dalrymple informed him.

Johnny eyed Dalrymple like he was planning some kind of surgical procedure on him. '"Volley in the crotch"?' He bristled. 'Highly unlikely. Anyway, a volley in the crotch might do some good; might wake things up a bit.'

'My things do not need waking up a bit,' Dalrymple insisted angrily. 'And I'll thank you to close the door on the way out.'

'What an attitude,' said Johnny in the corridor. 'A lucky escape there. The man's clearly a wimp.'

After classes, Johnny and Chizzie returned to the school to cast an eye over the school's football team at practice.

'There's two lads looking quite useful,' Johnny

observed. 'The stocky fair-haired lad and the silky black guy.'

'That's Ryan McKenna and Peter Oduah, who likes to be called Odu,' Chizzie informed him. 'Some scouts have been looking at Odu, apparently.'

When the practice was over, Johnny and Chizzie called Ryan and Odu over and explained their interest.

'Yeah, I heard about this,' said Ryan. 'A guy from Weever's outfit asked me if I was interested. But I said no. I'm not playing for Weever after he tried to buy up our playing field for his golf course. Yeah, I'll be very happy to be in your squad, Mr Bryson.'

Odu rubbed his chin thoughtfully. 'I heard Weever's signing up players from Millburgh and they're getting paid.'

'We don't have Weever's mountain of cash,' said Johnny. 'We're strictly amateur.'

Odu smiled. 'Right – sponsor me and Ryan for a hundred quid in the Millburgh 10k and I'm in.'

'We're running for Millburgh food bank,' added Ryan.

'We can't do that,' said Johnny.

'No,' agreed Chizzie. 'Not one hundred – we make it two hundred!'

'Augh!' spluttered Johnny.

'It's a deal,' said Odu. 'We're on it!'

Johnny and Chizzie thanked the lads, then made their way back into the school.

Passing the school library's glass doors, Johnny glanced inside, then stopped abruptly. 'There's a tall guy in there. Who's that?'

Chizzie took a look. 'Ah, that is Charles Thomson. Looks like he's giving a reading to some of the senior students.'

At first glance – and indeed every other glance – Thomson was not exactly what sprang to mind at the mention of Real Madrid or Manchester United, but he was a clever young man; a student studying for a PhD in English literature. In his favour was the possibility that he might prove valuable on the football field by being able to articulate his teammates' feelings towards the referee in a way that would avoid unnecessary conflict. He was currently residing at home, nursing shattered nerves following an unsuccessful seminar he'd delivered on the poetry of root vegetables at a symposium in Edinburgh. It had been a task as ill-conceived in the concept as in the presentation. Though, to be fair, English literature is a field very thoroughly explored, and to find new ground on which to expound is very difficult.

Charles Thomson had taken the instruction to find new ground quite literally. He'd not only found new ground; he'd got stuck right into it, delving directly into the world of root vegetables; a field where no student of poetry had gone before. Driven by sheer enthusiasm, Thomson had gained access to an allotment and gone rooting for root vegetables among his neighbours. Finding them, he'd sat down and contemplated them, mused on their place in the great scheme of things, then dug them up, felt them, smelt them, listened to them, devoured them, and even planted some. After one year, drawing on his wealth of newly acquired experience, he'd prepared a paper and a collection of poems for critical appraisal. It had not gone well; hence his current position as a convalescent on yeast tablets at his mother's home and his potential availability as a Lord Tulloh FC footballer.

Peering through the glass door, Chizzie was unsure.

'Problem is, I don't think he even knows what a football looks like.'

'Not necessarily a problem,' replied Johnny. 'Depends on whatever else he's got. Could be worth a try.'

'I should maybe add that he's a student.'

Johnny's jaw dropped instantly.

'And a poet.'

'A *poet*?' repeated Johnny, sounding like he'd just been told the man was awash with fleas.

'Nothing ventured, Father.'

Johnny shrugged, lost for words.

'But it could be he's keen to experience something completely new,' continued Chizzie. 'Looking to widen his horizons for the sake of his poetry. Extend his emotional range, perhaps.'

Johnny sighed. 'What is it with tall guys? First a hypochondriac and now a poet – wimps to a man.'

'Byron was a poet; he wasn't a wimp.'

'Byron who?'

'Lord Byron – he was no pussycat. Come on, let's see what the guy's got to say. Might be rousing stuff.'

They quietly opened the library door and crossed to the nearest aisle of books, where they secretly listened in to the reading as the poet waved goodbye to root vegetables and embarked upon his Romantic phase.

'So, "The Bells of Tannadee",' announced Thomson, before clearing his throat and adding, 'Though, I hasten to add, no school bells.' Thus eliciting a polite laugh from the audience.

'"The Bells of Tannadee",' Thomson announced again, and began:

Words fly high in Tannadee,
for bells are alive in Tannadee.
They ring out 'Hi!' and 'Welcome here.'
Or 'Where have you been? You're looking well.'
Or caught on the wind, sing of distant joy;
of love on the wing in wedding's flight;
hearts pealing open, brave with wanting;
young carillons sounding fancy,
sounding lovely, sounding lively.
But then... another day, another day.
Sorrow is tolling; tears are wringing,
casting down that beaten way,
where lumbering thoughts of deep intoning
are clarions of time not spent with you...
Hearts pine so long, in life so short.
Love's so dear, it leaves you hollow.
You were me, and I was you:
time came giving, and time came taking,
parting souls, now mere whispers.
But bells linger on, airy and free,
and words are forever in Tannadee.

Without a word, Johnny looked at Chizzie. It was a look that either held back an avalanche of opinion or swelled with a new sensibility.

Eyeing a couple of heads nodding off, Thomson struck up immediately with another poem. "'O, Break o' Day"!' he declared.

O, break o' day!
O, break o' day!

Stay thy greeting!
For I am ill with reasoning
the night away on love…

'What a prat!" growled Johnny. 'Who does he think he is – bloody Shakespeare?'

'Well, it might explain why he can't get up in the morning! His curtains are never open before noon.'

'I mean, who on earth talks like that?'

'It's poetry, Father. It's heightened language. Listen and you might… oh my goodness, he's finished.'

'He lost height helluva quick.'

'Shhh, he's got another one coming.'

'Aw, Gawd.'

'This one's called "Seasons", announced Thomson.

Tingle-tangle spring is here…

'Aw, Jesus! That's it! I'm outta here. "Tingle-tangle" – what next? "Bingle-bungle, Boulderhead's here"?' hissed Johnny. 'I came looking for a centre forward and I'm getting tingle-tangle; it's like a disease. Come on, we're off!'

They hurried along the corridor, then Chizzie stopped abruptly. 'Hang on, Dad. I say we at least find out what Charles could do for us.'

'Are you crazy? He's in a different world. A parallel universe.'

'You never know. Give him a chance; let's speak to him. Some of his audience were barely awake, but he battled on. He's a fighter – and that's a good thing.'

After lunch, Chizzie and Johnny sat down in their living

room to finalise their list of prospective team members. Yolanda joined them and listened in for five minutes while the men exchanged suggestions, few of which brought complete agreement.

In one of the moments of quiet reflection, Yolanda ventured, 'Have you considered recruiting from the Millburgh Women's Team?'

Chizzie instantly recognised it as a loaded question and flailed out a response. 'Oh yes… oh yes, yes,' he said, buying time for a more comprehensive reply and looking to Johnny for help.

But if Chizzie had a problem, Johnny had an even bigger one, and he quickly took out his handkerchief and blew his nose.

Then suddenly the problem was no longer a problem. 'Jenna!' declared Chizzie, like a prospector who'd suddenly hit gold. 'Yes, Jenna!' he repeated eagerly.

'And Karen Carnegie,' suggested Yolanda pointedly.

'You're right!' enthused Chizzie. 'Absolutely. Great engine, as they say in the game. Yes, thanks for reminding me, dearest.'

'And Caitlin,' continued Yolanda.

'And Caitlin,' agreed Chizzie. 'A very useful sub indeed. It's all up to our great manager here, of course. Over to you, Pater.'

The little discussion had given Johnny time to prepare. He drained his coffee cup and proclaimed, 'Yes, absolutely – our ladies might actually be key to winning the match. They're a surprise element – a lot better than the Millburgh guys will take them for. Jenna, Caitlin, Karen – they're all in the squad. So, Yolanda, if you will kindly ask them to join us, I'd be much obliged. And Chizzie, I've had second thoughts about that poet guy. He's got the height we need, and even if he is technically totally useless, that's not necessarily a problem. All we need is that he gets in the way of their tallest guy. We'll go see him after two o'clock – he'll be out of bed by then, surely.'

Chizzie shrugged.

As they approached Thomson's house, a relieved Chizzie observed, 'His curtains are open – a good sign.'

'At nearly three o'clock in the afternoon, you'd hope so!'

And indeed, the student poet was up and about. Near the door, they could hear the poet's voice issuing from an upstairs window which was slightly open.

'Gawd, he's at it non-stop,' Johnny whined.

'Tenacity, Father – a good feature.'

They listened in and were treated to some closing lines:

Swaddle me in beer bubbles,
cosset me in foam,
for I am a beer lover,
and I am come home.

'Gawd almighty, he's a drunkard too!' Johnny whined, and swivelled round, ready to march away.

Chizzie grabbed his shoulder. 'He's a poet who likes beer – perfectly natural. Almost compulsory, in fact,' insisted Chizzie.

'Ring the bell.'

The bell failed to ring.

'So much for "bells are alive in Tannadee", muttered Johnny.

Chizzie cupped his hands about his mouth and hailed the poet. There was no reply. Chizzie knocked on the door.

Moments later, Thomson's head appeared at the upstairs window. For a moment, the poet surveyed his visitors with a suspicious eye; then he declared, 'I'm not religious.'

'We're not here to convert you,' Chizzie replied. 'We just want to speak to you about an adventure you might like to experience. One that will broaden your horizons and enhance your perspective on the world.'

Thomson's look of suspicion faded to reveal one of cautious curiosity. 'What kind of adventure? Not illegal, is it?'

'Not at all,' replied Chizzie.

'Perfectly legal,' added Johnny.

'Hang on, then,' said Thomson before disappearing.

Johnny beamed. 'He bought all that balderdash of yours. Amazing!'

'Why shouldn't he? It's the truth.'

Some minutes later, Chizzie and Johnny were still waiting at the door while they were treated to the distant sound of hurried vacuuming inside the house. Finally, the door opened, and Thomson invited them in. With an apologetic smile, he explained that his mother was away on a Mediterranean cruise; hence the untidiness, which he would be attending to later that day. He failed to excuse the stale smell of last night's curry hanging in the air. Keen not to linger, Johnny got straight to the point.

A look of mild horror was Thomson's immediate

reaction. 'I'm not at all sporty,' he complained. 'Never played football in my life. Never even considered it. The very idea!' He shuddered as if to emphasise the point.

But Chizzie persevered, dangling the opportunity for Thomson to experience something entirely new to him: a rare opportunity for an adventurous, edgy, pioneering poet in the prime of youth. The allure of the new drew a silent reappraisal from the poet. Chizzie could almost hear Thomson's horizons expanding.

Then, as if touched by some divine spirit, the lofty poet smiled wistfully and uttered the magic words, 'Right, yes, I'll do it.'

'Excellent!' declared Johnny, offering his hand.

They shook hands.

'You'll need to tell me how to go about it,' said Thomson. 'All I know is, there's a field, a ball, and a bunch of men running about in shorts.'

'Well, it's not quite as simple as that,' Johnny assured him. 'Like the bells in your poem, there's a lot more going on in those shorts than meets the eye.'

Chizzie grimaced.

'Every player tells a story,' Johnny explained. 'And not just men – there could even be a lady.'

Chizzie added even more appeal: 'A drama of interweaving, eclectic characters played out in the red-hot arena of clan rivalry. Manna for the muse, I guarantee you.'

This evidently hit the mark, for Thomson's lips widened, almost smile-like – a brave gesture for a young poet defiantly risking mockery as a lightweight.

'Now, full name?' asked Johnny.

'Charles Robert Thomson.'

'Excellent – ageing teams like Millburgh are full of Chics, Rabs and Tams, and we can call you any one of those; in fact, all of them.'

'You mean I'm to be three people?'

'That's for the opposition to decide. Confusion's what we're after. With our guys shouting, "Chic", "Rab" and "Tam" around the field, there'll be total confusion in the Millburgh heads. You have that unique role. And in addition to that unique role, another very important one: you have the honour of being the decoy.'

'The what?'

'The decoy – the most important position on the pitch. While ordinary players are running after the ball, you're running away from it.'

'Is that difficult?' asked the poet, chewing on a fingernail.

'Only for the opposition. They have a decision to make. They're in two minds. You're magnetic, you see; you're drawing their attention away from the action. Mostly, you will attract the attention of their tallest guy. From time to time, he will expand your vocabulary with words and phrases you have never heard before. You'll see the world from a whole new angle.'

The poet rubbed his chin, apparently in two minds himself, or possibly even more.

Chizzie attempted to add yet more appeal: 'You're an enigma in the eyes of the other team. Semi-secretive – a unique opportunity to get a comprehensive view of the action.'

The poet stopped rubbing his chin, his interest rekindled.

'When we're defending,' continued Johnny, 'you'll be on the centre line. We'll show you where that is. And in attack, you roam at least ten yards away from the ball. That's the essence of the role. Wherever the ball is, you're somewhere else.'

'Could I have all this in writing? It's a lot to take in.'

'Of course, of course, and we'll also explain the offside rule. In the meantime, we'll get you some kit. What size are your feet?'

'What happens if I receive the ball?'

'You won't.'

...or will he?

CHAPTER 25

The team assembled at 5pm on Monday in the school's pavilion – a squad of fifteen including Yolanda, who'd offered her services to make up the numbers. Decoy Thomson had not been notified of the session for fear that he might run away if required to participate in physical exercise.

With no time to improve the players' fitness levels, Johnny focused his attention firstly on bonding. The players introduced themselves to one another. Florence McTaggart then arrived in tartan shorts and varicose veins to take them through an Eightsome Reel. A ramshackle affair, inevitably, but it achieved exactly what Johnny wanted: a good warm-up, plenty of laughter, and an opportunity to get the feel of each other in a way that would weld them together as a team. 'The team that dances together, bonds together' – that was Johnny's philosophy. Ms McTaggart had seemingly expected much worse and left with a smile... or perhaps she was just pretending she'd never been anywhere near the place. The rest of the session consisted of a seven-a-side football match, which gave Johnny an insight into who would fit in where.

The second and final training session took place on the following Wednesday, same time, same place, in a steady drizzle which, much to Johnny's pleasant surprise, did little to dampen the players' enthusiasm. They practised applying the offside rule, but it quickly became clear that the team had neither the discipline nor the relentless focus required, and the idea was abandoned. After practising penalties and set pieces, the players turned for home with instructions to get plenty of rest, and on Saturday morning they were to have a hearty breakfast. Poet and decoy Thomson would later be given permission to surface at 11am, early for him, before laying into his usual breakfast – namely, whatever was left in the fridge.

On the Saturday afternoon, shortly after 1.30, Chizzie and Johnny drove to the pavilion with a box of oranges, a crate of sports drinks, and a bag containing a sponge, smelling salts, plasters, and other bits and pieces, plus a few cooked sausages and chocolate bars for the likes of decoy Thomson, who might be having hunger pangs.

The local tourist office had seized on the match, proclaiming it to be the Battle of the Chiefs, and the local paper had featured it too. Even the local radio and TV news had highlighted it. The match had become an 'event', and the school car park was filling up with cars, some minibuses, and a coach. The Millburgh and District Pipes and Drums had even turned up to mark the occasion.

With half an hour to go before kick-off, all the players bar one had arrived; even decoy Thomson was there on time and his newly donated boots fitted nicely. The lady players had kitted out at the school. The one player yet to arrive was hard-tackling Danny Wylie.

Johnny looked concerned and asked, 'Anybody know why Danny isn't here?'

'He's superstitious,' Sven explained. 'He'll be waiting for the right omens.'

Johnny shook his head. 'Anybody else superstitious?'

Several hands rose.

'Under control?' asked Johnny.

They all nodded, guarding their secrets.

Johnny stepped into the centre of the room and tapped Ron Bailey on the shoulder. 'Right, Ron, you move to left back. Chico, you're on from the start.'

Thomson looked puzzled. 'Chico? I thought I was Chic, Rab or Tam?'

'Yeah, okay, sorry, whatever.' The pressure was getting to Johnny.

'Better keep your voice down, Dad,' advised Chizzie. 'The walls are thin.'

Johnny smiled slyly. 'Good thinking. Put your ear to the wall and listen in.'

Chizzie obliged, then reported, 'They're laughing... and singing... sounds like they think they've already won.'

Brian 'the Butcher' Muill growled, 'I've a good mind to put my boot through that wall. Give them a tasty surprise.'

In hushed tones, Johnny repeated his tactics. 'First half, every one of their players in our half gets an escort. You get between the ball and our goal. They get no space. Second half... we'll deal with that when it comes.'

Lord Tulloh knocked on the door and entered to thank everyone for their support. Then, sounding quite emotional, he embarked on a morale-boosting speech along classical lines. 'Gentlemen and ladies, I salute you—'

'Right, thank you,' Johnny interrupted. 'This isn't the

226

Battle of Waterloo. Let's get out there now and get jogging and stretching.'

As captain Duggie 'the Baker' Muill led his team onto the pitch, the players saw Weever and his security team arriving speedily in golf buggies, beaming like they'd just smashed the course record at St Andrews. All were clad in tartan of uncertain origin – probably pinched from some unwitting clan, since the McShellach tartan had yet to be discovered. And the clan crest on the flag flying proudly from Weever's buggy bore a distinct resemblance to the double-eagle crest of Perth and Kinross Council, though in fairness he had taken the trouble to change the colours. A ripple of sniggering delight swept through the Millburgh ranks when they caught sight of a woman in the Tulloh team. Clearly they were in for an easy afternoon. Team photos were taken; then the captains were called together by fifty-two-year-old George McPhee, a grocer wearing full black refereeing kit; the remnants of his heyday when he'd officiated at senior league matches. With his son and daughter assisting, also in all-black kit, the officials were arguably the most professional-looking team on the pitch.

Duggie Muill won the toss and elected to play with the slight breeze at his back. Millburgh, aka Weever FC, kicked off and passed the ball straight back into their own half, as normal, keeping the ball away from the onrushing enemy forwards. On this occasion, however, enemy forwards were not onrushing; they were thin on the ground, literally: none but the scrawny Thomson, and he was more like someone looking for a taxi. The great cheer that had erupted at kick-off now fell away, followed by an inquisitive murmur. You could almost see it materialise

227

into a giant question mark above the ground. What was this? Some kind of cowardice? Or some cunning strategy? An insult, possibly? Bravado, even, saying, *Come on ahead; do your worst, we can take it!*

The erstwhile Weever FC players looked as puzzled as the crowd, and simply took to stroking the ball around in the manner of a practice session while they thought things out. Johnny's plan had clearly opened like a dream: one minute gone and no score; only eighty-nine to go! Weever FC pushed the ball around in their own half for a few minutes more, until the captain and four of his teammates huddled together and came up with a plan. Out they came like hunting animals – advancing with menace; moving the ball quickly, slick and snappy; one-touch moves; give-and-go passing. Probing like timber wolves they came, seeking out the weak and the foolish.

The Tulloh FC players tightened up like a herd of musk oxen facing the predatory pack. The pack went first for Chizzie. All eyes were on him now. This was it. He stood on his toes and steeled himself. He had to do well; he had to inspire his team to something greater than the sum of their humble parts. He knew very well that his actions would affect the morale of his team. He could hardly breathe. The drums of war were beating loudly in his head. He must not be beaten! But the opponent came upon him so quickly that by the time Chizzie thought of tackling, the ball was away, and the nippy forward slipped it inside to an onrushing teammate. Fortunately, Billy Pung thudded into the tackle and booted the ball away into the Weever half. First blood to Tulloh! Desperate stuff, but a lot better than being a goal down after only five minutes. Johnny smiled quietly to himself and consulted his watch – only eighty-five to go.

Next, the probing wolves picked out Sven, assuming, no doubt, that the caber-tossing, hammer-throwing heavy would be too muscle-bound to keep up, but they were wrong: he was quicker than they were, and so again was Billy Pung, who pranged yet another of their forwards and forced him into a hurried pass, which was seized upon by Sven, who whacked the ball away with a massive kick that brought out the Weever goalie, who then caught it and promptly punted it back upfield. It was getting like ping-pong, and try as they might, the Weever forwards just could not find a way through. They hit the post twice and the crossbar once, and they got four corners, but the Tulloh defenders held out.

'Move it quicker! Move it quicker!' roared the Weever coach.

So they did just that, but no joy: the Tulloh players stood firm in their ten-man defence. Time for a rethink.

The Weever captain stopped, put his foot on the ball and appealed to the referee. 'We can't go on like this, Ref,' he pleaded. 'Tell them to come out and make a game of it – it's a disgrace, so it is.'

'Well, it's certainly unusual,' agreed the ref, shrugging his shoulders, 'but it's not illegal.'

'It's got to be – it's ungentlemanly conduct!'

'I'll have a word with them,' said the ref. And with that, he jogged over to Duggie Muill, custodian of the captain's armband.

'Our tactics,' explained Duggie, 'are to hit on the break, continental-style; it's just that we can't get any breaks.'

Truth, they say, is the first casualty in war; but, alas, not only in war – local football too, it seems.

'Fair enough,' said the referee, and he waved play on.

The Weever captain cursed under his breath; then suddenly, glancing upfield, he booted the ball high into the Tulloh goalmouth. Sandy 'the Cat' Paterson, the Tulloh goalkeeper, backpedalled a little, keeping his eye on it, keeping his eye on it, watching it, watching, watching, waiting... and down it came, straight through his outstretched arms, thudding onto the round, then bouncing up and hitting him on the chin. He staggered backwards. The ball trundled towards the line. Paterson, regaining some balance, dived for the ball but only managed to half-gather it, and it squirted onto the line.

'Goal! Goal!' shouted the Weever team. 'It's a goal!'

But the ref looked to his assistant on the line, and the assistant shook his head, so the ref shook his head. Weever players rushed to the linesman, and some to the referee, all of them complaining bitterly, but the ref waved play on as Paterson, still grasping at the ball, finally succeeded in getting it under control.

Of course, if the Weever players had been smarter they would've rushed in on Paterson, causing him to squirt the ball completely over the line, but no – drama's the thing; all the world's a stage when you're a serious footballer, and when a chance comes to rant and rave you take it – a chance to show off your new hairstyle and look professional. For all their furious heat, though, it was no goal and play continued with Paterson putting the ball out for a throw-in from a kick that was meant to be a punt upfield. Again, nothing unusual in that.

Now very peeved, the Weever players decided they too could play the waiting game, hoping to entice the bumpkins beyond the halfway line and so open up the game. But of course, they'd wait until hell froze over before the bumpkins ventured out of their shell. The bumpkins stayed put – though they were as confused as everyone else. The crowd began slow handclapping and whistling. A look of *What do we do now?* loomed on every Tulloh FC face. Johnny, seeing the need to freshen things up, shouted to decoy Thomson to go after the ball, which he gallantly did, but of course it was piggy in the middle as Weever's team passed the ball away whenever Thomson got near. Then when they saw him tiring, the Weever players got really brave and played the matador, letting Thomson all but touch the ball before drawing it away and passing it.

The crowd roared, "Olé! Olé!"

Weever FC were in a better mood now; the beast was getting one in the eye. But then it dawned on them that one in the eye wasn't actually good enough – they should be scoring. It was goals that counted. And if the mountain wouldn't come to them, they must go to the mountain. So, the Weever captain called for the ball and then booted it into the Tulloh half.

'There!' he bawled. 'You take it! See what you can do!'

More confusion in the Tulloh ranks. This wasn't in the plan. But big Duggie Muill called for it and booted it back into the Weever half. A Weever player gathered it and booted it back into the Tulloh half. It was getting like ping-pong again as the ball zoomed back and forward, back and forward. The crowd even started shouting, 'Ping' when Weever FC hit the ball, and 'Pong' when Tulloh FC hit it. Johnny looked at his watch – just twenty minutes to go in this half! But the crowd were losing patience and starting to shout insults. In every walk of life there can come a point when even the underdog loses the moral high ground and self-humiliation sets in. This was such a point for Tulloh FC. They had no option; they had to come out.

'Big lads up! Big lads up!' shouted Johnny. 'Duggie, Brian, Sven, up you go! Chizzie, you take the corner and come straight back!'

The four looked at each other. Then, shouting, 'Come on!', Duggie raced upfield and the other two followed.

Billy started off as well, but Johnny called him back. 'No, Billy, you stay put. Just stay there.'

Billy, clearly disappointed, nevertheless complied. The ref waited for the players to stop jostling in the goalmouth. Though no more than three, Sven and the Muills were creating a lot more trouble than the Weever captain had bargained for: players just bounced off these guys. Then the ref blew his whistle, and Chizzie sent the ball over with a surprisingly good curving kick towards the near post. Brian Muill ran in to meet it, got his head to it, and flashed it across the goalmouth, where Sven threw himself at it as two Weever defenders tried to knock him off balance – one even pulling his jersey – but he got to it, and headed the ball fiercely, striking the underside of the bar, from where it spun onto the line before a frantic Weever boot whacked it clear. Sven shouted for a penalty, holding up his torn jersey for the ref to see, but the ref waved the claim away, saying he hadn't seen it. As stunned as they looked embarrassed, the Weever players made to sweep upfield while the Tulloh big men were stranded in the wrong half. But the shock of so nearly losing a goal sent their passes wide and the Tulloh stalwarts had enough time to get back into position.

From now on, the ball was staying very firmly in the Tulloh half of the field. But the Weever FC advances were now tentative and unsure, until the captain had another idea; this one founded on the time-honoured principle: 'If you can't go round 'em, go through 'em.' Chizzie once again was first in the firing line. The Weever captain volleyed it straight into Chizzie's chest, all but winding him. When the ball broke to another Weever player, he followed suit and banged the ball off the side of poor Freddie Wang's head.

Duggie Muill protested. 'You can't let them get away with that, Ref – that's dangerous play!'

'I was trying to cross it!' shouted the Weever captain.

'Rubbish!' roared Duggie, advancing menacingly towards the Weever captain.

The ref stepped in. 'I'm giving Weever the benefit of the doubt,' he said. 'If your side just sit in their own half, it's difficult for everybody, so I suggest you come out and make more of a game of it.'

'Yeah, right on, Ref,' roared the Weever captain. 'About time too.'

'You mind your own business,' replied Duggie, angrily.

The game resumed with a bounce-up and the volleying continued, with Tulloh players taking heavy blows on the buttocks, backs, and even heads. The slap, slap of leather on skin, sounding almost like boiling porridge from a distance, filled the full fifteen minutes before half-time. If you were into S&M, you would be happy here. A former sheriff and a Minister for Rural Affairs were seen perspiring heavily before being helped away at half-time.

Half-Time

'You done great!' said Johnny, honouring his players with football-speak as he welcomed them back into the dressing room. 'We got them where we want 'em! They can't play for thinking. It's eating them up. And they're sweating – they're shocked! We got 'em, boys!'

'Yeah, they're tiring,' gasped Ron Bailey through the ice pack pressed on his lips as he lay sprawled on the floor.

'You're right,' Brian Muill agreed, applying a cold compress to his buttocks. 'They ain't hittin' so hard now.'

'Yeah, we got 'em psychiatrically,' said Sven. 'They dunno what hit 'em.'

'Well, I know what hit me,' said Chizzie, looking in the mirror and seeing the words 'butyl bladder' imprinted on his forehead. 'And to be perfectly honest, I don't know how much more I can take. It's tough out there. It really is.'

'It is,' said Duggie Muill, sporting various imprints on his huge head, including 'butyl bladder' and 'inflate to 10 psi'.

'I don't know if I can even get my feet back into these boots again,' Chizzie added. 'Look at these blisters on my feet, and I've got bruises all over the place.'

'Me too,' said Freddie Wang, applying some pungent lotion to his legs.

'We gotta change tactics, boss,' Duggie declared. 'We really got to; we can't take much more.'

'We will, lads, we will; just hang on in there for ten, maybe fifteen minutes more,' Johnny pleaded. 'Then they'll crack, believe me. Just listen to what's happening next door,' he said, pointing to the wall separating the two dressing rooms.

Everybody hushed and heard the terrible commotion going on next door as the Millburgh coach laid into his Weever troops, reading the Riot Act, kicking doors, punching the wall, stamping feet – altogether, not a happy sound.

'They're teetering, boys,' insisted Johnny. 'One little push and they're spaghetti; and that – that, gentlemen—'

'And ladies,' advised Chizzie.

'And ladies,' continued Johnny, 'is when we move upfield and start holding it up there, keeping possession, moving the ball – when they are psychologically crushed. Remember, a nil-nil draw and we're heroes, absolute bloody heroes! So, brave boys and girls, we can win this nil-nil!'

Emotion now got the better of him; he could speak no more – anymore and he would burst into tears. There they were, his own lads and lasses, his valiant team, so brave, steaming like a heap of streaky bacon – a team whipped, thrashed, bashed, belted, lashed, whacked and walloped, even damn near scalded, but still in the game, still defiant to a man and a woman. If only Winston Churchill could see them now, these scalded tigers. It was all too much for Johnny; he had to leave the room. And outside that door, a grown man welled up. Then the door of the other dressing room burst open and out poured Weever FC. Johnny pulled himself together and got back into the dressing room. Taking Duggie aside, he advised him to look out for further instructions as the game unfolded.

Duggie looked straight into his manager's eyes, and seeing the raw signs of emotion there, he very nearly spilled tears of his own. 'You bet, boss,' he answered through gritted teeth. 'You bet!' And with that, he turned and shouted, 'Come on, guys, up and at 'em! Let's stuff them zeros!' And off he went. Then back he came. 'Come on, guys, come on, for God's sake. Let's go!'

And then, as if emerging out of mud, the Tulloh team got to its feet and dragged itself into the sunlight.

Second Half

Having received the hairdryer treatment from their ranting, raving boss, the Weever players came out all fired up. This time they worked harder; they moved the ball quicker. And within a minute, a Weever forward broke through the forest of Tulloh legs and with only goalie Paterson to beat he aimed left, but, overeager, he sliced it to the right – just where goalie Paterson's face came diving and got hit with the ball. The ball rebounded to Sven's feet, and the muscleman kicked it mightily upfield. Paterson, the hero, staggered to his feet. Duggie Muill rushed over and wrapped his arms round him. Paterson, of course, was seeing only stars. And minutes later, a goal for Weever FC. Simple enough. They took a corner, an inswinger, Paterson lost it in the sun, and in it went. One-nil. A shock for Tulloh FC. but relief and cheer all round for Weever FC.

Twelve minutes later, further disaster: another goal

for Weever FC; this time it's from a deflection. Two-nil. Confident now, Weever FC took to showboating and teasing. It looked awfully like a drubbing was on the way.

'Focus!' bawled Johnny. 'Man-to-man marking!'

But the two-goal deficit had clearly knocked some of the stuffing out of the Tulloh players. The Weever players strolled about casually, aware that a barrowload was there for the taking. Their casual approach, however, gave Tulloh FC time to recover some of their morale, and it took until the seventy-third minute before a third goal loomed. From a corner, the ball swung into the Tulloh goal area. Paterson launched himself into the air, and at an altitude of two feet, he punched the ball away. But disaster! Paterson's lucky underpants went two feet in the opposite direction and wrapped themselves around his knees as the perished elastic, having taken one boil wash too many, finally gave out. Losing his balance, the goalie grabbed the nearest thing for support. Unfortunately, that support was an opponent of theatrical bent, and together they fell to the ground. Clear-cut penalty.

This was it. If Weever scored now, it would all be over; there'd be no coming back from three down. The Weever captain, Chic Rawlston, stepped forward with the ball, smiling assuredly. He picked up the ball, cradled it, and rubbed it with his sleeves – all part of his fussy winning formula. With the ball clean and shiny, he placed it meticulously on the penalty spot, turning the maker's name towards him at equator height. He then tapped it discreetly three times with his right forefinger. This ritual completed, he turned, put his heel against the ball, and paced out five yards. As he paced out the steps, his team joined him in a wink. His team knew – as he knew, as his supporters knew, as the po-faced Tulloh players knew, as their nail-biting fans knew – that this man did not miss. He was the penalty king; the killer: twenty-two penalties taken, twenty-two scored, no misses, no messing. And now it was number twenty-three, and what a time to score: the perfect time to suck the morale clean out of the opponents' souls.

Rawlston, now standing erect at the start of his run, eyed up the goalposts, then tested the wind with a wet finger – the kind of attention to detail that brought him all the goals. The Tulloh goalie, Sandy 'the Cat' Paterson, took a few spry skips, knowing that whatever he did, he couldn't lose. He was springy, he was buoyant, and he was booked for wasting time. Then the whistle peeped, and the deadly penalty ace began his fateful run towards the ball: one yard… two yards… three yards… But whoa! Whoa! Hold it! There's a streaker on the pitch!

'It's Tommy Neptune!' howled Weever.

'You're right,' replied Fairfoull. 'And he's stark naked!'

Weever exploded. 'The imbecile! What's he think he's doing?!'

Everyone else looked on, stunned, as Tommy Neptune picked up the ball and kicked it into the air. Then as he danced about, clutching his aching foot, a dog came running onto the pitch.

'There's a dog heading for Neptune,' declared Fairfoull. 'A French bulldog.'

'Good,' opined Weever. 'And there's a woman running after it.'

'She's shouting, "Boufon! Boufon!"'

'Yeah! Attaboy, Frenchie!' Weever yelled excitedly. 'Bite his boufon!'

'A boufon's a hairdo.'

'Agh, right. What's French for—?'

'He's been arrested! PC Tunnock's got him.'

'Right,' hissed Weever, 'if there's press about, the story is I'm looking after Neptune. He's gone nuts, but I'm gettin' him sane for free; gettin' him off drugs at my own expense.'

'Big-hearted Gordon to the rescue.'

'That's me.'

Young fans in the crowd now recognising Tommy Neptune went wild and ran after him as he was led away by PC Tunnock, who was nobly trying to cover the streaker's private parts with his police hat.

Eventually, the crowd calmed down and a hush settled over the scene. Rawlston took the ball and repeated his fussy preparations. The referee blew his whistle. The penalty king got on his way again, striding swiftly to the ball: one yard... two yards... three yards... four yards... Boom! Rawlston hit the ball with a thud like the sound of a coffin nail going in, and the ball flashed away, bullet-swift, straight towards the goalie's top left-hand corner – but over the bar it went, over the crowd, and clean out of the pitch. A shocked silence fell, and for a moment, it held like a photograph. Nothing stirred; nothing but the belated Paterson arcing across his goalmouth in a world of his own before plopping onto the ground.

And thus, in that hushed and bated arena was history made. For the tally now stood at penalties scored: twenty-two; penalties missed: *one*. And Paterson, the newly crowned shutout king, lying spreadeagled, was a legend; the great nemesis of the penalty king. The Tulloh players went leaping into the air and fell upon Paterson, the instrument of their rapture, hugging him and whacking him with sheer joy. When a miracle happens there's just got to be worship. Then again, maybe this was no miracle; maybe Paterson had really got to the guy; maybe he'd psyched him; maybe he'd sussed the guy. Whatever – witchcraft, sorcery, unwitting genius, bewildering incompetence – it had worked, and Tannadee were still in the game!

'Go for it, guys!' bawled Johnny hoarsely, pacing up and down the touchline and clapping his hands. 'They're down – hit 'em now! Hit 'em now!'

Freddie Wang took the goal kick and sent it straight to Odu, who turned sharply and threaded a superb pass out left, where Ryan ran on to it. Outpacing the defenders, he sent over a superb cross for Jenna, who came running into the Weever penalty area – but her heavy touch sent the ball straight into the hands of the goalkeeper. She yelled at herself and raised an arm in the air by way of apology to Ryan.

Five minutes later, Weever FC had learned nothing, but Jenna had, and this time her touch was immaculate. She slotted the ball sweetly into the net. The Weever players were stunned – to them, that goal was like the meteorite that wiped out the dinosaurs. They couldn't believe it, and nor could Johnny – this wasn't in his plan, but he sure took the credit.

'That's it, guys,' he yelled. 'Play the plan! Play the plan!'

What was happening was certainly not in the Weever FC plan. The blame game started. Losing goals to Tulloh FC couldn't possibly happen without somebody screwing up. Cliques appeared. Suppressed animosities reared their heads.

Johnny now smelt blood and started raving on the touchline. 'Get into 'em, guys, get 'em now! Go for it!' It was just like the old days. But a couple of his players were beginning to tire, so Johnny brought them off and put on Caitlin and Yolanda. 'I'm taking a big risk, ladies; don't let me down. Just keep pressing, pressing, pressing; you've got the engine.'

Caitlin and Yolanda did exactly as asked: they worked hard and gave the team a boost. As frustration mounted in the Weever camp, the wheels really came off when their goalie tried to dribble his way out of his own goal area, only to lose the ball to Jenna. She got it off him and slotted it home. Two-two! Abuse rained in on the poor Weever goalie as his teammates vented their anger. One tried to defend him, and civil war broke out as two of them squared up to one another, threatening blows. Their manager pulled them off, but no, they wouldn't go off – it was mutiny!

Gordon Weever made a move. He sent Fairfoull to his team's dugout with a big bonus offered to the player who scored the most goals. A mistake. Enter the messiah, the virtuoso, the chosen one, the one who would turn the game around entirely on his own, the greatest thing in football, the solo effort – the mazy dribble, beating two men, beating three men, rounding the goalie… and in the net it goes! The breakthrough! What a man! What a prat! Who did he think he was? Georgie Best? Pelé? Maradona? Did they play for an obscure Highland outfit? Reality check! But no – suddenly they're all stars, and off they went with the mazy dribble, trying to do it all by themselves, and no sooner gone than – bang! – straight into a Muill brother, and it's 'Ooyah!' and back down to earth.

With Billy Pung having, on his own initiative, taken up the role of sweeper behind the Muills, things were definitely not going well for the Weever men. And when their tricky little winger left the field on account of Brian Muill's boot having relieved him of some of his tricky little skin, tempers boiled over.

'They're trying to wipe us out!' bawled the Weever number seven into the ref's ear. 'Annihilation! That's their game!'

'Nothing of the kind,' replied the ref, taking a step back. 'It was an accident. These things happen – it's a man's game.'

'Accident? Accident?' roared the Weever captain. 'That was no accident – he skinned a man!' Which technically was true, but an academic point if ever there was one, because what really matters in a man's game, after all, is the spirit of the thing, and if you just happen to be one of those happy, gangling fellows blessed with the knack of accidentally skinning people, then who is to deny your natural, free-skinning ways?

And Muill wasn't the only one altering people's appearances: the two mutinous Weever players were at it again. This time it's fisticuffs: clobbering one another like mortal enemies. The ref had no option but to send them both off. Now it was nine prima donnas against eleven bumpkins.

Weever FC's fans began to turn ugly. A selection of groceries and household items came flying onto the pitch, led by the traditional mutton pies, and of course toilet rolls appeared, and a generous helping of fresh fruit salad arrived in the form of apples, oranges and bananas, topped off by that traditional pitch invader: the half-loaf. Whatever it is that keeps the modern football referee awake at night, it certainly isn't hunger or vitamin deficiency. But no amount of offerings could change the stark reality of Weever FC's position: two men off in a minute! They were shell-shocked. Panic flickered across their faces. The hunters now were the hunted.

Desperate to make amends for his earlier blunder, their goalie was playing a blinder. Until a thunderous shot from Billy Pung hit him in the testicles and rebounded straight back to Billy, who boomed it over the crossbar. The stricken goalie, though, now friendless and unforgiven, fell to the ground, and there he lay curled up, motionless and alone, keeping a lid on things while his testicles explored the full meaning of the words 'flattened and throbbing'. Biding his aching time as philosophically as he could was seemingly his way to a better future. And so he lay, biding and gritting, in the certain knowledge that one day this would all be over and he would once again walk throbless and fancy-free with everything neatly in proportion. It was simply a matter of time.

Billy Pung humanely went to the man and, drawing on his deep knowledge of the game, he broke forth with a rendition of the footballers' hymn, 'Abide with Me'. He sang from the heart. The words '*When other helpers fail and comforts flee,*' seemed to evoke particularly strong emotions in the stricken man, for there followed from him a noise like that of a distant seal, merging quickly into something like the tweeting of a skylark.

As the goalie eventually struggled to his feet, Billy took him by the arm and helped him. The Tulloh women stayed away to spare his blushes. Chizzie also stayed away, aware that helping the poor man would only confirm in some minds that the goalie had been nobbled financially as well as physically.

When play resumed, a sinister air hung over the field. Some of the Weever supporters were no longer shouting for their team; now it was crude words being shouted at their beleaguered players. And it was in this darkened atmosphere that the bumpkins attacked. Two minutes into stoppage time, Ryan and Odu worked the ball swiftly down the left again. Ryan sent over a looping cross, and Jenna came running in, but the ball was too high. But not too high for Billy Pung: into the penalty area he zoomed at just the right time. But he was blocked! Blocked by, of all things, Chic, Rab or Tam Thomson, who clearly had no idea what was happening but was evidently desperate, in the dying minutes, to play a material part in the dramatic poetry of the occasion. And he did, for luck shone on him: Billy pushed him hard on the shoulder blades, and as the poet fell his head struck the ball and it bounced into the net. A goal! A dramatic late winner! A poet's dream big enough to knock root vegetables for six. Minutes later, the ref blew full-time, and it was all over! Victory for Lord Tulloh and Tannadee!

Johnny, the mastermind of it all, scurried onto the pitch, falling over twice before joining his players in a hearty lap of honour. Lord Tulloh, in a daze of delight, wandered onto the pitch and got swept up shoulder high. After his lap of honour, Tulloh was lowered to the ground before Violet Wedderburn, who, looking very pleased, presented him with a blue bonnet sporting three golden eagle feathers. Lord Tulloh, quite overcome, bowed gracefully and Violet placed the bonnet on his head. They shook hands: the Clan McShellach had a new chief!

Weever, though, wasted no time in deserting the field. His convoy of golf buggies raced away to his golf course without so much as a 'Thank you, lads.'

While the Weever FC dressing room roared to the sound of recrimination and scuffling, the Tulloh dressing room was a haven of quiet jubilation. Johnny, hoarse and not a little emotional, let his players know that in all his pro career as a football manager he had never been so proud as he was now. Though, as only Chizzie knew, never in Johnny's pro career had there actually been anything to be proud of. Everyone knew that pride had every right to fill that dressing room that day, but the players were too tired for jumping and yelling, and they simply hugged one another; the warmth of the hugs more than compensating for any show of ecstasy. The hugs between Chizzie and Yolanda and Sven and Caitlin were particularly warm as Lord Tulloh announced a banquet for his victorious players, to be held next Saturday at the Tannadee Hotel.

Back at McShellach House, Tommy Neptune was the man to blame. Weever paced up and down in his office.

'If that crazy clown hadn't run onto the pitch buck naked, the penalty would've gone in, and that would have been it! Three goals up and it's all over and I'm chief of Clan McShellach.' He drained his whisky glass. 'Well, let me tell you this,' he continued, steely-eyed. 'I'm *still* chief of Clan McShellach. No way I'm taking this on the chin. We crack on. And first off, I want that Neptune rat out of my life once and for all. Get your heavies onto it.'

'The Gorries?'

'Yeah.'

'To do what?'

'Whatever. Just get that Neptune creep out of my life once and for all – wiped out; gone!'

CHAPTER 26

Fairfoull knocked on the door to Weever's office and entered. The great man was slumped in his chair, feet on the desk, and looking troubled.

'I need three golden eagle feathers pronto,' he said sharply. 'There's a gathering of clan chiefs in two days' time at Baltorran Castle. And I'm going.'

Fairfoull sat down. 'As what?' he asked.

'As chief of Clan McShellach. I'll get all the chiefs to back me; they'll count for more than old lady Wedderburn. I'm going to wow these guys off their feet. Now, I'm told all the really big clan chiefs wear three eagle feathers in their bonnets. So, I want three eagle feathers on *my* bonnet. And forget golden eagle: I want sea eagle – sea eagles are biggest. And that's what I want. The biggest and the best. I'm going to outshine them all.'

'Excellent choice, Gordon. And where do you get the feathers from?'

'Your problem, Charlie. I want the biggest, and I want them in two days.'

'Sea eagle? Two days?'

'Correct.'

'Any idea where I might start?'

'The sea?'

'Big place, the sea, Gordon.'

'Well, better get started right away. I need the feathers for the gathering. I only just found out about it from Erica.'

'Bit of a problem, though, Gordon: you're not actually a chief.'

Weever cast a withering look.

Fairfoull smiled. 'Yeah, okay – chieftain apparent.'

'Chief, Charlie, chief. And you'll come with me. You're my *fine*; that's the Gaelic name for the clan fixer. I've been looking things up. I'm quite an authority now on the Highlands. Heeeh-yooch!'

The following day, Fairfoull entered Weever's office with feather news. It wasn't quite what Weever wanted to hear.

'I spoke to a gamekeeper,' Fairfoull explained. 'He said it's illegal to kill a golden eagle or a sea eagle, but he knows an estate where a sea eagle was found poisoned. It's there for the plucking, if you like.'

'Poisoned? I'm not wearing poison. You want me dead too?'

'It took me a lot of effort to find it. But, okay, I have an alternative plan. It's a bit more iffy, though.'

'More iffy than poisoning? Not radioactive?'

'No, not radioactive. Acquisition by stealth.'

'Stealth? Stealing, you mean?'

Fairfoull shrugged impishly.

'Go to it, then,' Weever chirped. 'As long as the feathers are clean and healthy.'

'Might be a little dusty.'

'Lose the dust. Where are they coming from?'

'The Millburgh museum. They have the McTelfer

collection of stuffed birds in there. I asked the curator to lend us three sea eagle feathers, but he refused.'

'The loser! How much did you offer?'

'Three hundred pounds, eventually.'

'Should've made it five.'

'The curator guy said no amount of money would be acceptable.'

'Is he nuts?'

'Arguably.'

'Must be if he prefers dusty old feathers to three hundred pounds.'

'As dead and dreary as that museum is to us, it's heart and soul to that poor old curator.'

'Too bad! Get in there and get the sea eagle feathers. He'll never know.'

'Well, he just might. He might actually count them every night. He's that kinda guy.'

Weever smirked. 'We'll take the risk. Get in there, Charlie. And get it done. Get the Gorries on to it.'

'You sure?'

'We have to be. They're all we've got.'

A day later, as the sun set behind Baltorran Castle, the last of the sunlight threw long, turreted shadows across the car park, and the castle walls glowed amber in floodlit illumination. A distant babble of chattering voices drifted from the castle garden, while a flock of noisy crows flew overhead in the darkening sky.

A chauffeur-driven Bentley drew up at the gates. Out of the Bentley stepped first Charlie Fairfoull and then Gordon Weever. Both men were in Highland dress; Weever wearing just about everything going in the Highland chief's costume catalogue: big blue bonnet; three large feathers in the bonnet; plaid over the shoulder held by large silver clasp in stag's head shape; red dinner jacket; white shirt with ruff collar; red tartan waistcoat and kilt; large sporran of badger hair with six tassels on board; red-and-white diamond-patterned socks, each with a skean dhu and trim; and on the feet, stout black buckled brogues. While Weever's outfit explored the outer limits of Highland attire, Fairfoull's outfit was more conventional and came in at about half the weight of Weever's, having only a standard black bonnet with no feathers, black dinner jacket, white shirt, tartan bow tie, small leather sporran, white woolly socks, one skean dhu and standard black brogues.

At the castle gate an usher greeted them and respectfully asked to see their invitation cards. Weever presented his card.

'No, sir,' said the usher politely, 'this is your business card; I need your invitation card.'

Weever frowned, cleared his throat pointedly, and tapped his finger on the name shown on the card in flowing gold script.

The usher examined the card more closely. Now aware of the greatness before him, the man's eyebrows leapt and he issued a little gasp. 'Ah, Mr Weever! Of course. My apologies. I didn't quite recognise you for a moment in your Highland... Highland finery. Enjoy your evening, sir.' And with a sweep of the arm, he admitted the great man into the castle grounds.

In the small rose garden, Weever and Fairfoull met a sea of bonnets, each sporting three large feathers.

'More like a clone gathering than a clan gathering,' observed Fairfoull.

They listened to the conversation for a moment, waiting for a lull. When it came, Weever turned quickly to Fairfoull.

'Right, introduce me, then stand back.'

Fairfoull gently inserted himself between two of the smaller clan chiefs. All eyes fell upon Fairfoull, and the lips in the group fell silent.

Fairfoull greeted them and made his introduction in Gaelic. '*Ciamar a tha thu? Coinnich ri ceann-cinnidh Clann McShellach.*'

The result was yet more silence. Then a slight look of bewilderment grew on faces.

Fairfoull tried again, this time in Latin. '*Bonum vesperam. Hic est preesse multitudini Clan McShellach.*'

'Ah, Clan McShellach, *bonum vesperam!*' answered a tall, thin, bespectacled gentleman in olive-brown tartan.

'McShellac? Never heard of it,' bellowed a large, stout chieftain in bright red tartan, swaying slightly and clutching a tumbler of whisky.

A small chief in light blue tartan giggled. 'Shellac?' he exclaimed. 'Shellac – that's derived from an insect secretion!'

'The son of an insect secretion!' roared the large, stout chieftain, laughing himself into a sweat.

The laugh infected the others – but not Weever, of course. He barged in among the laughing faces, his own face reddening, almost as red as his tormentor's tartan. He moved towards the large man and thrust his face into his. 'Listen, buddy,' he advised. 'Call me "insect" again and I'll wrap your fat, hairy legs round your fat, hairy ears.'

The man gulped, then laughed nervously. 'Oh! A joke. Just a joke. No offence, dear boy.'

'I'm not a boy.'

'Of course – figure of speech. Do please accept my apology.'

'Accepted.'

Fairfoull stepped in and took Weever's arm. 'Thank you, gentlemen,' he said. 'Do excuse us; we have to circulate.' And with that, he led Weever out of the circle.

Weever was still fuming. 'What a bunch of cheeky *frieks*!'

'A right old mixture of accents in there, certainly. Some Old Etonians, by the sound of things. But not one Gaelic speaker among them. They got the Latin all right, though.'

Weever scoffed. 'Hah! There you have it. Anything but Scottish.'

'Yes, but you're in no position to crow, Gordon.'

'At least I can say "McShellach" properly.' Weever shivered. 'Brrr – you know, I just don't feel right here. I just don't like it here. I'm really not comfortable at all.'

'Yeah, me too. All that chatting and joking – feels so contrived.'

'The natural inclination of a clan is war.'

'And to your credit, Gordon, you're the only one who got anywhere near it in there.'

'Let's try another lot. What was that Gaelic thing you said?'

'It was "*Ciamar a tha thu?*" That's basically "How are you?" in the Gaelic language.'

Weever asked Fairfoull to repeat the phrase. Fairfoull

repeated the phrase several times until Weever finally got it. Then they approached a small group of clan chiefs.

Weever pushed his way in. '*Ciamar a tha thu?* McShellach. A McShellach!' he declared.

The others drew back as if the man was declaring some kind of medical condition.

But one smiling individual in green tartan recovered quickly. 'My, my, these are mighty big feathers you have there, McShellach.'

'Golden eagle?' asked another.

Weever smiled cockily. 'Sea eagle.'

'They're not sea eagle,' insisted a ruddy-cheeked chief. 'Sea eagles have white tail feathers. You've got vulture feathers!'

'What?!' yelped Weever. 'I beg your pardon?!'

'Yes,' continued the ruddy-cheeked chief. 'I've got some in my collection. They're off a bearded vulture!'

Weever gasped. 'Vulture? You... you're mistaken.'

'Not him,' answered the smiling chief in green tartan. 'He's an international birdwatcher – goes everywhere; he's written a book on it.'

'You've been mugged,' said the ruddy-cheeked chief.

'No, I haven't – tell him, Charlie.'

'Uh, well... yes... climate change!' blurted Charlie. 'Global warming! You see, as Scotland gets warmer, exotic birds arrive more and more often – big birds. You think the sea eagle is big? Well, you want to see the bearded vulture – the biggest bird in Britain these days, and it's only right that forward-looking chiefs put that bird's feathers on their bonnets. We're ahead of the game here, you see – no one more up to date than Clan McShellach.

Not that we're boasting, you understand; simply putting out the facts.'

'Is he right?' asked the chief in green.

'You know, I think he might be,' replied the ruddy-cheeked chief. 'From time to time these birds do come over from Europe.'

'From the French Alps in particular,' added Fairfoull.

'Good Lord!' exclaimed the ruddy-cheeked chief. 'You're a birdman!'

'I dabble. Environmentalist, really.'

Weever looked on, open-mouthed, but snapped out of his amazement quickly and got himself and Fairfoull away from the ruddy-cheeked birdman before Fairfoull's fund of bird facts was exhausted. In a quiet corner, the still-amazed Weever quizzed Fairfoull. 'How the hell d'you know about vultures?'

'Saw it all in the museum when I cased the joint.'

'Well, why didn't you tell the Gorries which one to hit?'

'I assumed they could read.'

'It would be dark when they were in there.'

'They had a torch, but apparently the battery failed as an earthquake rattled the place and a stuffed octopus fell on Dean Gorrie's head. He went hysterical. They panicked. Greg Gorrie made a wild grab at the biggest bird, then got the hell outta there. Not their lucky night.'

'An earthquake? In Scotland?'

'It's true, they happen here; magnitude three's not unusual in some parts round here. Glacial rebound. Ten thousand years ago glaciers pressed down the land, and now it's coming back up.'

'Well, you know what? We're rebounding. We're

leaving. I'm through with this. Lord Tulloh can have his clan, his meek and mild – they're all losers! They don't deserve me.'

'Wow! Gordon Weever quitting!'

'Not quitting – getting real.'

'Maybe so but think of Erica. What's she going to think? You won't set her buzzing again.'

'I'll set Erica buzzing again, don't you worry. Real business is where we're gonna be buzzin'. No more history of the past; we're gonna make the history of the future.'

'So, goodbye, Clan McShellach…'

'Hello, Clan Weever Corporation! We'll have our own tartan. And our clan motto will be—'

'"We put food on tables"?'

'Exactly. What's that in Gaelic?'

'Don't know.'

'Well, find out.'

'And you'll need some kind of logo.'

'You're looking at it. Heeh-yoooch!'

CHAPTER 27

A full day's teaching behind him, Chizzie returned to the Tannadee Hotel and found Yolanda in the new herb garden where she was working, quickly finishing up before the approaching clouds burst open over Tannadee. Seconds later, thunder rumbled, and big drops began to fall. Chizzie grabbed the wheelbarrow and they rushed into the greenhouse.

'That was lucky… thank you,' said Yolanda breathlessly. 'Got finished just in time. How was your day?'

'Hectic, as ever; barely a minute to think. But I did manage a few minutes' peace and quiet at lunchtime, and I got to thinking maybe the Gorries actually have a point: maybe we should consider some kind of deal with them. The way things are at present, no one's getting anything.'

'You mean you're back to thinking we just hand Peggy over and all's well?'

'No, no. I'm saying, if Caitlin simply wants her father to be seen as a reformed sinner, reconciled with his God and now at peace in heaven, then we can facilitate that.'

'Facilitate? You mean cave in. Give the Gorries all they want?'

'No. We divide the loot or whatever it is, and hand it in, or even put Caitlin's share to a good purpose.'

'And the Gorries walk away with the other half?'

'With the police on their tail. We inform the police.'

'Before or after the find?'

'After. If we inform beforehand, the Gorries could get wind of it, and they'll pull out.'

'They're not entirely naive, Chizzie – they'll know we'll put the cops on their tail.'

'That's their risk; we have ours.'

Yolanda took off her gardening gloves, kissed Chizzie on the cheek, and said, 'Let me think it over.'

A little while later, Chizzie was in the living room, sipping his coffee. Yolanda came in with a mug of coffee and a slice of carrot cake.

'I phoned Caitlin,' she announced, 'and she's thinking like you: she wants to meet the Gorries to see what's on offer.'

'Good. I'll call them when I've composed myself a bit. Don't want to appear too eager,' said Chizzie, before drinking the last of his coffee.

'The sooner we meet them, the better. I'll let Caitlin know.'

Chizzie phoned the Gorries, and to his surprise, the Gorries seemed in no rush to meet up. They arranged to meet in two days.

'Maybe they don't want to appear too eager now,' Chizzie wondered aloud. 'Could just be trying to secure a stronger negotiating position.'

Yolanda pondered for a moment. 'Or maybe they think they're on to something.'

'If they are on to something, they'll call off the meeting. Fingers crossed.'

The Gorries did not call off the meeting, so, with mingled confidence and apprehension, Chizzie, Yolanda and Caitlin duly arrived at the Gorries' door at 7.30pm as arranged.

'Welcome to our humble abode!' said Greg Gorrie, opening the door and bowing theatrically with a grand sweep of his arm. 'May I take your jackets?'

An invitation which, coming from a known criminal, unsurprisingly met with a negative response.

Greg smiled reassuringly. 'As you wish. Living room's straight ahead; turn right at the end.'

Not that Chizzie and Yolanda needed telling.

In the living room, Dean sat in a big leather chair with a bottle of beer as he watched TV.

Greg turned the TV off. 'Right, what would you like to drink? We offer a wide selection. You name it; I can make it.'

Again, there was a unanimous 'No thank you' from the visiting party.

Greg laughed. 'We won't poison you.'

'This isn't a social visit, Mr Gorrie,' said Chizzie pointedly. 'We just want to discuss what needs to be discussed.'

Greg motioned for all to be seated. Yolanda and Caitlin unzipped their jackets and took to the sofa, while Chizzie and Greg each took a high-backed easy chair. Dean remained in his big chair, drained his bottle of beer, gave a stretch, and then eyed Chizzie menacingly. Chizzie, out of sheer devilment, smiled, causing Dean's furry eyebrows to collide in confusion.

Greg rubbed his hands together keenly. 'Right, ladies and gentleman, what's new?'

Chizzie explained. 'We wish to come to some arrangement whereby we help you find what you're searching for, and we get half the proceeds, which we hand to the police.'

'Why the sudden change?' asked Greg with a smile.

Caitlin answered, 'I want my father to be known for the good man that he was. And that he repented his sins.'

'And very laudable; admirable, even,' agreed Greg. 'We can help you there. I promise you.'

'We need to know what it is you're searching for,' said Yolanda.

Greg frowned. 'Oh, come now, you don't expect me to tell you that.'

'Actually, we do.'

Greg shook his head with a wry smile. 'No, no, no. You see, the police aren't going to be interested in me and my brother if you simply approach them with some vague tip-off; but if, on the other hand, you give them specific details, that's another matter. So, no details.'

Chizzie complained, 'There has to be complete trust on both sides.'

Greg shrugged. 'We're all taking risks here. Any assurance I give you, frankly, is meaningless. You think we're criminals untrustworthy characters. But actually, we're not bad people: we've never physically hurt anybody.'

'I have,' complained Dean.

'But not badly,' said Greg.

'Only 'cause you stopped me.'

Greg winced. 'He's just a little rough round the edges.'

'More than the edges,' insisted Dean. 'I could—'

'Yeah, okay, Dean,' Greg broke in, 'nobody doubts

259

your roughness. We're all apprised of that, and we move on. So, Caitlin, you wish to clear your father's name. Very honourable, and, believe me, we're absolutely with you on that.'

'Yeah, honour among thieves, an' that,' opined Dean.

'We're not thieves, Dean, not anymore,' Greg maintained. 'We are reformed.'

'Ugh?' replied Dean, seemingly not entirely at one with the idea.

'Well, reform*ing*, let's say,' Greg revised. 'Our record, understandably, is a cause for concern. I get that. But we can only move forward if there's confidence on both sides. We need to trust that you won't shop us prematurely, and you—'

'Prematurely?' broke in Yolanda.

'You must give us twenty-four hours before you contact the police.'

'That puts us in a difficult position,' said Yolanda.

'Not half as difficult as the position we're in,' answered Greg.

'It wouldn't be right,' said Yolanda.

Greg shrugged. 'It's that or not at all. Your decision.'

'We've got our own sniffer dog,' said Dean brightly. 'He's good.'

Yolanda looked to Caitlin, who drew a deep breath, then pursed her lips and eyed Greg for a few seconds. Then she said, 'I agree. Twenty-four hours.'

Chizzie nodded. 'I agree too.'

'Right, you have twenty-four hours,' said Yolanda.

Greg smiled. 'Excellent! Now we get down to business. Dean, fetch the maps.'

'Fetch them yersel', growled Dean.

Greg sighed, got up, and fetched the Ordnance Survey maps and spread one over the coffee table facing his guests. 'Now, as we know', he continued, 'we're looking for a chapel. The red dots show where we've been without success. There's also farms and roads with "Chapel" in their name, so there's a lot to consider. We need to prioritise. So, Caitlin, where d'you think your dad would likely have put the stuff?'

'I don't know where he would've put your so-called "stuff", but among his favourite places to visit were the Rhynd, Findo Gask, Stormontfield, and the Loch Ordie area north of Dunkeld.'

'Right, let's look at Loch Ordie first,' Greg suggested, unfolding the other map. 'We don't know that area.' He studied the map quickly, then turned it round for the others to see. 'No chapel or anything there,' he said. He then folded the map and made a suggestion. 'Let's look at the Rhynd; probably a better bet.' He spread the other map out. 'There's a church-cum-chapel there. Let's do that tomorrow. Meet there at two in the afternoon – Dean and I have some other business in the morning.'

The others agreed.

'Are you sure my father said "chapel", not "church"?' Caitlin asked.

'Well, he was sedated,' said Greg, 'and a bit groggy at the time, but we're pretty sure he said "chapel". Might've been "church", though. We're keeping that in mind.'

'And a number,' added Dean.

'Yes,' said Greg, 'he muttered a number; very faint, but it sounded something like "Chapel A494". However, the A494 is a road down near Chester.'

'He was one helluva bloody cyclist if he put the stuff away down there,' opined Dean.

With that, the meeting ended, and the three visitors got up and left. They walked to their car in silence, but inside the car they could scarcely keep their feelings under control any longer.

Caitlin shivered. 'Oooh, I had goosebumps all the time in there. I've still got them now.'

Chizzie agreed. 'Me too. Yeah, I have to say I found that all very eerie.'

'Chapel A494,' said Yolanda. 'You think that was a devious attempt to get us out of the way?'

'If it was,' answered Chizzie, 'it was pretty crude.'

'They're crude people,'said Caitlin.

Yolanda asked the big question: 'Should we trust them?'

For a few seconds the silence of deep thought reigned. Chizzie even forgot to start the car. Then – wham! – something clattered onto the car and a nightmarish thing gaped in at the windscreen. Caitlin screamed. Chizzie recoiled. There, pressed hard on the glass, right in front of him, was a face like something escaped from a safari park! But it was no exotic creature.

'It's Neptune!' cried Yolanda.

And Neptune it was. He swung backwards, rolled off the bonnet of the car, and then spun round, pulled open a rear door and leaped onto the seat beside Caitlin. 'Get me outta here!' He yelped. 'Quick. I've escaped!'

Caitlin drew back; her goosebumps set to explode.

'Escaped what?' exclaimed Chizzie.

'Just go, man! Just go!' insisted Neptune. 'Just go!'

Chizzie hit the accelerator, his spinning wheels spattering gravel against the wheel arches. What condition Neptune was in, no one could be sure, but he did seem unusually coherent when he explained that he'd been grabbed by the Gorries and told he was being held in the house until they knew what to do with him.

'Then an old lady came to the room,' he continued, 'and she let me out, and I sneaked away. A nice old lady, she was, only she kept calling me Ben Gunn and asking if I'd had enough cheese. And people think *I'm* crazy!'

'Were they holding you for ransom?' asked Yolanda.

'No, they just said Weever wanted me gone – off the premises once and for all. By the way, if you're Chizzie, they're gonna double-cross you; I heard 'em say that. Take me to Lord Tulloh's place, will ya? Nice guy, him; he'll put me up till I can get away. I'm outta here. Crazy, crazy people.'

Having dropped Mr Neptune off at the Tulloh house, where he was made most welcome, Chizzie and Yolanda invited Caitlin to stay over and rest her goosebumps. Over bedtime cocoa, as they sat comfortably by the living room fireside, they discussed their thoughts.

Caitlin raised a concern: 'Did anyone else think Greg dismissed the Loch Ordie area rather too quickly?'

Chizzie nodded. 'Yes, I did. It was like he was in a hurry to rule it out. Maybe we should take another look at Loch Ordie ourselves.'

Caitlin reached into her bag. 'I found my dad's old maps and I've got them in my bag. They're a bit tattered but they still hang together.' She took out the maps and, finding the one she wanted, she spread it out on the coffee table and all three squeezed onto the settee to have a good look.

'You think maybe Greg blindsided us and intends to go there early tomorrow?' Chizzie wondered.

Yolanda leaned forward and pointed to an area just north of Loch Ordie. 'Look! Capel Hill; summit 494 metres!'

'Yeah!' cried Chizzie. 'Yeah, that could be it!'

Caitlin looked first amazed and then mystified. 'How on earth did we miss that?'

Chizzie thought for a moment, then answered: 'Maybe the new map's been revised.'

'Have we got a newer version of OS Map 53?' asked Yolanda.

Chizzie got to his feet. 'Indeed we have. I'll go and get it.' When Chizzie returned with the map, he had good news. 'You know what? Capel Hill's summit is 510 metres according to the new map.'

Caitlin raised her eyebrows: 'You mean the hill's grown sixteen metres?'

'Believe it or not,' said Chizzie, now in schoolteacher mode, 'the Highlands are still rising; rebounding from the massive weight of the ice sheet of ten thousand years ago.'

'Sixteen metres in thirty years?' exclaimed Yolanda.

Chizzie smiled. 'Yeah, a bit much – more likely it's been measured again with more accurate equipment.'

Caitlin sighed. 'Can't even trust the hills anymore.'

Yolanda looked thoughtful. 'The Gorries won't know about the 494. Do we tell them?'

'No!' said Caitlin emphatically. 'If Tommy Neptune's

credible, the Gorries are going to double-cross us. We need to go it alone.'

Yolanda agreed. 'Okay, but we'll need to be very careful. Greg Gorrie dismissed Loch Ordie very quickly, so maybe Capel Hill is actually in his mind, and he wants to throw us off the scent.'

CHAPTER 28

At first light the next day, Chizzie, Yolanda and Caitlin drove off with Sven and Peggy also on board. North of Dunkeld, they headed onto a leafy, narrow, unclassified road which – according to the map and Google Earth – offered a path to Capel Hill. On reaching a sharp bend, they came across a dark blue Maserati parked in a small clearing.

'Uh-oh,' groaned Chizzie. 'We have company.'

'I knew we couldn't trust them,' Caitlin hissed.

'And *they* can't trust *us*,' said Chizzie with a wry smile.

'But we go on,' said Caitlin. 'Jenna knows where we are.'

'And Florence, she knows where we are,' said Chizzie.

'Check phone coverage,' Yolanda suggested.

Everyone reported a good signal.

Sven was eager to get started. 'Let's go get 'em.'

'We proceed with caution,' advised Chizzie. 'Sven and I will go ahead. Ladies, best you stay a hundred yards or so behind with Peggy.'

'We can let their tyres down,' Caitlin suggested.

Yolanda shook her head, but suggested they park the car behind the Maserati so that it was boxed in. Chizzie presented Yolanda with the car keys, then he and Sven each took a spade from the car boot, and they set off.

Chizzie and Sven led while Yolanda, Caitlin and Peggy followed within shouting distance.

When they all arrived at Loch Ordie, through a light haze they could see that no one appeared to be on the summit of Capel Hill.

Then Sven pointed to a narrow path on their right. 'Look! Two guys!'

Two men, nearly a hundred yards away, could be seen bobbing about.

'They're fighting!' exclaimed Yolanda.

Chizzie recognised the familiar shapes: 'It's the Gorries!', he said ominously.

'Right,' said Caitlin, 'let's go round the back of the hill before they see us.'

'Too late – they've seen us,' said Sven.

Chizzie turned quickly to Yolanda. 'Right, Yolanda, you and Caitlin take Peggy and go back down the path a bit.'

'No,' insisted Yolanda. 'I'm staying.'

Caitlin nodded. 'Me too.'

Chizzie blew out his cheeks.

Sven eyed the approaching Gorries sternly. 'Any nonsense, I take the big guy. Chizzie, you get the other one.'

They waited in silence as the Gorries came striding towards them. Peggy whimpered and gave a little shiver. As the Gorries drew close, Chizzie eyed the broken spade being carried by Dean Gorrie and gripped his own spade tightly with both hands in readiness for a well-aimed swing.

'Well, well, well,' called Greg. 'So, you followed us, eh?'

Chizzie relaxed a little but thought it best to give nothing away. 'More to the point, what've you got there?' he asked defiantly.

'Nothing – there's nothing here,' declared Dean.

Exactly where he was talking about escaped Chizzie; he wondered whether to ask or not.

But Caitlin broke in. 'Nothing where?' she asked.

Greg looked thoughtful for a moment, then turned to Dean, then back to the others, then finally back to Dean again. 'They know what we know,' Greg said to Dean. 'Or if they don't, they soon will. Grid reference 494, ladies and gentlemen; or, more exactly, 4904, over there.' Greg pointed not to Capel Hill but to Deuchary Hill, about a mile to the south.

'There's no chapel around here,' Sven pointed out.

'We know,' said Greg, 'but there's Capel Hill, and Caitlin's dad might've got a bit confused.'

Chizzie's face flushed with anger. The Gorries had double-crossed him. He was desperate to claim the moral high ground, but the high ground behind him – all 510 or 494 metres of it – bore testimony to his own shortcomings. He couldn't resist being a little devious, though. 'Well, that's that discounted, then. We can all go home now,' he said.

Greg eyed him for a moment, like a wolf scenting the air. 'No you don't,' he said ominously. 'You've not come here to dig where we were. I can tell from your tone of voice.'

'You can't trick a con man,' said Dean.

'*Former* con man,' insisted Greg, bringing Dean up to date. 'You didn't come here for grid reference 4904. And come to think of it, I don't remember anybody following us. Do you, Brother Dean?'

'Not me, Brother Greg,' chimed Dean. 'And we know a lot about followin'.'

'There's something else,' said Greg sharply. 'You know something else, and you're not telling us.'

Dean fixed Chizzie with a glare. 'Yeah – see his face! It ain't natural. He's got somethin' we ain't.'

'Marbles,' suggested Sven.

Greg held Chizzie in a piercing stare. 'Looks like we've double-crossed each other.'

'How does that work out?' said Dean, a little puzzled.

'Square root of forty-five,' offered Sven, to the bewilderment of all, including himself.

'Okay, spill it,' Greg demanded. 'We told you about grid reference 4904.'

'Only after you'd plundered it,' said Yolanda.

'You're no better: you're here double-crossing us.'

Chizzie clarified as best he could. 'We thought you knew what we knew, and you were double-crossing us, even if you weren't actually because you were double-crossing us in the wrong place.'

Dean looked like he was going cross-eyed.

'We don't need you no more,' said Sven with a smile.

'Oh, but you do,' said Greg returning the smile.

'Oh yeah, yes you do,' parroted Dean.

'You need to know how to handle our stuff,' said Greg. 'Failure to handle it properly could have dire consequences, my innocent friends.'

'Needs proper handling,' agreed Dean, drawing a finger across his throat.

'We need to know what the stuff is,' insisted Yolanda.

'Yeah, you're right, you do,' Greg agreed. 'But we're not telling you.'

'Then we won't tell you where it is,' said Chizzie.

'We'll follow you,' said Greg.

Chizzie weighed up his options: push on up the hill quickly and grab the stuff before the Gorries got near or trust the untrustworthy and cooperate. 'Time out,' he said, and called a huddle several yards from the Gorries.

They hit on a compromise: they would let the Gorries follow without telling them exactly where they were heading. And so, the two parties set off, shrouded in mutual suspicion. Some flies proved a nuisance at first but, higher up, a fresh breeze drove them away.

After several stops to let the Gorries catch up, they all finally reached the summit of the hill, having weaved their way through heather, grassy tussocks, and rocky outcrops. Chizzie reflected that without the welcome breeze, the Gorries might never have made it. They certainly looked like they were in no condition to put up a fight if it came to that. The breeze swirled around the hilltop as several options swirled around Chizzie's head. Then Peggy let out several squeals. She pulled on the lead in the direction of some trees on the southern side of the hilltop. Chizzie let himself be led by Peggy. The others followed.

'Let it off the lead!' Greg shouted, but Chizzie ignored him; there was an awful lot of ground to get lost in.

As they approached a tree standing clear of the rest, Peggy could hardly contain herself. Up on her hind legs, she pulled hard on the leash to get to the tree faster and made for a rocky outcrop below the tree. Frantically, she scraped at the base of a boulder.

'Right, we're here!' roared Dean. 'Stand back!' He pushed the boulder away.

'Give me a spade,' Greg demanded, scarcely able to contain his excitement.

Chizzie gave him his spade. Greg then scraped away about six inches of soil to reveal a green baseball cap, which Peggy dived at and took away in her mouth. Greg continued scraping before pulling a thick black plastic bag out of the ground. He laid it gently on the ground and removed the several wire ties. Carefully, he put a hand into the bag and pulled out a smaller clear plastic bag containing some bits of paper.

'Where's the money?' Dean roared. 'The money! Let's see the money. Get the dog to find the money!'

Greg examined the bits of paper, then replied slowly, the colour draining from his face, 'There is no money.' He handed Dean some of the bits of paper he'd removed from the clear plastic bag.

'What's all this?' asked a bewildered Dean.

'It's receipts and letters,' said Greg. 'Receipts from some very grateful charities.'

'What?! You mean... you mean our money... it's gone?' yelled Dean.

Greg nodded weakly. ''Fraid so.'

'We've been robbed!' yelled Dean.

'Call the police,' quipped Sven.

'The bastard!' Dean roared, crimson faced. Then, looking around for someone to punch, his hateful eyes swept the onlookers. Then he thought again and grabbed a spade and, spitting obscenities, he beat the ground with it again and again.

'He'll sleep well tonight,' observed Sven.

Greg, looking stunned but keeping a lid on things, handed the receipts and several letters to Chizzie.

Chizzie leafed through the receipts to assess the value of the donations. 'Ten receipts – five thousand pounds each,' he announced.

'Gutting,' muttered Greg, shaking his head.

'But you've made a lot of people and a lot of animals very happy,' said Chizzie brightly. 'The letters are full of gratitude.'

Dean made a move, but Greg stopped him. 'Don't push it,' he hissed at Chizzie.

In silence, Greg reached into the big plastic bag and pulled out a smaller clear bag containing two golf balls, two tee pegs and a small piece of paper.

'What's that say?' asked Dean anxiously, pointing at the paper.

Greg read aloud, '"To help you on the straight and narrow fairway."'

'Cheeky bastard,' hissed Dean.

The final and biggest item in the black bag was a metal biscuit tin, which Greg opened to reveal a plastic bag containing items of jewellery wrapped individually in bubble wrap. Greg removed the wrappings and set the pieces on the ground. There were valuable bracelets, necklaces, rings, earrings, and some costume jewellery.

Yolanda broke the silence. 'That's some haul,' she observed.

'Butterflies and bees!' declared Sven in disbelief. 'They're all insects!'

'But valuable,' said Chizzie. 'We divide it here and now.'

'No,' replied Greg. 'We do not divide it, and I'll tell you why. These items are going back to their owners. My mother took them from her friends and some relatives. She has a little bit of dementia and a passion for a very particular item of jewellery.'

'Insects!' declared Sven.

Greg smiled. 'One insect in particular: the damselfly.'

'You sure?' asked Yolanda. 'I don't see any there.'

'No, you won't,' continued Greg. 'That's just the point. You see, my mother used to have a favourite brooch – it was a blue damselfly. But it went missing. We searched high and low, but we couldn't find it anywhere. Then it occurred to me that it was shortly after we declared it lost that she started acquiring other people's jewellery – all insects. So, I went online and found another damselfly brooch – one very similar to the original – and I gave it to her. She was ecstatic and she's worn it every day since, and she takes nothing from anyone anymore.'

'If it was a damselfly she wanted, why take all these other insects?' Sven asked.

Caitlin piped up, 'Maybe she believed that one day one of them would metamorphose into a damselfly.'

'Rather a tall order,' observed Chizzie.

Yolanda shrugged. 'Well, if she did believe that she wasn't entirely wrong, for in a way it did happen. After she took to acquiring other people's insects, her fine, reformed sons went and got her a damselfly.'

Greg smiled. 'And there's more yet to do,' he said firmly. 'When people found out it was Mum who took their stuff, they shunned her. She's been lost without them.

273

No friends to sing or dance with. We'll return the stuff and move on for the better. And before you say it, yes, we originally were going to flog the stuff, but we decided there was a bigger prize: our mum. And as I don't expect you to trust me, you can keep the stuff until we get the insurance companies and the owners to sort it all out. So, you take it.'

Dean, though, was of a different mind. He swung round to face Caitlin. 'It was you!' he bawled. 'You did all this. Your dad put you up to it! The receipts are fakes! You've got the money. Where is it?'

Caitlin stood aghast. 'No. I haven't got the money,' she insisted.

'They're real,' said Greg, indicating the receipts.

But Dean was not to be placated. 'They're fakes! She's lyin'! I know she is!' he yelled.

He strode menacingly towards Caitlin, who looked horrified and turned and ran away. Dean went after her. Sven took off after Dean. Dean, for all his power, was a lumbering runner and Sven quickly caught up. Taking Dean by the collar, he swung him aside. Dean wasn't down, though: he staggered a couple of steps, then regained his balance and got fully upright.

Sven stood facing him and glared. 'Cool it!' he snarled. 'Nobody's cheatin' you.'

'Liar!' Dean bawled, and lunged at Sven, who neatly sidestepped him. Dean shot past; then his feet hit something hard and with a nasty jolt he twisted and fell onto his back. 'Aagh, aw, Gawd! My knees! Agh!' he yelled, gasping.

'Serves you right,' said Sven, approaching Dean warily, clearly mindful of a trap.

Greg pushed past Sven. Chizzie followed. The stricken thug lay groaning and clutching his knees.

'Anybody know first aid?' asked Greg, running his fingers over Dean's shins.

'Nothing but problems, you two,' said Sven, eyeing Greg. 'Always in bother.'

Greg smiled ruefully. 'Actually, you don't know how right you are, mate. We were a problem family before we were even born. We're all from different fathers. Our oldest brother, Isaac, is from Mum's first marriage, I'm from the second, and Dean is a love child born after my father went crazy and gave up farming, then left us.'

'I'm a love child?' bawled Dean. 'What's that mean?'

'Quite literally, you're a bastard. Born out of wedlock. It's why you got called "bastard" at school – well, for that and other things. You always were a bit of a—'

'I had to be! People insulted me and our mum. Everybody hated us. I shut them up. And why you sayin' all this in front of people here? You shoulda told me. Fine thing to be tellin' me here in front of all them.'

'I didn't know how you'd react, but now you're laid out, it seemed a good time. Anyway,' replied Greg, turning to the others, 'some of you probably knew about us already.'

But they hadn't known. They shook their heads and offered sympathetic smiles.

Greg shrugged. 'Well, that's how it is. Isaac took over as man of the house. He's a clever dude – saw more money in crime, and we went stealing cars and burgling. It was good money, better than farming. Isaac's a preacher now, saving people, and we're moving on too. We're going straight.'

'Well, I'm straight out down here! And nobody's

botherin'!' bawled Dean. 'I need to get up, but I don't know if I can make it. I might need a helicopter.'

Caitlin went to Dean and bent over him to mop his brow. Then she kissed him on the cheek. Dean stiffened like he'd been electrocuted. His eyes bulged in amazement as Caitlin explored his thighs.

'I can't be certain,' she said, 'but I think nothing's broken; looks like you've probably strained some ligaments.'

'You're gonna live,' advised Greg. 'You're just a wee bit shocked. We'll get you back to the car and off to A&E.'

Caitlin kissed Dean on the forehead. 'Be brave,' she said.

Dean remained speechless. As Chizzie looked upon him, it seemed that Dean was undergoing some kind of material transformation; like some larval form emerging from a pond, casting off an old skin, just like a damselfly.

'He's never been kissed before,' said Greg solemnly. 'Not properly.'

'Well, he's a prince now, by the look of him,' Sven observed. 'Let's get him up and back on level ground.'

The following day, Caitlin returned to her father's favourite hill along with Chizzie, Yolanda, Sven and Peggy. She carried the casket containing her father's ashes. After checking the wind direction, she opened the casket and released the ashes into the air. Inevitably, a wisp or two blew back onto her, but rather than avoid them, she seemed to welcome them.

In the evening, Chizzie and Yolanda treated Caitlin, Sven and Billy to dinner at the Tannadee Hotel. The fresh air on the hill had made their appetites keen and conversation was sparse as they tucked into the main meal. Sven, not unexpectedly, finished his meal well ahead of everyone else. But what wasn't expected was Sven suddenly getting up off his chair, then going down on one knee and asking Caitlin to marry him: no ring; just the bended knee.

Caitlin, at first astonished, recovered and joined Sven on bended knee, and refused him with the words, 'Not yet', which confused Sven and put him off his pudding.

But he's a resilient lad, and the glint in Caitlin's eye persuaded him eventually to stop playing with his cherry pie, and he scoffed it in seconds and ordered another.

Jenna missed the meal: she was in Glasgow discussing terms with an agent who would be introducing her to professional football.

Some days later, Caitlin put her father's flat up for sale and she and Peggy moved in with Sven in the school janitor's house. Yolanda offered Caitlin the post of manager of the Tannadee hydroponics project, which was readily accepted, leaving Yolanda free to concentrate on her hydroelectricity project.

Desperate for a dog of his own, Billy asked Chizzie to accompany him to a dog rescue centre, where he fell in love with a young female collie called Tansy. He's thinking about training her to become a mountain rescue dog – 'Rescued to the rescue', as he likes to say. Peggy is no stranger, though, and she and Tansy run together along the lochside and splash about nearly every day.

Chizzie is still trying to win Gordon Weever's acceptance, if not his approval. Privately, he is taking golf lessons in the hope that one day he can play a match with

Weever, let the big guy win, pamper his ego, and win him over completely.

The 'borrowed' property found on the hill made its way back to its rightful owners. Greg and Dean sold their farm for a sum that meant they didn't have to work or steal again. The farm is now a care home with a small, sheltered housing estate, where Mrs Gorrie lives happily with people who know her for the kind and gentle soul she is. And her reformed sons now live mostly in Edinburgh, each with his own flat. The rest of their time they spend at their shared villa on the Costa del Sol, where they help to operate a miniature railway; thus allowing Greg to satisfy his passion for locomotives, while Dean satisfies his urge to punch by punching tickets rather than people. One can only hope that he continues to know the difference.

Tannadee

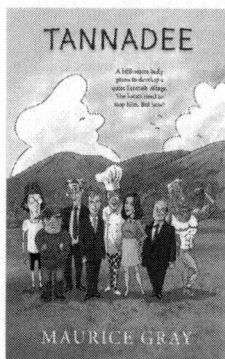

The village of Tannadee is a former Highland spa resort fallen on hard times, but billionaire Gordon Weever promises to turn its fortunes around. He wants to build an exclusive hotel at Tannadee. The locals, however, know that Weever has a record of using his power to go way beyond his planning approvals, and he might even go as far as destroying their village. The villagers band together to defend their way of life, but they need cash to meet the challenge. They find it in a uniquely Highland way, and traditional values go head-to-head with corporate power in a tale of drama, satire and farce.

An amusing, mildly satirical romp... with a cast of underdog misfits who... are all quite endearing.
(*The Herald*, Scotland)